ready or not

by J.L. BERG

Ready or Not
Copyright © 2014 by J.L. Berg

All rights reserved.

Cover Designer: Sarah Hansen, Okay Creations,
http://www.okaycreations.com
Editors: Jovana Shirley, Unforeseen Editing, www.unforeseenediting.com;
Ami Deason, www.bookglambyami.com
Formatting: Champagne Formats

Visit my website at http://www.jlberg.com

ISBN: 978-1503268272

Other Books
by J. L. BERG

The Ready Series
when you're ready
ready to wed (a novella)
never been ready
ready for you

within these *Walls*

For Jovana and Ami—Thank you for crossing my T's, dotting my I's and making each and every word shine. You are my rockstars.

Prologue

Twenty Years Ago

I stood on the large stage and quietly bent forward, smoothing the tiny wrinkles out of my pretty pink taffeta dress. The fabric glittered and shimmered as I moved under the bright spotlights. A simple satin bow sat high on top of my head, and dark ringlets curled down my back, reminding me of all the princesses Daddy would tell me about at bedtime.

Looking around at the crowded room and the large audience standing before us, I couldn't help but smile.

I guessed I was kind of like a princess now.

"Stop fidgeting, Olivia," my mother whispered next to me.

Her pale pink coat matched my dress, but it wasn't nearly as pretty. It made her look old and stuffy. I liked it better when she used to dress in shorts and sandals, and she'd dance with me in the sprinklers when the weather got too hot and sticky to stay indoors.

I heard a tapping sound as a microphone came alive. My attention turned to the front of the stage as the crowd exploded in applause.

Smiling, I watched my daddy step out from behind the curtain, grinning and waving, as he passed by a sea of red, white, and blue. Signs bearing his picture and name were bobbing up and down amid the crowd, and I soon found myself covering my tiny ears to block out the thundering noise.

Slender polished fingers wrapped around mine and tugged my hands back down to my sides. I looked up to find my mother wiping tears from her eyes. She gave me a tight hug, and then she whisked away salty trails that had made their way down her cheeks.

"He's no longer just ours anymore. Things are going to be different from this moment on," she said.

I glanced back at my father, who was now standing at the wooden podium. After thanking everyone in the room, he turned around and motioned for the two of us to come forward.

"I wouldn't be anyone without these two women standing beside me—my wonderful wife, June, and darling daughter, Olivia."

The crowd cheered, and I couldn't help but smile and blush a little.

I really did feel like a princess—or at least a senator's daughter.

Whatever that was.

My father always said that being a senator was a big deal. All I knew was, his face was everywhere, and soon, he'd start working at the Capitol building downtown. I'd once taken a field trip there. It looked like the White House, and everyone said it was very old.

"This is only the first step. We're making waves in Virginia ladies and gentlemen! Victory tonight, change tomorrow!" he bellowed into the microphone.

The crowd erupted once again as he wrapped his arms around us. My mother's tears continued to flow as I smiled out at all the people cheering for my father.

She was wrong.

Daddy wasn't different. He felt the same, and he certainly looked like the same goofy dad who would tuck me in at night and sing me songs about dinosaurs and princesses having tea parties.

It was just a job. Kara was one of my friends at school, and her father had gotten a new job. The only thing that had changed in Kara's life was that she got a bigger house down the street.

We already had a big house.

I looked up at my daddy one more time as he squeezed me closer to his side and waved to the crowd.

Nothing would change.

He'd always be my hero.

Chapter One

~Liv~

Late.

I was always late.

I didn't know how others managed their lives so effortlessly, especially when they had responsibilities outside of themselves, like kids and husbands and a few plants.

I had only myself to manage, yet I was always running around like a nut at the last moment, trying to decide things like if the teal or brown sandals went better with my dress.

"Teal. Definitely teal," I muttered as I stared into the floor-length mirror hanging on the back of my bedroom door.

Shoe decision made, I shifted into hyperdrive and began throwing on bangle bracelets and a scarf before finishing everything off with a spritz of my favorite lavender perfume.

I flew down the stairs and made it to the door before I came to a screeching halt.

"Brown!" I yelled to no one in particular as I ran back upstairs to switch my shoes for the tenth time.

I ran back down to the first floor of my historic little house and managed to grab my keys and purse before rushing out the door. I had just turned the lock when I noticed a beast of a moving van occupying the entire street.

"What the hell?" I mumbled, looking around in a daze.

My little blue Prius was perfectly blocked in by a red monstrosity of a moving truck.

Mike's Movers was plastered on the side, and two big, bulky men were slowly moving down a ramp with a large blue dresser.

"Excuse me!" I yelled, marching over to the beefy quarter-back-looking men.

"Yeah?"

"Are you aware your truck is blocking the entire street?" I asked, trying to ignore my high-pitched tone and the way my hand attached itself to my hip.

I looked like a bitch.

But I'm angry!

Beefy man number one's eyebrow arched in amusement. I had no doubt he found my annoyance cute and endearing.

"Sorry, sweetheart. It's a narrow road, and there aren't any alley-ways big enough. We're going as fast as we can."

"Listen, sweetheart," I replied, making his lazy smile falter slight-ly, "I'm late for something, and I really need to get out of my drive-way. So, if you could move your big-ass truck just a smidge and let me out, I'd be so very grateful."

Apparently, my attempt at politeness with a dash of southern charm hadn't worked. Not even a little.

The man looked at me blankly, before wiping his nose with the sleeve of his sweaty shirt. "Sorry, we're under a time crunch, lady."

"Ugh!" I cried out in frustration. "Is there an owner to all this crap?"

"There is, but he's not here right now. I think he got stuck in beach traffic on I-95. Moving here from down south, I think," he rambled.

"Awesome."

I took one last glance at the truck completely blocking in my car from getting on the road leading to my best friends' house—Mia and Garrett Finnegan.

I would be late once again.

An hour later, after whipping my car into gear and flying down the road as quickly as possible in the direction of Garrett and Mia's, I was finally on my way to the party.

Arguments with new neighbors and moving companies immediately vanished.

My little godson was turning one today.

It still amazed me to say that I had a godson.

When Mia Emerson had arrived on my doorstep four years ago, I'd found a shell of my former best friend. She'd looked much the same. Although older and perhaps a bit less naive than the last time I'd seen her, it had still been her peeking through those watery blue eyes—or at least part of her.

The other half she'd left behind eight years earlier when she walked away, broken and ashamed. When she'd found Garrett standing on a street corner in a farmer's market, it was like the entire world had righted itself that day.

It had taken time and a lot of healing on both sides, but eventually, they'd found a path back to each other.

Then, they'd found Asher, my beautiful little godson.

Due to a miscarriage gone wrong, Mia could never have children of her own. After their first couple of years of marriage, she and Garrett had decided to adopt and make a family of their own. Seeing my two best friends become parents was a joy I couldn't describe, and it'd made me believe that anything was possible.

Except the possibility of me ever being on time.

I glared at the stoplight that had been stuck in the annoying shade of red for what seemed like an eternity, and I silently willed it to turn green. Someone must have felt pity for me in that moment because the light miraculously turned, and I quickly made it down the last few blocks to the cute little renovated house where Garrett and Mia had been living since she returned to Richmond.

Since Garrett had moved in, the house had undergone several upgrades, and now, it was the showpiece on the block. Its fresh paint and beautiful landscaping made it one of the most sought after pieces of property in the area. But until little Asher needed more room or if they decided to add to the family, I believed the Finnegans were staying put.

I didn't bother knocking, and instead, I just entered through the front door, yelling, "Hello?"

Mia's golden retriever, Sam, came barreling down the hallway. Several small children followed behind, chasing his tail.

I gave him and the kids a proper welcome, and then I proceeded into the kitchen where the majority of the adults were crowded around the hors d'oeuvres.

"Hey, everyone. Sorry I'm late." I set down the veggie and hummus platter on the counter next to a large bowl of fruit.

"No problem." Mia grinned.

"What?" I asked, noticing the mischief in her eyes.

"Well, we're kind of used to it by now."

I chucked a kitchen towel at her head, and she burst out laughing.

"Shut up," I mumbled. "You have flour in your hair."

Her eyes widened as her hands flew up to her long brown hair, brushing away the white powder that had settled around her crown.

"I don't know how you manage to be on time for work every morning, yet you're late to everything else, Liv."

I shrugged. "Don't want to piss off my boss." I winked, which caused everyone to laugh. "Where's my—" I began asking just as the baby monitor went nuts.

Red lights started flashing as high-pitched wailing filled the room.

"Oh, there he is," I said with a grin.

"He took an extra-long nap," Garrett explained.

Mia motioned toward the stairs.

"Let me," I said. "I want to snuggle him."

My flowing teal skirt swished and floated behind me as I left the party and jogged up the stairs. I passed the master bedroom and walked down the hall until I reached Asher's nursery. Pushing open the door to the dimly lit room, I walked inside.

7

The soft light in the room washed out most of the bright colors, leaving only muted, somber tones. The yellow on the walls was barely recognizable with the black shade pulled taut, but I could almost make out the tiny star shapes I'd painted on the walls months before he was brought home.

My little peanut was standing in his crib as little tears trickled down his chubby cheeks. As soon as he saw me enter, his little hands flew up, making little pinchers, as he lost the last bit of patience he had.

"Okay, okay." I laughed. "I'll spring you free," I cooed, lifting him from the crib and nestling him in my arms.

He smelled like baby shampoo, so clean and fresh. Whoever had invented that particular scent was a genius. I had no plans of making a baby anytime soon, but just a whiff of that stuff even made my chained-up ovaries constrict just the slightest bit.

After a quick diaper change, I brought Asher downstairs to the rest of the family. His grumpy attitude was completely forgotten as he set his sights on his birthday cake. Blue with brown and white polka dots, it had a giant number one–shaped candle on top. After setting his wiggly body in his highchair, we all sang as Mia carried in the cake. As she placed it down in front of him, his eyes widened in delight as Mia tried in vain to keep his little pincher fingers from diving into the frosting. She and Garrett helped blow out the candle, and then they cut a small piece for the birthday boy. Everyone watched in delight and horror as Asher demolished the cake, coating his face and high chair in frosting and chocolate cake.

"He made a big mess!" Lily said to her mother, Leah.

A quick snort followed, and Leah answered, "Baby, you did the same thing. I was cleaning chocolate out of your nose for days."

Leah gave me a quick grin, and I laughed. I loved Leah. We'd grown really close over the years, and I considered her one of my closest friends. She was the best friend of Garrett's sister, Clare Matthews.

Somehow, I'd been pulled into this crazy family, making me one of them.

The Finnegans didn't define family as a last name or bloodline. Family was being with loved ones, and everyone in this room—whether the last name was Finnegan, James, Matthews, or even Prescott, like me—was considered family.

It was the only kind of family I'd had in years.

~Jackson~

"Good God, I forgot about the wallpaper," I muttered as I passed by the hallway bathroom. I dropped another box into the room that Noah had declared as his during our first walk-through.

"I'm kind of digging the toilet wallpaper, Dad," he said.

His young laughter filled the hallway as I found him leaning against the doorway, which led into the horrible bathroom.

"It's awful. Who does that?" My eyes roamed the floor-to-ceiling wallpaper that predated even me. It had probably once been a brilliant white, but it had faded into a dingy cream. The old antique toilets ranged from dusty blue to wrought iron and covered the entirety of the bathroom.

"Great Grandma," Noah answered. "Obviously."

"Yeah. She must have thought it was a good idea…in 1955."

He laughed again as I messed up his hair. Darting out of my way as he rolled his eyes, he did what I could only describe as a Justin Bieber hair flip to move his sandy blond locks neatly back in place.

I'd tried everything to talk him out of that ridiculous haircut.

I'd lost. The hair was cool, and I just didn't get it.

Gotta love tweens.

Noah was in those special years of development when he would be torn between the simple life of a kid and the alluring complexity of a teen.

My son was just about to enter sixth grade. I wasn't quite sure what had happened to him in the last few months of grade school, but it was as if the thought and anticipation of going to middle school had suddenly turned him completely upside down and backward.

That, or aliens had abducted my real son, and this was just a stand-in. I was still unclear.

He was constantly moody, going from one extreme to another. One minute, I'd find him in his room, playing Legos and singing to himself, and then the next, he'd be yelling and screaming over being treated like a baby.

We used to talk, from feelings to *Sesame Street* and everything in between. Now, I would get shouting and a door in my face.

Was it me? Was I coddling him? Or were these raging hormones that had suddenly infiltrated his body, and they were too much for him to handle?

Part of me always wondered if it had something to do with the lack of maternal presence in his life.

What if I'm not enough?

I always tried to be all he needed, but as awesome as I was, I couldn't be a replacement for a mother.

Standing in the hallway, I watched him shuffle off to his new room, no doubt in search of his phone or iPod, and I just shook my head. I didn't have time to sulk or ponder over questions I didn't have the answers to.

That blond hair, blue-eyed boy was the only thing I had in this world.

One way or another, I had to be enough.

~Liv~

I was pleasantly surprised to find my street free and clear of moving vans when I arrived home several hours later, stuffed full of food and high on the smell of baby Asher's shampoo. He was my fix. I loved that little monster. As usual, Mia and Garrett had to pry him away from me.

I was twenty-eight and had no plans of marrying anytime soon— if ever. Holding my godson every so often kept those baby-wanting tendencies down to a minimum. You might make a certain life plan and fully intend on sticking to it, but that didn't mean your hormones had to get on board with you.

I wasn't against marriage, nor did I have a horrible back story to defend my reasoning. I just didn't think I had that specific gene that allowed a person to mate for life.

One guy—forever?

It sounded so permanent.

Choosing just one would be like picking a favorite piece of jewelry.

I had this gorgeous turquoise pendant. I'd picked it up at a farmers' market from a jeweler who only made one-of-a-kind designs. It'd immediately become my new favorite thing to wear. The intricate silver and dark color of turquoise went perfectly with almost everything in my closet. I'd wear it so much that my friends forgot what I looked like without it. The pendant and I had become one—that was, until I'd found an amethyst and rose quartz necklace that outdid the turquoise one in every way. I would still wear the turquoise, but it wasn't nearly as special anymore.

Isn't it the same with men—the one you're with is like a turquoise pendant until something better comes along?

So, I had just decided a long time ago to have a very large jewelry collection.

I used the same logic on the men I dated—fun and casual while it lasted but nothing permanent. Life was too short to settle.

As I parked my car on the curb in front of my house, I snuck a quick peek into my rearview mirror, trying to catch a glimpse of my new neighbor.

I'd lived next door to Mrs. Reid for as long as I could remember. She was a sweet, grandmotherly-type woman.

She used to bake cookies every Sunday until the nurses had started coming every day, and then the cookies had stopped. She wasn't much of a fan of my all-natural version. I'd presented my plate of organic chocolate chip cookies and proudly boasted that I'd used applesauce instead of oil. She'd taken one hesitant bite and crinkled her nose.

"Cookies need fat, honey," she'd told me.

I'd laughed, not feeling the least bit offended.

She had grown vegetables and roses in her backyard up until she couldn't walk without assistance, and I'd been tending to her gardens ever since. Mrs. Reid was in her late eighties when she'd passed away.

When I finally stepped out of my car, a gasp escaped my lungs as my eyes lowered to the flower beds separating our two houses.

"Who would do such a thing?" I whispered, looking down at the decapitated and ravaged flowers.

The once beautiful display of multicolored perennials was now a churned-up disaster of footprints and soil.

My heated gaze settled on the lights glowing within the house. A shadow passed by an open window upstairs in what used to be Mrs. Reid's master bedroom.

I took one step forward, ready to march over, meet my new neighbors, and give them a piece of my mind.

A strong gust of wind sent the curtain into a tailspin and suddenly the shadow solidified, and I saw the finest bare back I'd seen in years. It was tanned, broad, and so muscular that the defined muscles could be seen from two floors down. Hard, lean arms reached out toward a box and grabbed a T-shirt as I begged him to turn around—until my eyes found his ass.

Dear Lord.

My new neighbor was hot—or at least the back of him was.

Turn around, turn around, I silently begged.

The weather took that moment to remind me of its mighty power and sent a strong gust of wind whipping through the two houses. The curtain settled back in place, and I was once again left with shadows.

As the first raindrop fell, signaling the impending storm, I looked down at the once perfect garden that I had painstakingly kept alive as a tribute to my longtime friend and neighbor. It had been trampled on and was now ruined, and I felt the rage boiling back up to the surface.

Hot or not, my new neighbor was a plant-trampling jerk, and when I got home from work tomorrow, I'd make sure he knew it.

I'd also take a moment to see if that face of his matched his perfect back and ass.

Shut up, Liv.

Chapter Two

~Jackson~

"You're taking me where?" Noah asked once again, his voice taking on that edgy whine I'd grown to hate.

"She's just someone you can talk to—besides me," I offered with a shrug.

"A counselor, Dad? You said counselor before."

I sighed. "Okay, yes. She's a counselor, but she's a very good one. She's not a shrink or a doctor. She's just someone other than your dad. Look, between the move and a new school, I know a lot is going on right now. This hasn't been easy for either of us, especially you. I just thought it might be a good idea for you to have someone neutral."

"Neutral?" he asked, his eyebrows furrowing together in confusion.

"Yeah, you know, someone who won't cringe if you say you want to keep wearing your hair like that man-child singer...or if you want to talk about girls."

"This is not a Bieber haircut, Dad!" he huffed.

A hint of a smile escaped him, and I couldn't help but laugh.

"It's a skater cut," he added.

I threw my hands up in defeat. "Okay, okay. It's a skater cut. It's cool." He gave me a doubtful look, and I grinned. "Promise."

"What is she like?" he asked as we made our way out the door and toward the car.

"I don't know exactly. I did a bunch of research last night after you went to bed, and she came highly recommended on several boards. I called this morning, and it usually takes weeks, but I managed to get you in right away because she happened to have a cancellation."

"Hmm," was all I got in response. He pulled his knees up to his chest and buried his head in his phone.

When I'd made the decision to move from our hometown of Charleston to Richmond, I had finally caved and bought him a cell phone. I'd known he'd miss his friends back home and need a way to keep in touch. I just hadn't realized how in touch kids stayed nowadays. I was surprised his fingers hadn't fallen off from overuse.

I also wanted to slit my own wrists for using a phrase like *nowadays*.

God, I felt fucking old.

Eleven years of single parenthood had done an amazing job of aging me past my years. At thirty-four, I felt a good ten years older most days, and that was even after running and going to the gym regularly.

Maybe this fresh start in a new city would be exactly what I needed.

As I set the car in park in front of a small office building and killed the engine, I looked up at the sign that read *Family and Child Connections* and hoped it would be exactly what we both needed.

"This place looks kinda hippieish," Noah stated in displeasure as we made our way to the front entrance.

"What do you know about hippies?" I asked, taking in the wooden wind chimes and pewter fountain tucked away in a neatly kept small garden. It was the cheeriest office front I'd ever seen. I'd give him that.

"I don't know, but Jake's mom always said their next door neighbors were hippies, and they had those weird wooden things on their porch."

I rolled my eyes. "They're just wind chimes. Stop listening to your friends' narrow-minded parents."

"You dated her," he reminded me as we stepped up to the door.

"Don't remind me." I shuddered. "Come on, let's go in."

Those two weeks were the worst of my life, and that was saying something.

Jake was a baseball player and a good one, too. His mom, Helen, was one proud Southern mama. There had seemed to be only two subjects Helen understood—well, three maybe—Jake, baseball, and Jake and baseball together.

Like most men, I'd watched my fair share of sports, including baseball. Since those two weeks, I hadn't been able to see a game without dry-heaving.

It was a damn shame, too, because she had been mighty good in the sack—once she'd stopped talking. Hearing her scream my name had been the only time I actually enjoyed the sound of that woman's voice.

After several hellish dates, I'd finally come to the conclusion that no amount of sex was worth that. Her tear-stained eyes, full of disappointment and hurt, had also led me to further realize that I shouldn't date the mothers of my kid's friends.

It was too messy.

That had been over two years ago.

Besides the random bar hookups here or there, my dating life had become a little dry. Sahara Desert dry, in fact.

Perhaps here in this new place, I'd finally find someone who wasn't crazy or heartless, someone who didn't care about baseball, and someone who would love Noah like I did.

Hell, I'd settle for someone normal right about now.

It was the exact opposite of what I saw when I turned my head and came face to face with Miss Prescott. She was wearing a long flowing dress that looked like an Indian sari, and her dark hair tumbled down her back in a loose braid. Noah's words from earlier came to me, and I couldn't help but grin as the word *hippie* flashed across my mind.

"Hi, you must be—"

"Jackson," I said as an introduction, holding out my hand.

She stepped forward, her multicolored skirt swishing as she moved. The many bangles around her tiny wrist jingled as her hand met mine. Her chocolate brown eyes looked directly into me, warm and inviting, as she smiled.

She is breathtaking.

"I apologize. My secretary had to leave suddenly—food poisoning. It wasn't pretty. So, I have absolutely no idea what is going on or who is coming in. I have a friend coming in to help, but it will be a few minutes. Please bear with me through all the confusion."

Her gaze drifted over to Noah, who had taken a seat on the plush green sofa. His phone was laying on his lap, but his attention was focused on the woman in front of us.

"And who might you be?" she asked, walking forward to sit next to him.

"Noah," he said.

"I like your haircut, Noah. It's pretty cool."

"Thanks," he replied. His cheeks reddened slightly as a small smile tugged at the corner of his mouth.

"So, do you want to hang out for a little bit?" she asked.

"Uh…" His eyes roamed around, and he hesitantly looked at me.

"Don't worry. We're just hanging out today. We can do whatever you want—just you and me. I've got a sweet Xbox in my office. Wanna see?"

"Really?" His expression shifted to pure adoration.

Hippie girl had all sorts of surprises up her sleeve.

~Liv~

Xbox worked every time.

I looked down at my new young client and smiled. He was cute with sandy-blond hair and light-blue eyes that lit up when he spoke. His dad wasn't bad-looking either.

"Yep. Why don't you go in there and set everything up for us? I'll be along in just a second," I suggested.

Noah jumped off the couch in search of the video games, relief clearly written all over his boyish face. He'd probably been afraid that I was going to drill him for an hour straight.

That was not my style, especially with kids.

I liked to get down to their level and hang out with them. Once they felt comfortable, really comfortable with the environment I'd created for them, they would open up naturally. Nothing closed people off and clamped down their walls faster than forcing information out of them.

"So, Xbox, huh?" Jackson said, as he rocked back on his heels in front of me.

His accent was thicker than what was considered typical for Virginia. It was full and rich, and the words *Southern charm* came to mind when I heard him speak.

"Yeah, it seems to help—the boys at least," I said. "I have half a dozen dolls and other things in there, too, if the Xbox fails, but it's usually quite the crowd-pleaser."

He nodded silently before finally opening his mouth again. "I'm here because I want to know why—"

I quickly held up my hands. "Stop," I advised.

His head tilted to the side, and I watched his left eyebrow arch. It was quite cute, and I had to fight the grin threatening to make an appearance.

Damn it. It wasn't cute. It was sexy.

Jackson—whatever his last name was—was hot.

I hated when the dads were good-looking. It made it so much harder for me to concentrate.

I quickly glanced down, noticing the lack of a wedding ring on his hand.

Double damn it. I also hated when they were single.

"I don't want to know anything at this point. I like to go in blind," I insisted.

"What?"

"I'll have you complete paperwork while you're waiting for us. During the first session, I like to have one-on-one time with your child to get to know him and learn about his life from his perspective. If you front-load me with information about him, it will make me biased. Right now, he's a blank slate to me, and at least for today, I want to keep it that way. After all, isn't that how everyone meets?"

"Huh. Isn't that dangerous?" He folded his arms across his broad chest.

The crisp green button-down shirt stretched beautifully, making me wonder exactly what lay beneath all those buttons.

He caught me mid-wander and grinned.

"Dangerous how?" I asked, my eyes jumping up to meet his silvery gaze.

"What if the kid has a single word that makes him go bonkers? Or what if he instantly goes into seizures if he sees a clown on TV?"

I gave him a doubtful look. "Do any of those things happen to Noah?"

"No." He smiled.

"Well, I think we'll be just fine then. Besides, most kids and families who come to me aren't that severe. If you are curling into a ball when you hear the word *tiger*, you should probably see a doctor."

I thought he was about to offer up another flirty comeback when the door jingled, and Mia stepped inside.

"Hey," she whispered, tiptoeing behind the front desk.

"There's my backup," I said. "She'll get your paperwork for you. I'm going to go play a game on the Xbox."

I felt his eyes on me as I turned away.

"Are you any good?" he asked.

I swiveled back around, smiling. "Guess you'll have to wait and see."

~Jackson~

After I finished the unholy amount of paperwork, I shook my sore hand and walked back to the front counter to deposit my completed stack.

"So, you're the friend, huh?" I said.

The woman took the papers and began sorting them into different baskets.

"Yep, that's me." She smiled. "I'm Mia. I sometimes fill in during the summer months when she needs an extra hand. I leave all the major stuff for the professionals, but I can sort papers and answer phones. It gives me an excuse to get out of the house."

"Stay-at-home mom?" I guessed from her exhausted expression.

"Close." She laughed. "I'm a teacher during the school year, but yeah, during the summer I become a stay-at-home mom. Who knew taking care of one infant would be ten times more exhausting than a classroom full of little kids?"

I chuckled, resting my arms against the counter. "Well, I've never taught, but I have had my fair share of experience with infants, and there were days when I swore I could sleep for a millennium."

A small giggle escaped her lips, and then she lifted her hand to cover up a yawn. I moved around the room, looking at the art adorning the walls, and then I picked up a magazine.

"So, how long has she been doing this?"

"Who? Liv—I mean, Miss Prescott?" she corrected.

I nodded as I took my place back on the sofa.

"Well, she's been on her own for about two years I believe."

I started to flip through the fishing magazine, barely paying attention to it as I listened to Mia.

"Before that, she was a family counselor with a large organization downtown."

"How come she decided to branch off?" I asked, digging for more dirt on the beautiful woman currently playing video games with my son.

"It was always a dream of hers, and she finally saved up enough money to do so." She shrugged.

The door opened, and Noah and Miss Prescott reappeared.

"Hey, Dad!" he greeted.

"Hey," I answered, amazed by his enthusiasm.

"Liv has a ton of games—even *Grand Theft Auto*. She totally beat me the first time around, but I won the second game."

I was stunned stupid for a second or two before I came back online. "Awesome," I replied, looking up at Miss Prescott for a reaction.

Her arms were folded across her chest as she leaned against the doorframe. She smiled sweetly down at Noah as if she'd just hung out with her own kid rather than a patient she'd been paid to see.

"Why don't you hang out in there and play another round for a few more minutes? It will give me a little bit of time to meet your father."

"Okay!" Noah disappeared back into the room behind her.

I watched her step forward, her long lean legs peeking out from a slit in her dress.

"Why don't we go for a walk." she suggested. "I have a little garden out back where we can sit."

I suddenly had a picture of the two of us sitting in a garden, holding hands and chanting.

That's not what we're about to do, are we?

I looked at her with a bit of hesitation.

"Just talking." She laughed, raising her hands in surrender. "It must be the long dresses or the tattoo, but I get a man in here with a Southern accent, and suddenly he's looking at me like I'm going to sprout wings."

Wait—did she say tattoo?

How did I miss that?

"We'll be back in a few, Mia." She said, briefly tapping the desk with her fingernails as she walked by.

As her flowery scent brushed past me, it was then that I saw it— an Indian floral design full of color and vibrancy running over her left shoulder and disappearing into the fabric of her dress.

How far down does it go?

I caught up to her and we walked silently, side by side, around the building along a little pathway that led to a small garden tucked between the office buildings.

"The dentist next door thought I was crazy when I told him I wanted to plant a garden back here, but I think he likes it now. I catch him back here, eating his lunch every once in a while."

I took a look around and admired the way she'd grown vines to creep up the building, creating an intimate atmosphere that made me almost forget where I was.

"It's great," I said.

She motioned toward a chair, and I took a seat, watching her do the same. My foot started tapping like a jackhammer in anticipation of what she might say.

Was there something wrong with Noah?

Had I done everything wrong?

Shit, I'm a terrible parent.

I felt her hand on my knee, and I steadied.

"Whoa there. You look like you're about to explode," she said.

"Sorry, I'm nervous."

She smiled. "You have nothing to be nervous about, Jackson. Noah is a great kid, a perfectly normal kid."

I let out the breath I'd been holding for probably months. "Are you sure?"

She nodded. "Yeah. Parents tend to forget that kids can be affected by stress just like adults can. Moving, leaving his friends, puberty—it's a lot for a young boy to take on. He's just confused and acting out."

"That's what I kept telling myself, but I was so worried—"

"That you weren't enough?"

"He told you?" I asked.

She smiled warmly. "It doesn't take a genius to figure out that his mom has been out of the picture for a while. He didn't mention her once."

"She left when he was a newborn, and she hasn't been back since."

Rather than saying *I'm sorry* or giving me those eyes that most people do—the sad ones that people always thought passed for empathy, but they were really just more pathetic than anything—she just leaned back in her chair.

"Don't ever think you're not enough. He's doing great."

"So, are you saying he doesn't need therapy?" I asked.

She laughed. "I'm telling you that Noah is simply stressed, and like all stress, it will pass. He needs to learn how to work through it. Whether you choose to let me help with that or not is your decision, but I would never pressure you into therapy."

I gave her a dubious look. "You're not a very good saleswoman, Miss Prescott."

"If I were in this for the money, I would have become a psychiatrist. But then, I wouldn't have this garden, would I?" She raised her arms and tilted her head toward the rays of sun filtering down between the buildings.

This New Age counselor looked like a Greek goddess, and she'd planted a garden behind her office.

What else would this woman surprise me with today?

Chapter Three

~Liv~

Considering my last patient had gone late, I wasn't at all surprised when my phone started buzzing seconds after I'd walked through my front door that night.

"Hi, Mia," I answered, shuffling around the bags of groceries in my arms.

"You didn't even bother checking caller ID, did you?" she pressed.

I could hear the slight edge of laughter in her voice.

"Nope." I set the cloth grocery bags down on the counter before rubbing my wrists where the straps had dug into my skin.

"Am I really that predictable?" she asked.

I stared at the bags boasting the words, *I recycle. I'm awesome*, in bright, bold green font.

"Mmm…yes," I answered. "But I still love you."

"Well, if I'm that predictable, why did I call?"

"The hot dad," I said in a deadpan voice.

"Damn it!" she shouted, causing me to laugh. "I really am predictable. Oh well, I can live with it."

"Live with what?" a deep male voice asked in the background.

"I'm predictable," she said, answering Garrett's question.

"That thing you did last night wasn't predictable," I heard him say in the background, his voice taking on a rough tone.

Mia's shrill laughter came blaring through the speaker, and I briefly pulled my phone away from my ear.

"Ew-uh…come on! I'm, like, right here!" I begged as a growl echoed through the phone.

Seriously? A growl?

"Down, boy." She laughed. "Let me talk to Liv. I'll be off the phone in a few minutes, Garrett!"

"Five minutes."

Those two words were so heated that I almost had to fan myself.

Lucky bitch.

"Okay, and then I'm all yours," Mia finally said breathlessly.

I laughed. "You called me, remember?"

"What? Oh, right! The hot dad!"

"Yeah. What about him?" I said, playing it off with a bit of nonchalance.

"What about him? He was gorgeous, and he couldn't keep his eyes off of you."

Really?

"He was probably staring at me like a person would look at a rare bird in the zoo. I was just something exotic and different."

"There was that definitely. I'm used to seeing people look at you in that way, but no, this was different. He was into you—or at least, he was attracted to you."

"Isn't that the same thing?" I asked.

"No, absolutely not. You can be attracted to someone but not be into that person. The sexy celebrity on the cover of this weeks' People Magazine? Yeah, he's attractive, but I'm not into him."

Note to self: Go back to store and buy People Magazine.

I found myself nodding even though she wasn't around to see it. "Okay, I get that. But none of this matters. I don't date my clients."

"Most of your clients are under the age of eighteen," she scoffed.

"You know what I mean—no entanglements. It's unethical."

"Yeah, yeah," she answered. "But you have to agree, he was hot."

A wicked grin escaped my lips. "He was the sexiest damn thing to ever walk through my door," I admitted.

"Good. Well, at least he'll make good eye-candy for a while."

Other than a noncommittal, "Mmm," I didn't answer.

Mia had signed a nondisclosure to work in my office. She understood that what happened in my office stayed there, but I would still make sure to keep all my clients' personal business to myself. Whether or not Jackson and Noah would come back to me was up in the air, but explaining that to Mia would require giving her more information on Noah than I was willing to divulge.

"Hey, you never told me about your new neighbors," she said, obviously catching on to my silence.

"There's not much to tell. I haven't met them yet. But I plan to— soon."

"That sounds ominous."

I huffed out a frustrated breath. "They destroyed Mrs. Reid's flower garden between our houses."

"The one you've been maintaining for her?" she asked.

"Yeah."

"That's awful. Who would be so careless? What are you going to do?"

"Put my groceries away. Have a relaxing nice dinner, and then I'm going to march over there and introduce myself to the smoldering asshole."

"Smoldering?" she questioned.

"Never mind."

~Jackson~

I was never going to move again—ever.

I'd die old and fat in this little old house with that creepy toilet themed wallpaper, and shag carpet. My ass was never leaving.

How did two people accumulate so much shit?

Just when I'd thought I cleared through a decent amount of boxes, I'd turn around to find more waiting for me. *Were they multiplying?*

"Hey, Noah! You want to offer a hand here, kid?" I hollered up the stairs as I arched and stretched my sore, stiff back.

There was no answer.

"Noah!"

"What?" he yelled back.

This was what life had become in our house—screaming between floors.

"Come down and help unpack some of these boxes!"

He miraculously appeared at the top of the stairs with his phone in hand. "Do I have to?"

"No, it was just a suggestion. Carry on," I remarked sarcastically.

He rolled his eyes and trotted down the stairs.

"Do me a favor, and put the phone away for ten minutes. Do you think you could manage that?"

"Yeah, okay," he answered as he swung his dark blond hair out of his eyes.

"So, how was your meeting with Miss Prescott?" I asked as I cut open another box labeled *Living Room*.

"It was okay." He sat down next to me and started shuffling through a box.

Kids are so descriptive.

"Okay? Just okay? You nearly bounced out of there like you'd just visited an Xbox convention."

"She's just fun to hang out with. She's easy to talk to I guess."

"Well, what kinds of things did she talk to you about?" I pressed, pulling a few knickknacks out of tissue paper and placing them on the mantel.

"I don't know. Stuff."

"Like?"

"Like, just stuff, Dad, okay?" He popped up to a standing position, shoving his palms in his pockets.

I held my hands up, waving my white flag, as I tried to calm him. "Okay, no more questions. Sorry."

"I'm gonna go back upstairs," he mumbled.

I nodded, feeling defeated, as I watched his lanky frame flee from my presence.

Taking a deep breath, I tried to remind myself of what Miss

Prescott had said earlier that day. Everyone handled stress differently—even kids. I had to believe he'd come around, and I'd eventually
see a glimpse of the carefree boy I once knew.

I began to break down the box I'd just unloaded when the doorbell echoed throughout the house.

That was something else to add to the list of things that needed
to be fixed.

My grandmother couldn't have gone with a standard buzzer or
even one of those normal ding-dong chimes. No, she had gone all out
and bought the most annoying doorbell ever created. Every time the
little button was pressed, a classical symphony would play through
the tiny electrical speaker. If Mozart knew his music would one day
sound that horrid, he probably would have burned every last sheet of
paper he owned.

"Coming," I called, putting the blade back into the X-Acto knife.
I set it down on the couch and jogged over to the door just as silence
finally filled the house once again.

Grabbing the ornate handle, I pulled the door open and found
myself face-to-face with an armful of flowers—and legs that went on
for days.

"Do you have any idea how much time I spent on these?" a shrill
yet somewhat familiar voice shouted from behind the flowers.

"Um..."

"Don't you have any respect for the former owner of this house?"
she asked.

That piqued my interest. "What do you mean?" I reached out
my hand and slowly lowered the flowers to try to find the face that
matched the long legs I'd been admiring.

I got about halfway when recognition blossomed across the mystery woman's face.

Flowers and soil crashed to the entryway, and I found myself gazing down at the raven-haired beauty I hadn't been able to stop thinking about.

"Miss Prescott? I didn't realize you made house calls...and
brought flowers," I joked, looking down at the mess she'd made on
my doorstep.

This further cemented my beliefs that I needed to stick with my plan of finding a nice, normal girl-next-door type. This was what happened when I sought out something different and exotic. I ended up a single father with a pile of dead flowers at my front door.

"You!" she exclaimed. "You're my new neighbor?"

Confusion suddenly spiraled through me, and I looked around the neighborhood like it would spring forth some clue I hadn't noticed. "You live…here?" I asked.

She turned slightly and pointed to the house directly next door. "Right there."

Our eyes met, and I felt the blood draining from my face. "We're next-door neighbors?"

"It appears so."

"Fuck me," I whispered.

"What?"

"Nothing," I said, shaking my head. "Why don't you come inside? We obviously have some things to discuss."

She glanced down at the flowers strewed all over my front stoop and proceeded to step over the mess with her head held high. I couldn't help the slight chuckle that escaped my parted lips.

"Oh, shut up," she said. A tiny grin appeared as she passed me.

"Sorry about the mess. I'm starting to think I might never unpack everything." We passed through the entryway into the living room and I watched her eyes take everything in.

Swimming in their depths were genuine emotions I had yet to understand. Her fingers trailed over the wood trim of the furniture and ornate fireplace mantel lovingly as if they had memories and tenderness. "Why does it all need to be unpacked at once?" she finally asked. "Is there any reason it all needs to be put away right this minute?"

"No."

"Then, take some time to settle," she suggested, finally picking a place on the old love seat my grandmother had owned for decades. Once again, her fingers quietly traced the floral pattern, over and over like a prayer.

"I just thought it would be better for Noah if everything had a place right away," I admitted, not really sure why I was telling this woman anything. She'd just accosted me with plants.

"What Noah needs is you, plain and simple. If you are stressed, he will be stressed. Take a moment, and enjoy this new life of yours."

"I thought you came over here to yell at me?" I quipped,

"Occupational hazard," she admitted with a shrug, before adding, "Has he ever been to Richmond?"

"Only when he was younger and then briefly this year for my grandmother's funeral. This was her house."

"You're Mrs. Reid's grandson?" she asked, her eyes round with surprise.

"Yeah. Why? Did you know her?"

She smiled sweetly, looking downward as if seeking out a fond memory from the recesses of her mind. "Yeah, Mrs. Reid and I were very attached to each other. I've lived in this neighborhood for several years, and…well, let's just say she became like a grandmother to me."

Her eyes lifted once again, and I watched her wipe away a lone tear.

"I didn't know. I'm sorry. I haven't been around much and I don't remember much of the funeral. It's all a blur."

"I wasn't there," she answered. "My practice, as well as most of my clients, was still fairly new. I hated the idea of having to cancel on them. I felt terrible about missing the funeral."

"I'm sure she would have understood," I offered, finally moving across the room to take a seat across from her. Leaning forward, I folded my hands and took a deep breath. "Sorry about the flowers," I said. "I'll replace them."

She waved her hands in front of her, shaking her head. "No, it's all right. I'll take care of it."

I nodded and watched her fiddle with the bracelets around her wrist. They caught the light from the lamp, sending shimmery streaks across her face and skin.

"I guess this puts a kink in our former relationship, doesn't it?" I finally asked.

She looked up at me, and I was once again startled by her natural beauty. Her rich dark brown eyes were the color of cocoa, and her hair fell across her shoulders like ebony waves of silk. The desire to reach out and touch her was nearly beyond my control, yet I somehow managed to stay put.

She might be the girl next door, but she was definitely not my girl next door. I needed normal and Liv with the vibrant tattoo and crazy flower beds seemed to be anything but.

"Unfortunately, yes. I'm sorry. I think it would be wise for you to seek other counseling options for Noah, if he is still in need of them. Having me next door will only confuse him of my role in his life. If I had the choice, I'd rather be his neighbor and friend than his counselor."

I chuckled briefly. "You just really don't like to be paid, do you?"

She laughed. "It's not about money to me, Mr. Reid. I've had money, and it does nothing for the soul."

"Call me Jackson, Miss Prescott."

"Only if you call me Liv."

"Deal."

"And what do you do, Jackson, to feed your soul?" she asked, her sculpted dark eyebrow rising in challenge.

"I'm a lawyer," I answered.

She grinned as she rose from the love seat. I followed her to the door and watched as she stopped and turned toward me.

"That feeds your wallet, not your soul, Jackson. Figure out the difference."

As I clicked the lock in place, her parting words swam around in my head, reminding me of a time when I'd sworn to make the world a better place. Through my law degree, I was going to change the world one client at a time.

Unfortunately, single fathers didn't have time for such lofty dreams.

Chapter Four

~Liv~

I loved Saturdays.

There was nowhere to go and nothing to do. When the weather warmed up like it did during the summer months, there was nothing better than waking up to a window full of sunshine and a day full of opportunity.

Before I'd started my own practice, my life had been less structured. My schedule had been up in the air and never the same. I enjoyed the regular schedule that having my own practice provided. I did, however, miss running errands at eleven thirty on a Tuesday morning when no one else was out but tired stay-at-home moms and other random people like me. Now, I instead had to do my shopping late at night, or risk going on the weekends when the lines were out the door, and patience was nearly nonexistent.

But not today.

Today, I had nothing planned but some serious time with my latest paperback and a little sunshine.

After grabbing my purple robe off the back of my door, I loosely wrapped it around my body. I walked downstairs and ran my hand along the polished wooden banister, loving the way the old grain felt against the pads of my fingers.

This part of town was historic, dating back over one hundred years when Confederate soldiers roamed the city. My own home still had the original hardwood flooring and much of the tin ceiling the first owners had put in when it was built. I'd added my own touches here and there, bridging the modern and old together with bright colors and funky artwork, but it still had its old-world charm.

Stepping into the kitchen, I pulled out a tin of one of my favorite blends of loose tea. It was strong and black with a hint of fruit for the morning, and it was the perfect way to wake up. I set it aside and fired up the kettle, and then I pulled out some Greek yogurt and fresh fruit for breakfast.

With my freshly brewed tea and yogurt, I sat down in my favorite spot—a cozy little armchair I'd rescued from a secondhand store—and I grabbed the book I was eager to finish. Snuggling down in the red velour chair, I sighed contentedly.

This was heaven.

I got about five seconds of heaven before it was all jacked up.

Boisterous loud laughter and shouting echoed from outside my window, causing my Zen-like calm to transform instantly into annoyance.

Pushing the curtains back, I found the root of my problem. Several men clothed in ratty jeans and T-shirts that all displayed the same faded logo were moving around with what looked like pitchforks, digging up dirt and mulch.

"My flower beds!" I screamed, suddenly realizing what they were up to.

Leaving my tea and breakfast behind, I marched out my front door, dressed in only a flimsy nightgown and robe, ready to defend the flowers I'd so painstakingly maintained.

Again.

"What the hell are you guys doing?" I shouted, rushing over to stop them.

Four sets of startled eyes settled on mine. No words came as they looked me up and down, obviously trying to figure out why a crazy half-naked lady was standing in front of them.

My hip jutted out, and I folded my arms across my chest in annoyance. Mia would call it my bitch stance.

I looked down, noticing the bags of chemicals and horrific mulch that was dyed an unnatural bright red color.

Horrible.

One of the men, the oldest-looking one, took a step forward, his hands going up, as he tried to explain what they were doing.

I got very little other than they were hired to do a job, but when he pointed to the house behind him, I knew exactly who to blame.

This was Jackson's doing.

I quickly apologized, smiled, and walked off toward the front door of my new neighbor.

If he was going to interrupt my perfect morning, I would return the favor.

After several loud knocks on his brass knocker, I heard his voice moving closer.

"Hold on a minute!"

He sounded annoyed.

Good. That made two of us.

When the door opened, I was ready for battle. I was not, however, ready for Jackson to be half naked. The speech I'd written, edited, and perfected in my head as I stomped over and waited for him to appear suddenly disappeared from my brain as visions of sculpted abs and perfectly defined pecs danced in my head.

Dressed in a pair of loose-fitted linen pajama bottoms that were low enough to be nearly illegal, I found myself almost leaning forward, hoping to catch a glimpse of what might follow that gorgeous V that disappeared into the waistband of his dark blue pants.

My gaze meandered up his body, and I realized he was returning the favor as his eyes wandered over my thin robe and the abundance of bare skin peeking out.

"Can I help you, Liv?" he asked in a slow Southern drawl that seemed a whole lot sexier with him standing there, shirtless.

"Um…" I answered.

He smiled lazily and leaned against the doorframe. Masculine thick arms folded across his chest as he tucked one leg across the other.

I thought the slow cocky smile was what tipped me over the edge, reminding me of my cup of tea that was currently getting cold on my coffee table and the uneaten breakfast I hadn't touched because this man with the crooked grin couldn't follow simple directions.

"You," I said, pointing a finger toward him, "were supposed to let me handle the flower beds."

He looked down at my accusatory finger and burst into laughter. "Is that what this is all about? A thank-you card would have sufficed. You didn't have to march over here first thing in the morning." His eyes moved quickly down my body as his smile intensified. "Although, I don't mind the view."

"Ugh!" I yelled. "You really are a lawyer, aren't you?"

His smile faltered as his arms dropped to his sides. "What the hell is that supposed to mean?"

"It means," I said, angrily pushing my finger into his chest, "that you are overbearing and arrogant, and you think everything can be fixed with a little money."

Grabbing my finger with his large hand, he stepped forward, getting close to me. I could smell the woodsy scent of his aftershave.

"Look, I know you think I trampled those flowers, and I'm sorry. I have no idea what happened, but I'm guessing it was the movers since they were the ones here the day of the move—not me. You were upset, so I fixed it. I really thought you would appreciate the help."

"But I didn't need you to help me. I was going to take care of it. It was my thing, and you are currently ruining it with chemicals and tacky mulch."

"You're kind of a pain in the ass," he said slowly, his eyes blazing with fire.

"You're exasperating."

He stepped inside, his smug grin firmly back in place. "I hope you enjoy your flowers, sweetheart."

"You're not going to fix them?"

"Why, I believe I already did," he answered in a sweet voice, his accent thicker and high-pitched. "You have a nice day."

With that, he shut the door in my face.

~Jackson~

"That woman is a menace!" I shouted as soon as I saw her door slam closed from my perch behind the curtains.

"Whatcha doin', Dad?"

I stood and turned to find Noah standing in the entryway of the living room, looking at me with a mix of curiosity and amusement.

"Nothing," I muttered. "But that woman," I said, pointing toward her house, "is insane. Do you know what she did?"

He shook his head and plopped down on the love seat. His hair fell in his eyes, and he brushed it away before adjusting his bright blue skater shirt and kicking off his shoes.

"Who? Liv? It's kind of awesome that she turned out to be our neighbor, huh?"

"Yeah, really awesome."

"So, why is she crazy? I thought she was really nice—and pretty," he added shyly.

"The pretty ones are always the craziest," I warned. "I called the best landscapers in the area and paid extra to have them come out at the last minute on a Saturday to fix her precious flower bed that the movers had messed up. And what did she do?"

"Uh—" he managed to say before I cut him off.

"She yelled at me. She told me I was overbearing and…and a lawyer!" I threw my hands up in the air in frustration before finally sitting down on the sofa across from my son.

"Well, you are a lawyer. She was right about that," he chimed in.

"That's not the point."

"Okay."

"We need to find a gardening store," I announced suddenly. A wicked genius idea started to formulate in my head.

"Um…okay. Why?" He glanced out the window to catch a glimpse of the men still working outside.

"Because we are going to do a bit of gardening of our own today," I answered. "Come on, let's go."

I may have received a few odd looks as we roamed the aisles of the gardening store, and I tried to keep the maniacal laughing to a minimum.

I said I tried.

When I told the staff member who had pulled the short straw and was sent over to help us what my plan was, he eagerly agreed to help us.

An hour later, we had enough supplies to fill up my entire truck bed.

Catching Liv's stunned face as Noah and I began hauling bag after bag of bright red mulch out of the truck onto the grass of the backyard was worth every goddamn penny.

"What the hell is this?" she asked as she stepped off her patio and began walking toward the edge of the fence.

I thought seeing her in that flimsy robe had been a treat. Watching her walk up to me in a bikini had me nearly swallowing my tongue.

But this woman was the enemy now, and I had to keep my wits about me.

That meant keeping my thoughts to myself and my dick in my pants.

But damn, she was swinging her hips with her sun-kissed tan breasts peeking out of her bright orange top. Then, there was the belly-button ring, glinting and winking at me with each sway of her hips.

Focus. Must focus.

I shook my head and stared straight ahead, making sure my eyes wouldn't waver again.

"We're gardening," I answered sweetly.

"Again?"

"Yes. Your love for gardening really brought out a side of me that I didn't know existed. So, I decided to just go for it, you know?" I motioned toward the stacks of mulch and rows of various flowers that Noah and I had picked out. Nothing matched—seriously, nothing. There was no rhyme or reason to the plants we'd selected. I was betting half of them would die in a matter of weeks.

I was actually hoping for it. It would make the victory of this day so much sweeter.

"Is that what I think it is?" She pointed to my crowning achievement of the day as it was peeking out of a plastic bag.

"Oh, yes," I answered, grinning. I bent down, pulled my new friend out, and firmly planted him into the lawn.

"Oh my God, that's hideous. You're not actually going to put that in your yard?"

I looked down at the bright pink plastic flamingo. "Oh, yes, I am. And he has an entire family in the truck. We couldn't separate him from his mama." I grinned.

"You're insane!" she screamed.

"Right back at you, babe."

With that, she turned around and stormed off, and I enjoyed the view of her ass and hips swaying all the way back to her house. The slamming of her door and the high-pitched scream were priceless.

Game, set, match.

Chapter Five

~Liv~

Good friends were always there to listen and lend a helping hand.

Great friends did all of the above but also showed up at your doorstep bearing wine and food.

I had great friends.

I pulled my front door open and found my three best friends standing there with beaming smiles on their faces. "I am so glad all of you managed to find babysitters tonight!" I exclaimed with excitement.

"Babysitters?" Leah replied. "Who needs babysitters when we have husbands?"

"And grandmothers!" Clare chimed in, raising a bottle of merlot in enthusiasm.

"Well, let's get this party started!" I said, ushering them in.

Mia followed the others inside and gave a wink as I helped her with her load of food and beverages.

They gathered around the kitchen island, and they all sat down on the comfy barstools I'd picked out from an eclectic boutique down the street as I began popping corks and setting out trays of food.

"So, we're all mad at you, Liv," Leah said, her fingers grabbing a handful of chips.

"Yeah, totally mad," Clare agreed, pulling handfuls of cheese off the tray.

"Why? What the hell did I do this time?"

Being the only childless, single one, it could be anything really. Shaving my legs two days in a row could elicit a riot among them.

"Your hot new neighbor?" Clare said, raising an eyebrow. "We saw a glimpse of him as we were walking up. He was shirtless while working up a sweat. Don't tell me you haven't peeked outside your window."

I sensed my change in color because I could already feel the heat of anger radiating through my pores.

"That neighbor," I stated, "is a jackass."

"Did you see that back, Liv?" Leah asked. "I think I need to go to the window to refresh my memory again!" She hopped off her chair and took off running.

"Don't you dare, Leah James! I'll tell your husband you were checking out other guys!" I screamed, threatening her.

"Ha!" she shouted. "Declan is too cocky to care. He knows he's better-looking than any other man out there."

"He's not wrong," I muttered.

Leah's husband was a god among men. A former movie star turned director, he had once held the hearts and panties of nearly every woman in America. He had been the quintessential untamable man until he'd met Leah. Now, he only had eyes for her. Their love was like a fairy tale—well, the R-rated, super-sexy kind. But still, it was a fairy tale of sorts.

"I mean, seriously, Liv. Look at that eye-candy you literally have right out your window. Why aren't you glued to this plate of glass, eating popcorn and posting Instagram photos?"

The others joined us at the window, and they'd even brought the snacks and wine. Apparently, my sweaty, half-naked neighbor had been chosen as our form of entertainment tonight.

"Because he's a jerk."

"So? Does staring require talking to him?" Leah asked.

"No."

"Then, it doesn't really matter."

"I still hate him."

"Didn't this guy move in, like, a few days ago?" Clare sipped from her glass of water.

"Wait a hot second," Mia said, her eyes narrowing, as she took a step closer toward the window. "Holy shit!" she exclaimed, causing me to nearly spit out my wine from the rare use of profanity vacating her lips. "Is that the hot dad from your—" She stopped, turning to me, unsure if it was okay to finish.

I nodded. "Yes."

Clare and Leah turned toward the two of us in obvious confusion.

"A little update would be appreciated," Clare said sweetly.

"I met Jackson, my neighbor, and his son, Noah, at my office yesterday—before I knew they were my neighbors." My face went blank as I waited for the two of them to piece everything together.

Their eyebrows furrowed in confusion, and I watched Clare's gaze cast downward until her eyes suddenly shot upward.

"Oh my God! The son was a patient of yours?"

"Bingo!" I said.

"Well, that's slightly awkward, but it doesn't explain why you feel such an immense hostility toward the father," Leah commented.

Setting my wine glass down on the bookshelf below the window, I pointed. "There? Do you see what I'm pointing at?"

"The flower bed? Did you redo it? It looks different from the last time I was here," Clare said.

"No, I did not redo it," I muttered. "His movers trampled all over it and ruined it."

Mia's hand fell on my shoulder. "I'm sorry, babe. I know those flowers meant a lot to you. So, I'm guessing the talk didn't go well?"

"I thought it did, but I guess we didn't exactly understand each other. He's Mrs. Reid's grandson, so I assumed he would appreciate the idea of restoring it back to its former glory. Apparently, money is all that matters to him, and I woke up this morning to find my flower bed being completely redone with chemicals and this horrid red mulch. It looks nothing like it did before. I could have saved some of those poor plants."

"I'm sure you could have," Leah echoed, giving me a warm smile.

"That's not all," I said softly.

"Of course not." Mia laughed.

"I might have marched over there and yelled at him—a lot."

They just laughed, not surprised at all by my reaction. I guessed I wasn't known for tact.

"Perhaps I was a little rude," I admitted. "But then, he called me crazy, and went out and did that!" I pointed to his backyard.

Mia snorted. "Is that a flamingo?"

"Yes, and there are about five more back there somewhere. Oh, and more red mulch."

"You know, it's really doesn't look that—" Clare started to say.

"Don't finish that sentence if you want to live past your first trimester, Clare," I said.

Everyone's eyes widened as Mia and Leah spun around to face Clare.

"How did you know?" Clare asked me.

"I uncorked a bottle of that chocolate wine you love so much, and you haven't touched it. Add that to the fact that you're stuffing cheese in your mouth at an alarming rate…it can mean only one thing."

Her eyes moistened with unshed tears. "We just found out this week," she gushed, her voice becoming heavy and full of emotion.

This would be Clare's third child.

Lucky number three.

Clare and Logan had gotten married before I knew them, but I'd been told the harrowing story of how they came together. Clare had lost her first husband to brain cancer, and she'd been left to raise their infant daughter, Maddie, on her own. Several years later, in an ER room, she'd met Logan, and the rest was history. They'd had their own share of ups and downs, including Logan's own battle with cancer, but they'd managed to pull through. Several years and another child later, they were still solid and strong. They constantly amazed me with the enormity of love they had for each other and their growing family.

"How's Dr. McSteamy doing with the news?" I asked as we all huddled together.

"Like any doctor would with the same news. He's over the moon and going slightly insane." Clare laughed.

"Triple-checking your vitamins again?" Leah asked.

"Oh, yes," Clare answered.

"Well, you know what this means?" Mia said.

"What?" we all responded in unison.

"We have a heck of a lot more wine to drink now!"

Laughter filled the house as we made our way back to the kitchen where we celebrated the newest addition to our growing family.

A few years ago, I'd had hardly anyone left in the world I could turn to. The little old woman who lived next door to me had become the closest thing I had to a friend or family member. Now, thanks to Mia and Garrett and the women surrounding me, I had an entire support system. The Finnegan family had a way of taking in strays like me and making them feel almost whole again.

It was a feeling I hadn't experienced since I walked away from my own family years ago—or actually, they'd walked away from me.

Either way, the lines of communication had been severed for far too long.

Much wine and food was consumed as we all sat around the kitchen, catching up on our lives and families. As the merlot began to buzz in our system, the conversation came full circle.

"So, how are we going to get back at Mr. Hot and Sweaty?" Leah asked picking up a brownie from the picked over tray.

I stuck to my veggies and hummus, throwing in some cheese for protein. "What do you mean?"

"You can't let him win, Liv."

"It's a contest?"

"Obviously. Don't you see that? He's goading you with the backyard crap, and now, the ball is in your court. You have to do something."

"That is seriously childish!"

"Well, what do you expect? He's a man!" Clare laughed.

"So, if I don't respond, I lose?"

"Yep," they all answered in unison.

"Men are idiots."

"What if you replaced all the gas in his car with water?" Clare said, excitedly clapping her hands together.

We all stared at her blankly.

Her ivory white complexion blushed as she looked back at us. "What?"

"That's just evil and also probably illegal." Leah just shook her head. "It's always the quiet ones you have to worry about."

"Okay, anyone have an idea that won't cause permanent damage and land us in jail?" Mia asked.

Clare's head fell to the counter as she laughed hysterically.

"We could TP his house tonight! Declan and I have done that before," Leah offered.

"Whoa there. Hold up. Is this something you two do on date nights? Do I need to set up security cameras?" I laughed.

She grinned. "It was when we were dating. We TP'd my ex-boy-friend's house."

She sighed dreamily, as I rolled my eyes and snickered.

"Okay, toilet paper party it is!" Mia exclaimed. "Let's go to the store! Clare is driving because the rest of us are wasted!"

Oh boy, this is going to be a disaster.

~Jackson~

My backyard looked like a landscaper's worst nightmare.

It was fucking awesome.

As I finished cleaning up and putting things away, I couldn't help the grin spreading across my face. I hadn't had this much fun in far too long.

I should probably be focusing on the fact that the current shift in my rather boring life all revolved around the type of woman I swore I'd never pursue, yet I couldn't seem to stop thinking about her.

Yeah, I should be thinking about that.

Instead, I continued grinning like a damn fool.

Throwing the last empty bag of bright red mulch into the trash, I threw the lid on top, grabbed my shirt off the patio chair and headed for the back door.

Liv's house was lit up, an inviting warm glow coming from the first floor. Female laughter seeped out of the walls and into my ears as I caught a glimpse of women standing around her kitchen.

They probably had no idea that I'd seen them out of the corner of my eye, all huddled together by the window while watching me rake out the last of the mulch.

Liv had been no exception. Her eyes had been glued to me as I worked under the hot sun. It had taken every last ounce of my will power I had not to turn around, walk over to the back door and show her just how neighborly I could be.

But every path that started with Liv or any woman like her would end in disaster.

I should know. I was a survivor of one, and I was never going back for seconds.

Letting the storm door swing close behind me, I walked past the laundry closet and dropped off my sweaty shirt that I'd abandoned hours ago into the washing machine. Then, I headed for the stairs and climbed two at a time.

I came to a halt at the first door. "Noah!" I yelled.

There was no answer. I looked around at the clothes scattered across the bathroom floor and the mess of toothpaste and hair products all over the counter.

"Noah Wilson Reid!" I hollered again.

"What?" he answered back, poking his head out of the dark cave he called a room.

"What is all this?" I pointed to the floor and countertop.

"A bathroom?" he answered sarcastically.

I was not amused. "Clean this up—now." I stalked off into the master bedroom, which was still decorated in pink rose wallpaper, and I began stripping off my shoes and shorts. Walking into the adjoining bathroom, I turned the water on as hot as I could stand it and stepped into the spray, letting it pound against my aching muscles, as I waited for my anger to abate.

It was just a mess, not the end of the world.

I braced myself against the shower wall as memories of my little boy came rushing in. I could see him stacking little wooden blocks in neat piles.

"Why do you do that?" I'd asked as I watched him organize his toys.

"Because I like to know where all my favorite things are," he'd answered matter-of-factly.

He'd been the neat and tidy one. I'd been the envy of every parent around because the words, *Clean your room*, never had to be said in our house. His room had been as neat as a pin. He might have been borderline OCD maybe, but my little boy was very particular.

It was no longer like that.

And he wasn't my little boy anymore—or at least he was trying desperately not to be.

This growing-up thing was driving me into an early grave, and it was ten times harder going through it all alone.

I quickly finished showering and threw on a pair of jeans and a T-shirt before heading downstairs.

This was our first Saturday night in our new home in a brand-new city. I should have planned something.

Instead, I was boiling water for mac and cheese and flipping through the channels, looking for a movie we could watch.

I'd get my shit together next week. After I got settled into my new firm and had a few more boxes unpacked, we'd properly introduce ourselves to the city we'd adopted as home.

For tonight, it looked like comic book characters would be our entertainment.

"Hey, Noah, *The Avengers* is on!"

That one sentence managed to get him downstairs quicker than anything I'd said in days.

As he settled into the sofa, completely immersed in what was going on in front of him, I shook my head and walked back to the kitchen to assemble our meal.

"Guess I did something right," I mumbled, feeling proud I'd stuck to my guns and never allowed a TV in his room.

If I had, he'd have no reason to come down here, except to eat. At least I could hold *The Avengers* over his head, so I could manage to squeeze a few hours in with him even if no talking was involved.

After finishing up in the kitchen, I handed him a large bowl of mac and cheese, and we both dug in. Once we were both equally stuffed, I returned the empty dishes to the sink and began to load them into the dishwasher.

"Hey, Noah, can I get you to take out the trash?" I asked, poking my head out of the kitchen.

"Do I have to?" he whined, his eyes never leaving the TV.

"Would I be asking otherwise?"

He huffed and pressed the pause button on the DVR remote before shuffling his feet all the way to the trash can. After several more frustrated puffs of air, I heard him shuffle out the back door.

Finishing the dishes, I dried my hands and shook my head. *Oh, the woes of being a child.*

I took the few seconds of quiet time to quickly check my email and go over my agenda for Monday. Although the first reason we had moved up to Richmond was because my grandmother had left this house to me in her will, the second reason was the number of job opportunities awaiting me here.

We had moved from Charleston, South Carolina. It was a fairly large area, and since passing the bar after law school, I'd had a great job there, working as an attorney. But I had itched for more, and I'd felt like I was suffocating. I'd wanted something bigger and better. Being from an area where everyone had known my name since before I was born, there had seemed to be this unwritten hierarchy to how life worked—you had to pay your dues, honor your superiors, and wait your turn. Hard work paid off. That was what my parents had always taught me. Then, somewhere along the way, I'd discovered it didn't always work that way.

During my senior year, my best friend had managed to land the coveted scholarship to one of the top schools. Maybe it was a coincidence that he was also the football coach's son, but when putting the two of us side by side, I'd beat him every time. Last year, I had been up for a major promotion, and I'd watched as it was handed to one of the cousins of a judge from a few counties over. That was probably another coincidence.

I was sure coincidences like that happened everywhere, in every county and every walk of life, but I wouldn't be the same person after moving outside of Charleston. Here, I wasn't the son of Mr. and Mrs. Reid, and I wasn't the guy who had gotten screwed over by the one girl everyone had warned him to stay away from.

In Richmond, I was a blank slate.

It was exactly what I needed.

I just hoped it would be what Noah needed as well.

I looked up from the papers on my desk and found the couch empty and the TV still paused.

How long did it take for one child to take out the trash?

After walking toward the back door, I turned the knob and stuck my head out, looking for signs of Noah. The faint sounds of laughter whispered through the wind, and I immediately perked up, stepping outside as my eyes danced around the backyard.

I snuck around the edge of the house and then came to an abrupt halt. Under the cover of night, Noah and Liv were huddled together. The moonlight cast a soft glow on her face, illuminating her smile, as she looked down at my son.

"You're going to TP our house?" Noah asked.

"Well, we were." She laughed quietly. "Do you…maybe want to help us?"

"No way! Could I?" he asked.

I shook my head in disbelief. *Traitor.*

"Of course you can! Have you ever TP'd a house?"

He shook his head no, and I saw her smile shine back at him under the moonlight. "Okay then, we need to teach you how to do it first."

I leaned against the house and watched them.

She was going to TP my house, like a middle school adolescent girl, and now, she was bringing my son in on it. She handed him a large white roll, and he looked down at it, his face lighting up like he'd never seen toilet paper before in his life.

"There's a certain way to do it?" he asked.

"According to my friend Leah, yes. I'm a first timer as well. Come on, let me introduce you to everyone!"

She took his hand and pulled him along to join her gang of misfits while I continued to lean against the house in amazement.

I had two options. I could follow them, break up the fun, and thus ruin my son's night. Or I could go back into the house and deal with the royal mess in the morning—and lose to a girl.

I let out a huff as I trudged back into the house.

Liv might have won this round, but it would be her last.

46

Chapter Six

~Liv~

"What is that horrible light shining through the window?" I groaned. Squinting, I pulled the sofa pillow over my head and buried my face further into the cushion.

"That would be called the sun, babe," Clare replied brightly.

"Someone make it stop!" Mia whined from somewhere across the room.

I lifted the pillow and looked up to find Leah shuffling into the living room.

"I'm seriously regretting that last bottle of wine," Leah said as she haphazardly pulled her messy blonde hair into a bun. She ducked down to peek out the kitchen window, and a wide grin curved across her face. "But I definitely don't regret that. Ladies, come look at our masterpiece."

We all jumped up, even the three of us who were sporting epic hangovers made our way to the window. The Reid house was now a brilliant white spectacle, covered in two-ply as far as the eye could see.

"Damn, we did a good job." I laughed.

"I can't believe his kid helped us," Leah chimed in, shaking her head.

"Helped?" I said. "He was practically the ring leader by the end."

"He really is adorable," Clare commented, a warm smile spreading across her face.

"Yeah, he is. He's really sweet," I said.

"I can't wait to hear his dad's reaction," Leah chimed in. Someone's stomach growled loudly and attention quickly turned from the window to breakfast.

I moved around the kitchen, opening several cupboards and pulled out a variety of cereal boxes.

"I'm sure I'll be hearing from him soon." I grinned. *Maybe he'll show up shirtless.*

"For someone who can't stand to be around him, you look awfully happy about that," Mia said, a yawn cutting through her words and making them almost inaudible.

I scoffed, "No, he's still a jerk. Besides, I don't have time for annoying Southern boys."

"Of course not. You have Victor." Mia rolled her eyes.

"Who's Victor?" Leah and Clare asked at the same time.

"Her flavor of the month," Mia said.

"He's not my flavor of the month!"

"Well then, what is he?" she asked, her eyebrows rising in amusement.

"He's just a guy I'm enjoying some quality alone time with," I stated with a slight grin.

"Oh, please!" Leah laughed. "We might all be married, but we're not dumb."

"Okay, fine! He's my flavor of the month. We met in the gourmet cheese aisle at the market. He's intense and foreign. When he speaks, I can't understand half of what he's saying."

"Bonus!" Mia laughed.

"We have fun."

"Well, you keep having fun with your mysterious foreign man.

Just keep us updated on your hot neighbor, okay?" Clare requested.

"Deal."

"And one more thing," Clare added quickly.

"What?" I sighed.

"What the hell is that cereal you're trying to feed us?"

I looked down at the boxes of all-natural, organic cereals and laughed. "Toast?" I offered.

"Did someone order breakfast?" a male voice bellowed as the front door swung open.

The husbands had arrived.

We all turned to see Logan, Declan, and Garrett walking through the front door, carrying bags bearing the logo of our favorite local café, Phil's.

"Oh my God, you're lifesavers!" Clare screeched. "She was about to serve us that weird toast again! I would have starved!"

"Well, we can't have that," Logan said.

With a sly grin across his face, he looked up at all of us before returning to Clare. She nodded her head, obviously granting permission for something.

"Gotta keep my girls healthy." Logan placed a gentle kiss on Clare's cheek as his hand tenderly cradled her flat stomach.

"Just because you were right about Ollie's gender doesn't mean you are a guru at it. We could be having another boy."

"It's a girl. I know these things." He kissed her temple and smiled. "I'm a doctor, remember?"

"You're crazy."

"So, what exactly happened next door?" Declan asked, giving his wife a wicked grin.

"Why, I don't know what you're talking about, Hot Shot." she answered sweetly.

"I know my wife's work when I see it."

"We might have been a little intoxicated." She held her thumb and pointer finger close together as she scrunched her nose.

He laughed a rich, sexy deep laugh. "Well, you did a good job. He'll be cleaning that up for days. Do I want to know what he did to deserve it?"

"How do you know it was a he?" I asked, pursing my lips together.

He cocked his eyebrow and gave me a lazy grin as an answer.

"Fine," I lamented. "He's a know-it-all lawyer who destroyed my flowers,"

"You could have just said lawyer." Declan grinned.

"Hey, where are all your kids?" I asked suddenly, realizing how rare it was to have all of them in a room without a child present.

"With my mom," Garrett answered not bothering to wait on anyone else as he dove into the bag of bagels and began tearing it apart.

"You left her with all of them?" I asked, feeling very bad for Mrs. Finnegan.

"She offered." He shrugged, finishing off an entire bagel in a matter of seconds. I didn't know whether to be amazed or horrified by Garrett's ability to consume massive amounts of food.

"My dad will be over there helping, I'm sure," Mia added.

I raised my eyebrow at that, but I quickly dismissed it. Whatever was or was not going on with Laura Finnegan and Derrick Emerson was none of my business.

I really wanted it to be though.

Soon, the house became quiet as plates piled high and orange juice and freshly brewed coffee from Phil's were passed around. Everyone began filling up on bagels, croissants, and muffins. Once everyone's bellies were full and breakfast was cleaned up, the house began to empty once more.

"Thanks for hosting all of us last night," Mia said, giving me a hug. She was always the last to leave.

"Anytime, babe." I smiled. "Bring my godson over soon. I need some snuggle time."

"You got it."

Garrett wrapped his arm around her waist, and I watched the two of them walk slowly to the car. Her head curved toward his shoulder, and I smiled as the sound of her laughter filled the air.

Closing the door behind me, I headed upstairs and entered my bedroom, removing my clothes as I went. I quickly showered, and then I took time in selecting a conservative, flowery dress with very little jewelry. I curled the ends of my hair, and I kept my makeup light.

Today wasn't about me.

Silently, I headed out the door and drove the familiar route I'd come to memorize recently. Over the years, I'd worn a path between our houses, and now, it seemed I was doing the same as I drove through the familiar neighborhood each and every Sunday.

Sundays were the unofficial day for families. Dads would fire up the grills while teenagers emerged from their slumbering caves to spend a few hours with their parents. Kids would play in the yards as mothers read while lounging in the sun. Sundays were for spending time with the ones you loved.

Today, I was spending the afternoon with the woman who had been my only family for years.

She was the one woman who had loved me when no one else had.

~Jackson~

I walked through the gate and already felt uneasy.

I hated cemeteries.

They creeped me the fuck out, especially this one.

My nana loved American history. It was the reason she'd refused to move into a retirement home even though the doctors and the entire family begged her to reconsider.

That house had been her life.

It had been a cockroach or two away from being condemned, and every realtor this side of the James River had told my grandparents that they were crazy to even consider buying it, but they hadn't listened. Nana and my granddad had spent every cent they had to buy it, and they'd built it up from the heap of rubble it had formerly been.

"It's history, Jackson," Nana had explained. "And all history needs to be preserved and cherished."

And they had done just that. They did most of the repairs before I was born, but never seemed to stop working on the endless list of repairs and projects the house required. With their love and time, the formerly forgotten piece of history was restored to its former glory. I had spent many summers in that house—polishing banisters and mantels, cleaning out closets that had been long forgotten, and discovering treasures in the attic that hadn't been seen by human eyes for decades.

Her love for history was the reason they'd chosen to be buried in this particular plot of land. It was the oldest cemetery in Richmond, and therefore, in my opinion, it was also the most disturbing.

It was juvenile, but I couldn't help the shudder going through me as I walked along the curved pathway, dreading the moment I'd have to step off it to get to Nana's and Granddad's graves.

I hated stepping off the pathway.

I looked around, noticing the perfectly arranged flowers on the headstones, and suddenly, I felt like an ass.

Here I was, at my grandparents' gravesites, and I was so focused on everything else, I hadn't even taken a moment to consider the real reason I was actually here—and the fact that I hadn't been here since the funeral.

I should have come sooner.

I should have sent flowers.

I should have visited them more before they'd died.

I should have done a lot of things.

I took a deep breath and stepped off the path onto the grassy earth. As I made my way to the fourth headstone down the row in front of me, I wondered how much regret was felt within the gates of this place.

How many people walked these pathways, knelt in front of these stones, and wished for one more day, one more hour, just to make things different or right?

In life, there really wasn't such a thing as a second chance. Life remembered, and it would move on. All you could do was move on with it and hope for the best.

As I approached the matching headstones, I immediately saw the small clusters of flowers scattered around the base of the granite.

Tons of them, white lilies and purple lilacs, were beautifully cradled between the two stones. Some were showing age while others were new and bright.

Who would do such a thing?

I looked down at my empty hands and felt like a failure.

"You can have these," a small voice said.

I turned to see Liv quietly standing behind me, carrying two bouquets of flowers. One was white lilies, and the other was purple lilacs.

"It was you?" I motioned to the flowers at the foot of the headstones.

She nodded, stepping forward. She handed me the lilacs, and we both knelt down together, setting the bouquets side by side in front of the others.

"I come here every Sunday," she said.

"Why?" I asked, completely stunned by her admission.

"I told you, she was special to me."

"I guess I didn't realize how special."

Looking down, my gaze settled on the engraving, *Etta Reid—Beloved wife and mother. Loving grandmother and friend.*

"I should have visited more. I should have been here," I said softly, settling down onto the grass in front of the granite stone.

"She knew you loved her. She always talked about her Jax," Liv said, giving a wistful smile.

"She's the only one I ever let call me that."

"Really? Why? I kind of like it. It's mysterious."

I shrugged. "Sounds like I belong in a motorcycle gang."

She laughed and gave a wink. "Exactly."

We got up and said our good-byes to Nana and Granddad. I stepped back, allowing Liv a moment alone with Nana, and I waited.

She touched the top of the stone and smiled before saying, "See you next week, Etta."

We walked back to the pathway in silence before I decided to lighten the mood.

"Did she ever bake those cookies for you?"

"The ones with the dried cherries and toffee pieces?"

I nodded, grinning.

"Yeah, she did," she answered. "They were like an orgasm in a baked good."

I laughed, shaking my head. "They're damn good, but if that is your comparison to an orgasm, you've been with all the wrong men."

"And just who is the right man? You?" A wicked smirk spread across her face.

Reaching the entrance, I stepped in front of her, causing her cool confidence to falter slightly. Inching forward, I breathed her in, nearly molding our bodies together. I could feel her breath against my neck.

"Babe, a night with me would be better than all the fucking cookies in the world."

Her eyes widened, and I watched her lips part and her chest rise. *Perfect. Be flustered, Liv. You fluster me constantly.*

My mouth curved upward, forming a large grin, just as I abruptly turned around. "Sorry, but I've got to get home. I have quite a mess to clean up. Someone TP'd our house last night. You wouldn't know anything about that, Liv, would you?"

Looking over my shoulder, I saw her collect her composure once again.

"No, I wouldn't know anything about that." She grinned.

"Hmm…of course not."

Recognizing her little blue car next to mine, I unlocked my doors and waited for her to do the same. "You know, I'll have to retaliate, right?"

Her eyes lit up before she slowly slipped on a pair of shiny black sunglasses. "Oh, I'm counting on it."

Chapter Seven

~**Liv**~

My weekend finished much like it always did—dinner for one and a quiet night of reading. I might have been the only single one left in my small group of friends, but that didn't mean I had the most exciting life either.

Despite my job and love for my friends, I was actually quite reclusive. I could flirt and mingle when the occasion demanded it, but most nights, I'd rather be home, curled up on the sofa or making something in the kitchen.

I'd spent every last dime I had left from my old life on this little piece of property. The money was a parting gift I'd tried to refuse from my parents when we were torn apart. The sizable sum could have paid to further my education for a PhD, but I had chosen stability instead.

It was the best decision of my life.

This house had allowed me to take the job downtown at the counseling center for a wage that I probably never would have been able to survive on otherwise. Not having to worry about a mortgage had given me the freedom to save my earnings and tuck it away until I was able to finally fulfill my own dream and go into business alone.

This house was more than a home to me. It was where I felt connected—to myself, my friends, and even my family and the life I'd once had.

After my quiet weekend ended, I fell back into the weekday pattern, rising early to exercise and then meet clients before they went to school. My hours were long and sometimes grueling, but I loved what I did. Children were always easy for me to connect with. Maybe it was my weird clothes or the bright tattoo on my back, but they always found me interesting and different, and I would use it to my advantage when counseling.

Every young boy who passed through my doors that week reminded me of Noah and the way his face had lit up like a Christmas tree when I invited him to play in the fun night of debauchery.

Days had passed since I last saw either of them. I knew Jackson had started his new job. I'd hear his car leaving around the same time as mine, and the other night, I'd caught a glimpse of him in a suit and tie.

I would be lying if I said he'd looked horrible.

The days had flown by, and it was now Thursday evening. After arriving home late from work again, I frantically raced around my room, trying to make myself presentable for my date with Victor.

I looked in the floor-length mirror and frowned at my dress choice. *Too frumpy.*

Running back into my closet, I picked out a little black number and held it out in front of me. It was sexy, tight, and hugged my curves in all the right places.

A sly grin slowly spread across my face as I pictured *Jackson* taking it off.

What the hell?

Okay, that was going back in the closet.

Instead, I slipped on a summery dress that was slightly fitted, and I paired it with coral wedges. Just as I was putting the finishing touches on my makeup, the doorbell rang.

I looked at the clock on my nightstand. "Right on time, and I'm not late!"

After slipping on my jewelry, I hopped down the stairs, trying to focus on the fact that I was going on a date with Victor, not Jackson.

I opened the door, plastering a large happy smile on my face, and I came face-to-face with my handsome date—and Jackson.

Huh?

Both men smiled back at me as I stared blankly at them. I was so confused by the scene in front of me that I nearly reached up and scratched my head like one of those large gorillas in the zoo.

"Um…hi?" I finally said.

Maybe I also had the IQ of a gorilla as well.

"Olivia, so good to see you again," Victor greeted in his smooth Brazilian accent. He stepped forward and touched his lips to my cheek, slowly and possessively. "I was just meeting your neighbor," he added, giving Jackson a less than friendly look.

Jackson, seeming unfazed by the death stare, just smiled and turned toward me.

I ushered both men inside, not feeling the least bit uncomfortable.

Nope, not at all.

"Yes, I was tending to my flowers because I wouldn't want any-thing to happen to them," he said with a wink. "I saw this particular flower, and it reminded me of you, so I felt the need to come right over and give it to you. It is the neighborly thing to do after all." His accent became thicker and sweeter as he spoke.

I couldn't help but laugh.

"So, where's the flower?" Victor grumbled, looking around with annoyance clearly written across his face.

"Sorry?" Jackson asked, turning toward Victor.

"Where is the flower you just had to bring over?"

He brought up his empty hands and sighed. "Oh, I must have lost it along the way. What a damn shame. And I interrupted your date, too!"

I had no idea why he was here, but it really was quite adorable, seeing him ruffle Victor's tail feathers so easily.

"Please don't let me hold you up any further," Jackson pressed.

He grabbed my purse off the kitchen counter and handed it to me. I felt his warm hand press into my back as he ushered us to the door.

The heat zinged down my spine, sending shivers to my core.

"I'm sure you have places to be," he insisted.

"Reservation," Victor mumbled.

"Of course, of course. Hurry along!"

We all exited out the front door.

Jackson raised his hand in the air, waving good-bye. "Y'all have a good time, ya hear!"

What was that man up to?

~Jackson~

I ran through the front door after watching that douche bag's car drive away with Liv tucked inside. "Noah! Quick, throw on some shoes! We're running to the store!"

"What?" he replied from the top of the stairs, shoving his phone in his pocket.

"We're going to the store! Quick!"

I made hurried motions with my hands as he rolled his powdery-blue eyes.

He finally trotted down the stairs. "Okay, okay! I didn't realize groceries were such an emergency."

"Oh, we aren't getting groceries." I grinned before grabbing my keys off the counter. "We're getting our revenge."

Ten minutes later, we were standing in front of the balloon aisle at the local party store.

"Why are we here exactly?" Noah asked, looking up at the rainbow of balloons spread out before us.

"This is called payback." I picked up a pack of assorted balloons. There were one hundred and fifty to a pack, and that wouldn't be nearly enough. I needed a basket, a really big basket.

"You're using balloons?"

"Yep," I answered. "And you're helping. Don't think I don't know who helped them figure out the new latch I had installed."

He gave me a sheepish look and grinned. "Are you mad?"

"No. You helped clean it up, and there are worse things you could be doing late at night besides hanging out with Liv."

I ran to the front of the store and returned to the aisle with a large basket and began shoving bags of balloons into it.

"So, you don't hate her?" he asked.

"No, I don't. I thought I would, but she's not that bad."

"So, why the balloons?"

Thinking back, I remembered the overwhelming feeling of jealousy that had sparked through me when I saw another man walking up to Liv's door this evening. He'd looked over at me and nodded, a smug grin spreading across his face, as he'd smoothed out his hair and straightened his shirt. Every muscle in my body had tightened as I'd wanted to leap over the fence and show him the way back to his car.

She wasn't mine to claim, which meant I'd have to deal with the endless parade of men who came knocking at her door. But that hadn't meant I couldn't ruin this one's evening a little.

"You'll understand when you're older."

The sun had barely risen over the horizon when I heard a faint knocking coming from my front door. It increased in volume as I lay in bed, trying to figure out who would be crazy enough to visit at this ridiculous hour.

The night before suddenly flashed before my eyes, and I grinned.

Jumping out of bed, I didn't bother with throwing on a T-shirt before racing down the stairs to answer my early morning visitor.

"Good morning, Liv," I said after opening the door and serving her a megawatt smile.

She stood before me in tight spandex shorts that hugged her muscled trim thighs and accentuated the curves of her body. Her hot pink sports bra nearly had me coming unglued as my eyes settled on the perfect little valley of cleavage between her breasts.

"I believe this is yours," she said, holding a bright red balloon in her left hand.

I smiled, leaning languidly against the doorframe. "Hmm…looks familiar. Where did you find it?"

Her eyes roamed up my bare chest before she thrust the balloon at my head. "You know exactly where I found it, asshat! In my house—

along with its five hundred brothers and sisters!"

"Actually, it's eight hundred and forty-three. We counted—for fun," I added.

I saw a grin tugging at her bottom lip before she tried to straighten it.

"How the hell did you get into my house?"

"Well, I was the last one out," I stated, playfully waggling my eyebrows at her.

Her eyes widened. "That whole charade with you coming over was just so you could get into my house later?"

"Well, that, and I got to see you in your pretty dress," I said with a wink.

She shook her head. "You're impossible. And you roped your son into breaking and entering? Terrible."

"In your professional opinion, is that better or worse than teaching him how to vandalize a home?" I questioned.

Her face went blank. "That was totally different."

I laughed. "Of course."

We reached an impasse, and I could see her hesitating, her eyes darting around, as she tried to grasp for something else to say. I watched her beginning to form a word, and I knew she was about to leave, so I did the only thing I could think of. I stopped her.

"Hey, are you about to go for a run?" I asked, pointing down at her shorts and running shoes like an idiot.

I'm so smooth.

"Yep."

"Mind if I join you?"

She looked me over once again, and I smiled.

"Just give me a minute to write a note for Noah and change?"

She nodded, and I motioned for her to come inside. I watched her take a seat in the same spot where she'd sat when she last visited. I briefly wondered what it had been like when she visited Nana.

Is that where she sat? What did they speak about over those long visits for so many years?

I should have been jealous of the woman who had spent so much time with my grandmother, but instead, I was grateful to her. I was thankful Nana had had someone like Liv around when I hadn't been there.

When my world had been turned upside down with the news of Noah, I'd become driven and focused on one thing only—my child.

From the moment he had come screaming into this world, everything revolved around him. Even my career had become about him. I wanted to be someone he could look up to and respect. I'd worked hard to get to where I was, finishing college by night and taking classes in between working forty hours a week. Nothing I'd accomplished was ever easy, but I'd managed it all. I hoped he would one day see that anything in life was possible if he tried hard enough.

I jotted a few words onto a sticky note and stuck it on his door before racing into my room to change. The note would probably go unnoticed since he tended to sleep until I'd pull him out of bed and force him to get ready for the day camp where he went while I was at work.

He'd tried to persuade me that he was old enough to stay home by himself, but I wasn't quite convinced.

A couple of minutes later, I was back downstairs in a pair of running shorts and a T-shirt, ready to go.

"No shirtless running today, Jackson?" she mocked as we walked out the door.

"Wouldn't want to cause a riot." I grinned as we stretched.

We started out slow, jogging down the street at a leisurely pace, as our muscles warmed and lengthened.

"Do you run every morning?" I asked as my feet hit a steady rhythm.

"No, I try to mix it up. I ride my bike some days and do yoga on other days. I get bored easily."

"And what about Don Juan DeMarco? Are you bored of him yet?"

She slightly turned her head, smirking at my reference to her ridiculous date.

"Hmm...I don't know. Our evening got cut short. He didn't have the same reaction to the balloons as me, so he went home early."

I couldn't help the smug look of satisfaction spreading across my lips.

"That's too bad," I commented.

"Mmhmm..."

"What do you see in a guy like that anyway?" I asked.

Our speed slowed slightly as we curved around a turn and crossed the road.

"What do you mean?"

"He was unlike you in every way."

"You mean, just like you?" she goaded.

"I mean, in the ways that count. He didn't seem genuine or caring. He didn't look at you the way you deserve to be looked at."

We all but slowed to a stop as her eyes found mine.

"And what way is that?" she said.

"Like the sun was made just for you," I said. "You deserve more."

I didn't realize that we'd stopped. Standing face-to-face in the middle of an empty street, her eyes met mine, budding with promise before she blinked, and I watched the moment drift away with the wind.

"And you got all this after a two-minute meeting with him?" she asked, trying to bring our conversation back to light and casual.

"I'm very wise," I answered, smiling.

"A wise lawyer? That's a new one."

"Smart-ass."

"Race you back to the house?" she yelled before taking off in a hard sprint.

Trying to catch up, I chased her down the street.

Somehow, I didn't think it would be the last time I chased after Olivia Prescott.

Chapter Eight

~Jackson~

Liv was in the forefront of my mind the rest of the morning.

While I showered, I pictured her beautiful bikini-clad body walking toward me as the glint of her belly-button ring winked and sparkled under the sunlight. I thought of her smile and quick-witted sense of humor as I flipped eggs and poured cereal for Noah before quickly scurrying out the door for work. It was her face I thought of as the elevator climbed up to the fifteenth floor, bringing me to Jeffrey, Morgan, and Stein—one of the most prestigious law firms in the area, and my new employer.

It had been roughly two weeks since I first walked through these glass doors and took my new position as associate attorney. I had a long road ahead of me and a lot of ladders to climb, but for once in my life, I felt like I was being judged for my merit and not for which people I knew. Being the new kid on the block was never easy, but so far, I'd earned several gold stars. I had a fierce, ready-for-anything attitude and zeal for success.

"Good morning, Mr. Reid," a sweet voice greeted me from behind.

I turned to see my secretary moving toward me with a fresh cup of coffee in her perfectly manicured hands.

"Good morning, Kate," I replied. "You know, you can call me Jackson."

She smiled sheepishly as I took the cup from her, my fingers briefly brushing hers.

"It just sounds so intimate," she admitted, her eyes turning away, as a blush stained her cheeks.

Kate was everything a single young lawyer like myself could hope to find in a woman. She was beautiful, smart, and charming. Her body could bring a man to his knees, and I was nearly there, but something was stopping me. Something was keeping me from taking the plunge on what I knew would be a sure thing with Kate, and it had little to do with our work situation.

In the back of my head, I already knew.

Kate was exactly how I'd envisioned my perfect girl next door. She was everything I'd wanted but exactly the opposite of what my body craved.

I'd found that girl next door, and she was nothing like what I'd expected.

"Well then, I guess we can stick to formalities for now," I responded politely.

Her blush quickly faded as she straightened and regained her professional composure.

I had no idea where things were going with Liv, but I knew where they were not headed with my secretary.

Kate was perfect for someone else maybe, but she was definitely not for me—at least not anymore.

At work, my dick would stay firmly in my pants.

At home—well, the verdict was still out on that. I'd made the same promise regarding Olivia Prescott, but damn, if I didn't want to break it. I'd never met a woman who could drive me insane and set me on fire at the same exact time. It was a recipe for disaster, but I couldn't stop myself from wanting to try, even for just a night.

Looking around, I walked to the row of windows highlighting the Richmond skyline. Rays of orange and yellow sun streaks were making their way through the clouds, heating up the early morning air. As I looked down at the city, everything still felt so foreign, so new. I'd spent many childhood summers here, but places had looked different through the eyes of a child. Gazing down at the city now as an adult, it was as if I had just arrived for the first time.

We'd been here for two weeks, and I still hadn't found the time to take Noah anywhere. We hadn't even been out to eat.

He must be bored out of his mind.

"I think I'm going to work until noon today and then take a few hours off," I suddenly announced as I made my way to my office door.

"Okay, Mr. Reid. I'll clear your schedule. Anything special planned?" she inquired.

"I think my son and I need to spend some time getting to know our new city," I answered.

"You picked me up early?" Noah said in amazement as he got into the car.

"I did," I said as I did the same.

"You never pick me up early."

His stunned and confused expression left me feeling happy and ashamed in the same breath. I was glad my job was flexible enough that I could take a few hours of my day to finally spend some much overdue time with my son. At the same time, I was sad that it had taken me so long to realize how necessary it was.

Had I really neglected Noah so thoroughly that an afternoon off from work was that much of a shock?

"So, what are we going to do?" he asked, his eyes trained on the leafy green trees whizzing by.

"I thought we'd walk around, check out different areas of the city. Liv said we'd never feel at home here until we explored and made this place our own, so that's what I thought we would attempt today. Sound good?"

"Better than craft time at camp. Crafts are for babies…and girls," he answered.

I tousled his hair and laughed as he ducked away from me.

As we turned onto the block leading to our street, he turned to me in question.

"We're just stopping at home, so I can ditch the suit. Ten minutes, tops."

He gave a nonverbal answer as we pulled up next to the curb. His car door flew open, and I watched him bounce down the lawn toward the front door. Within seconds, he had his key out, and he was walking through the front door.

A car drove past, and I turned to find Liv parking her little blue Prius along the curb. She pushed the door open and stepped out, her eyes colliding with mine instantly.

"Playing hooky today, counselor?" She smiled.

"Might say the same thing about you," I replied, stepping through the grass to meet her halfway.

"I had taken a half day to spend the afternoon with Mia, but her son, Asher, came down with a cold, so it looks like I'm flying solo."

"Can I hire you as a tour guide for the afternoon?"

Her eyes darted to our front door where Noah had just reappeared.

"Finally taking my advice I see?"

"Yeah," I answered, "but I have no idea where to start."

Taking a leisurely gaze down my body, she grinned. "Start by stripping off that monkey suit, and I'll handle the rest."

"Deal."

~Liv~

As soon as I saw Noah meandering out of the house in his *I Heart Football* shirt, I knew exactly where I wanted to take them. First, I wanted to make a few stops and show them the Richmond I loved.

We also needed to eat. I was starving.

Our first stop was one of my favorites, second to the farmers' market. I loved Carytown. Here, you could shop the world, eat pretty much anything, and spend hours discovering new talent. It was the heart and center for art, music, and food in the area, and it was where

I felt most at home. With brightly colored buildings and funky shops on every street corner, it was the one place in the city I never felt different.

"So, what do you boys feel like eating?" I asked as I took the first available spot in the parking garage.

"What's good?" Jackson asked.

Everyone hopped out of the car, and we began our journey.

"Pretty much everything. There's an awesome Thai place a block or so that way." I pointed down the street. "Oh, and there's a killer Mexican place right there," I said, motioning to the brightly painted sign.

Noah squinted his eyes and frowned. Jackson didn't look too excited either.

"Sushi?" I asked.

Their faces fell further.

I was beginning to guess my Charleston neighbors were not the adventurous eaters.

"Um...pizza?" I suggested.

Their eyes instantly lit up, and I couldn't help but laugh.

"Okay, pizza it is!" I announced.

We headed to the right in search of pizza. The place I selected was well known, a Richmond tradition for years, and had some of the best pizza in the area. I hoped my guys wouldn't be disappointed.

Once we were seated, a hush fell across the table as everyone's attention fell to the menu.

I peeked up over the top of mine and stole a glance at Jackson. His eyebrow rose, and a small smirk appeared at the corner of his lip.

"Stop staring at me," he whispered.

"What are you ordering?"

"A cheese pizza."

I snorted and shook my head.

"What?" he asked.

"I just would never have believed the super fancy lawyer ate like a five-year-old."

"I do not. I just enjoy basic food."

"You mean, boring food?" I quipped.

"As opposed to whatever the hell—heck," he amended, looking

quickly over at Noah, who was still buried in his menu, "you eat. What was it you suggested? Thai food?"

I nodded. "Just you wait, Jackson. I'm going to get you to love Thai food."

"Not in this lifetime, sweetheart."

Whenever he said *sweetheart*, his accent would grow thicker, and my panties would simultaneously grow wet.

Smug bastard.

The waitress came by to take our orders, faltering when her eyes stumbled on Jackson. She quickly righted herself when she saw me. She must have assumed Noah, Jackson and me made a happy little family. I didn't bother correcting her. She could keep her eyes to herself.

She needed to learn to be professional. That was the only reason I wanted her to stop eye-fucking Jackson, and damn it, I was sticking to that lie.

Both men ordered a slice of cheese pizza, and I managed to keep my snicker to a minimum.

"And for you, ma'am?" Miss Perky asked.

"I'll have the veggie calzone," I answered.

The waitress finished up and walked away. I couldn't help but look up to see if Jackson was watching her very obvious saunter into the kitchen.

His eyes were trained on me, and it gave me chills.

"So, you don't eat meat? Like, ever?" Noah asked, breaking our connection.

"Um…what? Oh no. I haven't for years."

"Why? That's kind of weird," he said.

I laughed. I loved the raw honesty of a child. While most adults kept their opinions to themselves, only to voice them when in the restroom or after leaving for the evening, kids would be upfront—no pettiness, no games. It was refreshing.

"I guess I just don't like it," I answered.

"Not even steak? My dad makes the best steak."

"I bet he does, but no, especially not steak."

"Someday," Jackson said, "I'll get you to eat one of my steaks, and when I feed it to you, it will be the best damn meal of your life."

His voice deepened, and I wondered if the offer came with the option to lick his fingers clean as well.

"Better than Thai?" I asked, trying to keep my brain out of the deep gutter I'd created.

"Way better than Thai." His lopsided grin nearly had me but I refused to be charmed.

"Sorry, sweetheart," I mocked his pet name from earlier, "never going to happen."

Our food arrived just then, and the conversation quickly died to a minimum as food became the main focus. I did manage to get Noah to talk about school a bit.

"Are you excited?" I asked between bites.

"I guess." He shrugged.

"That's about all I can get out of him, too," Jackson said.

He had already managed to polish off his extra-large slice of pizza while I was still only three bites into mine.

I gave Jackson a wink. *He's just playing it cool*, I mouthed.

We finished up lunch, and being the Southern gentleman he was, Jackson insisted on paying.

"Are you sure? I can pay for my part," I said.

He stole the check out of my hand right after the waitress had placed it on the table.

"I asked you to join us, so it's my treat," he pressed.

"Okay," I relented. "Thank you."

His eyes met mine once more, and he gave a brief nod.

"Where are we off to next, tour guide?"

"If our next stop doesn't amaze you, I don't know what will."

~Jackson~

Liv pulled the car into the parking spot and cut the engine.

"Is this what I think it is?" I asked.

"It depends on what you think this is," she mocked.

"Are we at the training camp for the Washington Redskins?" I looked around, watching families pile out of their cars, covered in burgundy jerseys.

"Why then, yes, Jackson, this is in fact exactly what you think it is." She smiled.

"Holy shit," Noah whispered from the backseat.

"Noah!" I scolded even though I had been about to say the same thing. The little nut had just beaten me to it.

"Did you not know the team trained here during the summer?" Liv asked.

We climbed out of her tiny car, the one she'd insisted on driving because mine was, as she'd put it, "a gas-guzzling ozone killer."

I helped her pull a few things from the trunk. The woman had come prepared with blankets, a few chairs, and even a picnic basket and cooler.

"I knew. I mean, I heard from a few guys at work that the team practiced here."

"It's a big thing for the local fans. They've only been training in Richmond for a couple of years, and it's become one of the biggest events of the summer. We just need a ticket to get in," she said, waving her hand in the air, "which we have." She dove into her tiny purse and produced a printed piece of paper from its depths.

I grabbed it and saw it was indeed the golden ticket to get us in. She stole it back just as we reached the gate and as if the gates of heaven were opening up, they let us proceed forward, and make our way to the field.

"Whoa! Dad, look!" Noah exclaimed, pointing ahead, as the first string made their way across the grass.

"This is amazing, Liv. Seriously. I would never have thought of this."

"I know. All the chemicals in your brain from that crappy food you eat clog the thought process."

I looked over at her and watched the serious face she was trying to uphold melt into a fit of laughter.

"I'm kidding!" She giggled. "Mostly. Come on, let's go, counselor."

Watching a training practice was light years different than seeing an actual game. There was no stadium or huge jumbotrons advertising various sponsors and vendors. It was simple and gave real fans the opportunity to see behind the scenes.

We found an open spot of grass with a great view of the field. Together, the three of us spread out the large blanket and set up the two chairs for Liv and me while Noah lounged on the ground.

"What do you have in here?" Noah asked, peeking in the basket.

"Fruit and crackers. Some cheese as well as some water is in the cooler."

His face scrunched together in displeasure, and I laughed. Noah was not a fan of health food.

"Some cookies might also be in there somewhere," she said in a sweet tone.

That kid's cookie radar hadn't lessened with age. In three seconds flat, he found the chocolate chip cookies, and he was stuffing one in his mouth.

"Hmm...not bad," he mumbled between bites.

"Are they as good as my grandmother's?" I asked her, taking one to try for myself.

"No, definitely not. She had a way with cookies, if you remember me telling you."

Oh, yes, I did.

We spent the next hour watching numerous drills and plays being practiced over and over across the field. The coaches worked the men hard, and by the time the whistle called for break, the team was dripping with sweat and gasping for air.

Some chose to make their way into the locker rooms while many others walked across the field to the fence where their eager fans awaited for a moment or two of attention.

Noah watched and nearly vibrated with excitement as several of his favorite players stepped up to the fence. Children and adults alike swarmed them, asking for s and pictures. They were gracious and signed everything and anything shoved in front of them, from pictures to notebooks, and even in their exhausted state, they still posed for pictures.

Liv and I stood with Noah and waited our turn, finally making it up to the front.

I looked over at Noah, who appeared to have temporarily lost the ability to speak.

"Hi, this is my son, Noah. He's a big fan."

His head bobbed up and down, but still, no words came.

The guy in the middle smiled, turning his head from me to Noah and then finally stopping on Liv. "Beautiful family you've got."

"Oh, thank you, but I'm just a friend. Noah and Jackson are new to the area, so I'm showing them around. Couldn't do a tour of Richmond in the summer without stopping here."

His eyes roamed down her body, and I felt my knuckles tighten.

"No, definitely not. We're always glad to have fans." His attention finally focused back on my son. "How about an autograph and a picture with my boy, Noah?" he asked, as Noah's eyes went wide.

"Okay," Noah managed to say before stepping in front of the towering giant.

Both Liv and I pulled out our phones and snapped a few pics. Noah didn't have anything for him to sign, but he had some fancy app that allowed him to sign his phone. He could save it like a picture.

I just shook my head, wondering how long it would be before he knew more than I did.

He probably already did, and I was just in denial.

I turned to thank the guy for being so generous, and I found him leaning over the fence, talking to Liv.

"Since you seem to know the area so well, would you mind showing me around sometime? I don't get out much and would love some…one-on-one time with a local."

The way he said it left no room for the imagination, and I rolled my eyes at his very obvious tactics for picking up a date.

Reaching my arm out to aid Liv, I fell short when I heard her utter the one word I'd assumed she never would.

"Sure," she replied.

"Great. Give me your phone," he instructed.

She willingly handed her phone to the no-name football player, and I watched as he punched in a series of numbers.

"I just programmed my number into your phone and called myself, so now, I have your number. I'll be in touch."

I didn't talk much to Liv for the remainder of the day. I would say only just enough to get by. She'd obviously picked up on my annoyance. Whether or not she knew the source of it was a mystery.

By the time we packed up and made it back to the car, I was about to explode.

"What will Don Juan think of your date with the football star?" I seethed.

She pulled out of the parking spot. "I guess I will never know since I don't plan on telling him. We aren't exclusive, Jackson," she answered, her voice clipped and short.

My head fell back on the seat, and I closed my eyes in frustration.

Exclusivity—is that what I want with Liv? Can I see myself building something solid and long-lasting with her? Or do I just want to take her away from everyone else?

Chapter Nine

~Jackson~

My sour mood didn't abate as the weekend dragged on.

On Monday, thoughts of Liv once again dominated my mind as I rode the elevator at work, but this time, they were anything but pleasant. I imagined her beautiful body wrapped around that hotshot football player after he'd wined and dined her all over the city. I was pining for a woman who was the opposite of everything I needed.

This had to end—now.

The elevator door slid open, and I stepped out on the fifteenth floor. Breezing past the front desk in the direction of my office, I already knew what I was going to do—the one thing I'd sworn I wouldn't.

But desperate times called for desperate measures.

And I was desperate. I needed to move on from this…infatuation with Liv—and fast.

"Good morning, Mr. Reid," Kate greeted as I rounded the corner and stopped in front of her desk.

"Again with the formalities, Kate. What am I going to do with you?" I grinned.

"Oh, um…I just thought—"

"Call me Jackson, please. Why don't we go out to lunch today? That way, we can get to know each other, and you won't feel so awkward about it."

She nodded with enthusiasm.

God, I even hate myself right now.

"Great. It's a date," I said.

"Are you sure you don't want to come in, Jackson?" Kate asked, seductively leaning back against the doorframe.

It was Friday night, and after an evening with a woman who looked good enough to eat, I should have been jumping at the chance to walk through that door and find out exactly how good she tasted.

Instead, I was trying to think of any excuse to do the opposite.

"I'd better get back home. It's my first night out since the move, and it's a new babysitter. I'm getting a little antsy, wondering how they're doing," I tried to explain, throwing out words faster than my brain could process.

"Of course." She nodded, rubbing her hand over my shoulder in a comforting manner.

I looked down at it, forcing myself not to back away from her touch.

"Tonight was amazing, Jackson," she started.

She'd gotten over formalities fairly quickly after our initial lunch date, and she now used my first name in such abundance that I was even beginning to hate it.

"Glad you had a good time," I responded lamely.

"Call me tomorrow?" she asked with expectant wide eyes.

Dear Lord, what have I done?

"I have a busy weekend with Noah lined up, but I'll be sure to catch up with you on Monday, okay?" I suggested, seeing her face fall as the words tumbled out of my mouth.

"Sure. Monday then." She gave me a small peck on the cheek and turned, stepping into her apartment.

I watched the door shut behind her perfect little body.

God, I am a grade-A asshole.

But it didn't stop me from fleeing to my truck like a man running for his life the moment the lock had clicked into place.

What have I been thinking?

Kate was indeed everything I had hoped to find when I began this new adventure in Richmond. She was smart, beautiful, and came from a similar background as me.

She was also the most boring woman on the entire planet.

Her life could be summarized in a few paragraphs. She was a carbon copy of probably a dozen other women I'd dated in the past. There was nothing special about her, nothing that made her stand out in a crowd. I was left to wonder if there was anything that made her unique at all.

I'd learned one thing while sitting through my torturous hours with Kate. It didn't matter who I dated—whether she was smart, funny, interesting, or downright gorgeous. None of them would ever be what I wanted.

Because no one could hold a candle to Liv.

Driving home that night, I knew I wanted Liv for more than just reasons of some silly territorial game. Somewhere along the way, between our fighting and battles, I'd begun to fall for my crazy neighbor.

I just had no idea what I was going to do about it.

After paying the babysitter and sending her out the door one hundred bucks richer, I found myself standing by the window, staring at Liv's house.

There was a single light on.

Was she alone?

Did she have company?

Was it the Latin guy or the clueless football player?

Or someone new entirely?

I was going to go clinically insane while living next to this woman.

"Dad," Noah said from the couch.

"Yeah?" I mumbled, not breaking contact with Liv's window.

"Can we go school shopping sometime this weekend?"

"Uh…sure. Does this mean you're excited about school?" I questioned.

The news that Noah was to attend a private school had not been well received. It had, of course, resulted in a fight, in which he'd asked why I was sending him to a "stuck-up preppy school" now.

I had to worsen the news by adding the tidbit that he was required to wear uniforms as well. Our little argument had gone nuclear and he refused to talk to me for the rest of the evening.

I wanted him to receive the best education possible, and I had the means to do so. The school I'd picked out was one of the top in the area, but it required uniforms. His last school had no such rule. He had been struggling with it since I broke the news weeks ago.

"Maybe," he said.

Liv was right. He was playing it cool, and I guessed I should just bide my time until he decided he wanted to open up.

Several minutes later, footsteps sounded across the wooden floor, and Noah joined me at the window. "What are you looking at?"

"Nothing," I lied.

"You know, Dad, it's okay if you want to go out with Liv. I don't mind her. She's actually pretty nice."

I looked down at him as he stared out the window.

"What do you like about her?" I asked, curious to see what stuck out in his mind.

"She's different. I thought it was weird at first, the way she dressed and how she acted, but I like it. She's always the same with everyone. And she treats me like a person rather than a kid."

"I like that, too," I admitted.

"Dad?" he asked.

"Yeah, buddy?"

"How do you know when a girl likes you?"

Oh, here we go. Time to put my parenting hat on.

"Well, I guess it depends on the girl. Some girls will follow you around and try to talk to you. Others are shy and quiet, so they might not be as aggressive. Some might even act a little crazy."

One of those must have reached home because he smiled.

God, I hope it's the shy, quiet type.

"Thanks, Dad."

"Anytime, kid."

~Liv~

My phone pinged again, signaling another text message.

I didn't bother checking it. I already knew who it was from—the same person who had been blowing up my phone all night.

It was Travis, the football player.

Why had I agreed to go out with him? Why had I handed over my phone like some airheaded groupie?

I didn't want to date him. Hell, I didn't even want to share a meal with that meathead of a man. I didn't even like football!

His proposition had honestly taken my by surprise. Getting hit on at a bar was one thing. Getting hit on at a football field with a bunch of ankle-biters jumping up and down was another. I had been shocked by his blatant boldness and cocky attitude.

As I had been formulating the nicest way possible to let the giant of a man down gently, I'd felt Jackson's hand brush the small of my back. I hadn't known whether he felt sorry for me and was trying to come to my rescue or if it was some macho, territorial thing. Either way, the gesture had pissed me off.

I was not a woman who needed to be rescued by a man. I was independent and completely in charge of my own destiny. So, I'd taken matters into my own hands.

My cell phone buzzed again, rattling around on my coffee table. I sighed as my head fell back against the sofa. I'd beautifully handled the situation without Jackson's help.

Obviously.

One week and several different avoidance tactics later, I was still dealing with my horrible decision. I watched my cell phone light up, notifying me I had three unread text messages.

Didn't this guy have anyone else to bother?

I grabbed my phone, typed my password in, and pulled up the messages.

Hangin' at a bar downtown. Wish you were here.

I set the phone back down and shook my head.

No, thanks.

I could only imagine what constituted as a good time for a twenty-three-year-old professional football player—shots lined up down the bar, girls dancing everywhere, and music loud enough to make my ears bleed.

That image alone made me feel as old as the beams holding up my historic house.

The further I stepped away from my college days, the less I found myself needing that type of entertainment. A girls' night out was different, and I still enjoyed getting tipsy with my friends, but I found myself loving fuzzy socks and paperbacks far more than high heels and body shots these days.

Picking up the phone once again, I sent a quick text, hoping it would sever all communication with Travis, the football player.

Sorry, Travis. Stuck at home with my daughter. She's only thirteen months old, and she has a cold. Snot is everywhere. Maybe next time?

I snickered as I pressed Send.

That should do it.

Dropping the phone on the coffee table, I decided a bit of fresh air was in order, and I headed out the back door to my patio, immediately feeling the humid warm breeze hit my face. I took a deep breath, wrapping my arms around my chest, my eyes darted from one corner of the yard to the next, chasing fireflies.

"Nice night, isn't it?"

I looked over to see Jackson standing in a similar position on his patio. His gaze was locked on me.

"It is," I answered.

"Mind if I join you?"

I began to shake my head, but I realized he probably couldn't see much of me.

"No, I don't mind."

I watched the moonlit silhouette of him move closer to me. He opened the gate that separated our two yards and stepped through. A few moments later, he was at my side.

"Hi," he said, his smile shining through the darkness.

"Hi. Busy week I guess?" I asked, searching for something to say.

He nodded, rocking back on his heels. "How is the football star?"

No pussyfooting around tonight.

Jackson's eyes sparked with anger, making his motivation on that field days earlier very apparent.

"Why does he bother you so much?" I asked, stepping closer as my own anger began to rise.

"For the same reasons Don Juan, or whatever his name is, bothers me. Neither of them are good enough for you. And they aren't me."

His confession caught me completely off guard, and my anger seeped away.

"And you are good enough?" I asked softly.

His intense gaze met mine, sincerity pouring out of his memorizing stare.

"I'd damn well try to be."

Like a flash, he was on me—his lips, his hands, and his entire presence. My breath hitched in surprise as my body melted into his, molding around him as if I'd been made to do so.

My mouth opened, and his tongue found mine, caressing and moving together like we were long-lost lovers. His fingers twisted into my hair, pulling me closer. I felt every hard inch of his body pressed against mine.

Holy shit, I am kissing Jackson Reid.

I was making out with my asshole neighbor.

My body went rigid with panic. Feeling the shift in my demeanor, Jackson slowed, pressing sweet kisses to my lips and cheek.

"You're pulling away," he stated.

"Don't you think we should talk about this?"

His eyebrows rose, but his position didn't change. His arms remained firmly wrapped around me. "Sure, but don't pull away from me, Liv."

"I just need to know, what are we doing, Jackson?" I looked up at him and watched his expression turn mischievous.

"As in right now? Or a couple of minutes ago?"

I playfully slapped his arm, causing him to laugh.

"I mean, in general. This. What is this?" I made a motion that encapsulated the two of us.

"I don't know," he answered honestly.

I sighed, slightly stepping back. His playful attitude faltered as his fingers moved up my arms.

"It's just that I don't do this well."

"And what is *this*?" he asked.

I threw my hands up in frustration. "I don't know. I thought you would know."

He laughed. "Then, how do you know you do it so poorly?"

"Because I do. Intimacy and relationships," I said, nearly shuddering over the words, "I suck at them. I've never managed to stay in one longer than a few months."

"Maybe you're just dating the wrong guys?"

I looked up at him and smiled. "Maybe."

"Besides, Liv, so far we've only just made out a little on your patio. Lay off the doom and gloom. Aren't you the therapist? Shouldn't you be spouting off this ridiculous crap?"

A smirk tugged at the corner of my lips. "You know how they say, *Never marry a chef if you love to eat*?"

"Uh…no. I don't think I've ever heard anyone say that."

"Well, they do," I said. "And the reason is, chefs rarely cook for themselves. It's like a housecleaner with the dirtiest house on the block. Didn't you know counselors are the most screwed-up people of them all?"

He shook his head. "Well, that's reassuring."

"I'm kidding—mostly. But you're right. I'm jumping way ahead of myself. You might not even want to date me," I said.

"Hold up," he replied. Stepping forward, he slid his hand around my waist and pulled me tight against him. "I want to date you," he whispered.

He kissed the nape of my neck, which sent shivers up and down my spine.

"Only you, Liv. Okay?"

Words failed me, so I nodded.

"But I'm going to need you to get rid of the football player and Don Juan."

"There is no football player," I said softly.

Pulling back, he looked at me in confusion. "What?"

"I didn't go out with him. I never wanted to."

"Then, why? Never mind, it doesn't matter. Only me, Liv, okay?"

"Yes."

"Good. Then, we will figure out the rest later. Right now, I just want to kiss you again," he said right before his lips melted back into mine.

I'm okay with that.

Chapter Ten

~Liv~

"You're going on a date with your hot neighbor?" Mia squeaked into the phone.

I moved around the kitchen, preparing breakfast for one. "Yeah. Am I crazy?"

"To go out with a hot guy on a Saturday? Wait—he's taking you out during the day?"

I laughed, putting the last smear of almond butter on my toast, as I took a seat on the sofa.

"Yeah, that's the plan—or at least the only part I am privy to. He won't tell me where we are going or what we will be doing. He only said to wear comfortable clothes and to be prepared to get dirty." I shook my head, remembering his early morning phone call.

"Hey," he whispered, his voice coming in clear and vibrant across the airwaves.

I stretched, brushing my legs across the silky sheets. "Good morning," I greeted, my voice still hoarse from sleep.

"Did I wake you?"

"Yeah, but I don't mind."

"Good. You need to get up," he commanded.

Laughing, I asked, "And why is that?"

"Because we have plans."

I didn't usually go for the bossy type, but on him, it looked good.

"Dirty, huh?" Mia commented. "I want details and pictures—unless they're kinky. You can keep those to yourself," she laughed.

Asher's babbling rang through the phone line, and I heard Mia coo back.

"Someone misses you," she said.

"Tell him I miss him, too." I paused for a moment as I looked down at my untouched cup of tea that was turning cold. "Are you sure I'm making the right decision, getting involved with someone so close to me?"

"Isn't that the whole idea? Getting involved with someone we're close with, Liv?" she asked.

"You know what I mean."

She huffed. "Let me ask you something. In the nearly four years since I've been back in Richmond, have I ever met a single guy you've dated?"

I sat my plate down on the coffee table as my mouth opened to answer. It hung there, wide and empty, as I thought, but I was unable to come up with a single name.

"Well, there was…" I started but stopped.

"No, Liv, there hasn't been one. We've never double-dated. You haven't brought any of them over here for dinner. Nothing. Why is that?"

This was a jaw-dropping moment.

"I don't know."

"You want to know what I think? I think you're purposely dating the wrong men."

"Why would I do that?" I asked.

"Honestly, I think you've been biding your time."

"For what?" My eyes suddenly drifted over to the small house next door.

"Now, isn't that the question of the day?"

Our phone call finished up soon after that, and I spent the next hour staring at my closet, wondering why it seemed like everyone in my life had suddenly decided it was their life mission to counsel me.

Did they have degrees to do this kind of shit professionally?

I sighed audibly as I sunk further into my closet, bending over in search of denim.

Why didn't I own more jeans?

Jackson had said to dress comfortable. On most days, that was my normal attire. Light, airy dresses and skirts were the epitome of comfort. But he'd also said to prepare to get dirty, which required an entirely different outfit.

I needed denim and a T-shirt—two items that were scarce in my closet. While most women could live in jeans, I personally hated them. They were tight, constrictive, and stiff.

My girlfriends thought I was nuts, too.

Biding my time? That was ridiculous.

Mia clearly had no idea what she was talking about.

It was almost as ridiculous as saying I purposely dated the wrong men because I feared they would all leave me like my father.

I froze, nearly tumbling head first into the darkened depths of my closet.

"Oh crap," I muttered.

Did I really do that?

I stood upright, my eyes becoming unfocused, as I let my mind wander back to all the men I'd dated and dumped over the years.

I was always the one who had broken it off. I was always the first one to walk away.

Holy shit, I am a nut case.

In an attempt to move past my own self-realization and instead of diving headfirst into denial, I began digging through my closet with gusto. I managed to find a couple of pairs of jeans that didn't scream soccer mom or that didn't magically time travel me from the '90s, and I threw them on. They actually looked pretty good and hugged my hips and ass nicely. Paired with a black tee and some old boots, I was nearly ready to go by the time the doorbell rang. I threw on a pair of earrings, spritzed on some perfume, and high-fived myself in the mirror for being almost on time.

How about that?

I resisted the urge to throw a couple of bangles on my wrist or to accessorize my plain black shirt with a scarf, and I forced myself down the stairs. Jackson had been waiting long enough.

Stopping at the door, I took a deep breath and pulled it open.

Jackson was dressed in similar attire, and I allowed myself a moment to appreciate the way his T-shirt molded to his upper body, outlining every defined muscle.

"I will never look at denim the same way again," he said as his eyes traveled back up to meet mine. "You look hot."

"These old things? Really? I pulled them out of the back of my closet." I turned toward the kitchen to grab my purse, feeling his eyes on me.

"That's what all women say."

"No, I'm serious. I literally pulled these out of the back of my closet. I hate jeans."

"Well, they definitely don't hate you," he said, his Southern drawl growing thick and sultry.

The corner of my mouth twitched as I tried not to grin. I didn't usually give in to cheesy lines like that, but damn, he could read the phone book with that Carolina accent, and my clothes would probably melt away before the end of the first page.

"So, where are we going?" I asked, snatching my purse from the counter.

We headed out the door, and I locked up.

"I'm not telling, but I will guarantee that it will be a dating first for you." His grin was cool and so very confident.

"And how exactly can you guarantee that? I've lived here my entire life, and I've probably done every cliché first-date thing you can imagine."

"I know, which is why we are doing something completely different."

He held his hand out toward me and raised his eyebrow. "Are you ready?"

"As I'll ever be," I answered, placing my hand in his.

"Good. Let's go get dirty."

~Jackson~

"If you're taking me to a NASCAR race, then I hate to burst your bubble, but that's already been done," Liv said as we pulled away from the curb of our street.

"No car racing," I answered.

Out of the corner of my eye, I saw her nibble on her bottom lip as we took a left toward downtown.

"Rodeo?" she guessed.

"Around here?" I couldn't help but laugh.

"I don't know—I'm sure it comes to town every once in a while. I was going to guess a hike, but then you turned the wrong way, so I'm clueless."

Placing my hand on her bouncing knee, I steadied it.

"Then, stop guessing. You don't have to be in charge all the time, Liv. Learn to enjoy the passenger seat for a change."

Her eyes briefly met mine before I set my sights back on the road. I heard her shift back in her seat, relaxing into it. Her leg remained steady, and her breathing evened out.

"Picnic?" she whispered.

"Shut it." I laughed.

Ten minutes later, I was parallel-parking a block away from where we were supposed to be.

She nervously looked around. "Um…you know this isn't a great part of town, right?"

"I'm aware."

We stepped out of the car. I made sure the doors were locked, and nothing was in plain view. It was daytime, and my truck was by no means new, but I didn't want to tempt anyone.

"Okay," she answered. "I actually used to work down here, a few blocks back that way." She pointed the opposite way we were headed. "It has a bad rap. There are lots of drug dealers, and it's a run-down neighborhood, but there are still families who need help and children who just want someone to talk to." She looked around, taking in the buildings, as we walked down the sidewalk, hand in hand.

"It was here where I really discovered my love for what I do. I always knew it was something I was interested in, but here—working with families and getting to know them and the lives they lived—that was when I truly knew it was what I was supposed to be doing."

"I honestly don't know what that's like," I confessed.

She stopped and looked up at me. "You don't like being a lawyer?"

"I do, but when I hear you speak about the love you have for your profession, I realize I don't feel that—or at least I haven't for a long time. I remember the feeling from when I first started long ago."

"What changed?"

"Money." I shrugged.

She nodded, understanding seeping through her expression. "Noah," she simply stated.

"Yeah, the curse of a single provider I guess." My thoughts drifted back to the memory of my little man arguing over whether he needed a babysitter this afternoon. He was adamant that I could trust him to be alone. It was never a matter of trust, but more an issue of my nerves lasting through the ordeal. I knew I would have to give in soon, but in the meantime, he was stuck with a sitter.

We continued our short walk down the street in silence until she asked, "If income wasn't a factor, what would you do?"

I thought about it for a moment. "I'd probably still be a lawyer, honestly, but I'd focus more around the ideals I value most—family and helping people who need it most."

"Maybe someday," she offered as we crossed the street

"Maybe someday," I agreed.

I slowed down my gait until we came to a stop in front of the soup kitchen. She looked around, taking in the building and small sign.

"Okay, if we're doing what I think we are, then yes, this is a definite first for me." Her voice was excited and full of anticipation.

It was exactly what I had hoped it would be.

"How do you feel about doing a little volunteer work?"

"This is awesome, Jackson!" she squealed, throwing her arms around me in a giant hug.

I laughed and lifted her off the ground, loving the feel of her body in my arms.

"Okay, come on. We need to get inside. They start preparing dinner hours in advance."

For the next few hours, we slaved away in the kitchen—chopping, slicing, and mixing—until our backs ached, and our fingers were ready to fall off. We talked about everything. I told her about what it was like growing up in Charleston, and she reciprocated with stories of growing up in Richmond. She also asked me about Noah. We fell into a natural rhythm. By the time the last onion was cut, we were both exhausted, but it was all worth it when the organizers placed us side by side and allowed us to help serve the meal we'd assisted in preparing.

Liv was in her element, meeting and greeting everyone, even those I'd rather she wouldn't. She had no fear when it came to people, and she managed to break down even the hardest-looking individuals, earning a smile from them by the time their macaroni and cheese had been dished up.

After we finished, we said good-bye to the other volunteers and thanked the coordinators for letting us participate. Then, we hobbled back to the truck.

I drove us to a quaint little diner not too far from where we lived. We found a booth toward the back where we could rest our feet and not distract others with our awful appearance and funky food odor.

Liv looked over the menu and groaned. "I want all of it, all the food."

I laughed. "Order whatever you want. I think I'm getting double of everything. I'm starving."

Our waitress came by and didn't falter or even raise an eyebrow as I ordered two hamburgers and a double order of fries. Liv stuck with a veggie burger and sweet potato fries, but she added an Oreo milkshake on as a treat.

"You're sharing that," I said as the waitress walked away.

"Because your two meals aren't enough?" she quipped.

"I'm a growing boy."

"No, you're not." She laughed. "But I'll still share because this has to be the most original and best date I've ever been on. Kudos to you, Jackson."

I mimicked the motions of tipping a hat in her direction. "I wanted to prove to you that I was different."

"Why?" she asked.

"Because I know you have...how shall I put this?"

"Been around the block?" she guessed.

I smirked and shook my head. "I was going to say dated a lot, but whatever floats your boat, sweetheart. I'm sure those other men took you out to fancy restaurants and moonlit picnics—believe me, I want to do that, too—but I wanted to show you that I understand you."

"No one has ever done anything like that for me. It was exhilarating."

"I knew it would be, because I know you, Liv."

"How? We've only known each other for a few weeks, and we've spent the majority of that time fighting like cats and dogs."

I leaned forward, resting my arms on the table. "Tell me something about myself, something you've learned about me in the last few weeks."

"Besides the fact that you like pink flamingos?"

A smile tugged at the corner of my mouth. "Yeah, besides that."

"You're an incredibly good father. Everything you do revolves around Noah."

My chest ached, hearing her say those words. I knew it in my own heart, but hearing someone else confirm it meant a lot.

"See? How do you know that after only a few weeks, Liv?"

"Because I know you," she said softly.

"Exactly. Look, I don't know what we're doing. We don't have to put a label on it. Call it whatever you want, but all I know is, I'm not going anywhere. I'm going to stick around until there's nothing new I could possibly learn about you, and even then, I'll probably still stick around just to annoy you."

A laugh escaped her throat as the waitress returned with her milkshake. She unwrapped the straw, dropped it in, and stirred it briefly before leaning forward to close her lips around it.

She finished and then pushed it forward. She watched as I took a long sip through the straw.

"This scares me, Jackson," she said, raw honesty written all over her face.

"Not as much as it scares me."

"So, what do we do to make sure we both don't run away in fear?"

"Take each day as it comes and hope that they're all like this," I said, pushing the milkshake back to her.

"And if they're not?"

"Then, we come back here, order an Oreo milkshake, and remember."

Chapter Eleven

~Liv~

Making the final touches on my long braid, I wrapped the tiny black band around the end and slipped on my sandals before heading to the door. It was Sunday morning, and I was going through the motions of my morning ritual, preparing to make my weekly visit to Mrs. Reid.

Still in a bit of a haze from yesterday—post-date bliss I guessed— it took me a second to recognize the quiet knock coming from the front door.

I ambled down the stairs and walked to the door. I turned the handle and opened the door to find Noah standing before me. He looked nervous, his eyes downcast, and he seemed shorter, with his shoulders sinking down. It wasn't the normal kid I was used to seeing.

"Hey there," I greeted.

"Hey," he answered back shyly.

"What's up? You want to come inside?"

He nodded as I stepped aside to let him pass.

He looked around briefly before turning back to me. "My dad said you go to visit my great-grandma on Sundays?" His expression was hesitant as if he were unsure he should be asking.

I smiled warmly, trying to set his mind at ease. "I do."

"Could I come with you maybe?"

"Of course you can. Whenever you'd like, Noah."

He visibly relaxed.

I turned my head to the side. "I always like to eat before I go. Have you had breakfast yet?"

"Yeah."

"What did you have?" I asked.

He shrugged, and his light-blue eyes that nearly matched his father's met mine. "Lucky Charms."

I laughed, ruffling his hair as I moved past him. "Come on. I'm going to make you a real breakfast."

I turned briefly to find him in the same spot where I'd left him in. "And you're going to help, so don't just stand there!"

He grinned and came racing up behind me. "You're not going to make any of that hippie food, are you?"

I pulled open the refrigerator door. I began pulling things out and then set them on the counter.

"Hippie food?" I laughed. "What exactly is that?"

"I don't know. Plants and nature stuff?"

"That just sounds like food to me, weirdo. Come on. We're going to cut some veggies—you know, nature stuff."

We chopped up some bell peppers and a few mushrooms. I even threw in a little bit of onions when he wasn't looking.

I cracked a few eggs into a bowl, and had him scramble them while I began sautéing the veggies.

"Is that spinach?"

He grimaced as I threw in a few leaves to wilt.

"Yes, and you're going to love it. Promise."

"Okay." He didn't sound convinced.

I let him pour the eggs over the cooked veggies. I tossed in a small handful of cheese and let it melt, and then I flipped it over and cut it in half. After only a few minutes, we had a perfectly cooked omelet.

I pulled two plates from the cupboard, and I poured some freshly squeezed orange juice.

"Do you want some salsa on top?" I drizzled a fresh mix I'd bought from a local grocery store over my half of the omelet.

"Is it spicy?" he asked, eyeing the container with suspicion.

"Nope, not at all."

I handed it to him and watched him mimic my motions, taking a few spoonfuls and placing the salsa on top of his eggs. I waited for him to take his first bite, and I held my breath the entire time he chewed.

"Wow, it's actually good!" he exclaimed.

"See? I told you!"

"Can I come over here every morning?" he asked.

He meant it as a joke, but I could see the little boy inside him, peeking out from behind those light eyes and begging me to say yes.

"Absolutely, Noah. You can cook me breakfast any day of the week," I answered with a wink.

We cleaned up, and Noah even helped me load the dishwasher. As I grabbed my purse, I sent a quick text to Jackson.

Taking Noah to the cemetery. Is that okay?

He immediately replied back.

Yeah, it's great. Thanks for checking in. X

The *X* at the end of his text made my stomach flutter as my memory raced back to our good-bye kiss the day before.

He slowly walked me to my door as if we had all the time in the world. I just wanted to drag him by the hand all the way up to my bedroom where I could discover every delectable inch of Jackson Reid. He cupped my chin, tilting my head, as he leaned forward and tenderly placed his lips against mine. I moaned, long and low, as he deepened the kiss, pushing me against the solid wood behind me. Every masculine hard inch of him pressed into me. It was divine.

"Come inside," I whispered.

"No."

I pulled back and found him smiling.

"Why?" I was pretty sure I was pouting.

"Because that's exactly what everyone else would do."

And that was exactly how he'd left me, a wanting mess of need, on my doorstep, which had probably been his evil intent from the beginning.

Stupid, sexy jerk.

"What?" Noah said as we made our way out the door and toward my car.

Shit, did I say that out loud?

"What? Nothing."

"Adults are weird," he said, shaking his head and smiling.

"Oh, Noah, you are so right."

Both of us were quiet as we walked the curved path to Mrs. Reid's final resting place. Noah's attention moved from name to name as we passed aged gravestones, weathered through the decades. Finally, we stepped off the path and found Etta lying next to her husband, Theodore.

"Do you want some time alone?" I asked.

He looked back and forth between the two stones. "No. Please stay."

I nodded, watching him bend down to trace his fingers over the words etched in the stone.

"I didn't know her that well. Dad wasn't able to take much time off when I was little," he confessed.

"Well, that doesn't mean you didn't love her."

"What was she like?"

"Kind and giving. She loved her garden, and she baked the best cookies and pies."

He smiled. "She used to send us cookies on Christmas. They were good."

"Yeah? What else do you remember about her?" I asked.

"She would always send me a card on my birthday with a ten-dollar bill inside. It always looked new, like she'd gone to the bank especially for me."

I grinned, remembering Etta's love for cards. "She did. She loved sending you those birthday cards, and she would always make sure she went to the bank a month in advance, so she could send it out in time. When she got really sick, I would take her."

"How come you liked her so much, Liv?" The tiny pads of his fingers briefly touched the wilted flowers I'd brought last week.

"I guess it's because, for a while, she was the closest thing to family I had."

"You don't have parents?" He looked up at me from his position on the grass.

"I do, but we haven't spoken in a long time. We don't…get along well."

"That's too bad," he said. "I don't have a mom. I mean, I guess I do, but I think she hates me."

I stepped forward as the protective instinct in me took over, wanting to shield him from such thoughts. "What makes you say that, Noah?"

"She left right after she had me. She must not have loved me much."

I knelt down, so we were eye-to-eye.

"No one could ever hate you, Noah. Whatever reason she had to leave had everything to do with her and her own problems. It had nothing to do with you. Like you said, adults are weird. But kids? Kids are easy to love. You are probably the easiest one of all, so please don't think she left because something is wrong with you, okay?"

"Okay."

"Ready to head back now?" I brushed the dirt from my skirt before helping him up.

He nodded, and we made our way back to the trail.

"Oh, and, Liv?"

"Yeah?"

"You're pretty awesome, too."

~**Jackson**~

"That's just disgusting," Liv said, pointing and shaking her head.

I used the tongs to gently lay the two steaks I'd been marinating all afternoon onto the hot grill.

"No," I argued, "this is culinary perfection. When I'm done, this meat will melt in your mouth. It'll be so tender that it could make babies weep."

She gave me a wry but amused expression.

"A little overboard?" I asked.

"A little bit, and that definitely won't be melting in this mouth."

Her laughter filled the backyard as I finished up putting the food on the grill. I took care when I placed her veggie burger down, making sure it was far away from the meat. I might not understand how she could choose a life without steaks and bacon, but I certainly respected her decision.

Setting the grill's lid down over everything, I walked over to the wicker chairs that had definitely seen better days. My grandmother used to love the outdoors. Her backyard had been a testament to that—at least, when she'd had the energy to keep it up. In the end, I'd been told she had barely been able to venture across her own house, let alone go outside to tend to her plants. If it weren't for Liv, everything would have died. The worn, unused furniture was proof of that.

"I think I need to go furniture shopping," I said, sitting down and looking at the blue paint that had mostly faded to a dull gray. I ran my fingers over the textured pattern, wondering what Nana must have thought about when she'd sat in this same chair.

"She loved to sit out here and watch the fireflies in the summer, and then she'd wait out here for the first snowflake in the winter. I'd yell for her to get inside before she froze." Liv paused and rested her hand on mine. "But she'd want you to make this house your own, Jackson. It's why she gave it to you and not anyone else."

"Out with the old and in with the new?"

"How about a mixture of both?"

Nodding, I looked up and found her brown eyes in the last few remaining sunbeams of the day. "I think I could live with that."

Rising, I moved back over to the grill and checked on our food, flipping the steaks and veggie burger over.

"Noah was quiet when you two came back today. Was he okay?" I added the vegetable skewers Liv had brought over onto the grill.

"Yeah." She smiled. "I think it was good for him to go. He was curious about her, and it gave him a chance to get to know her through my eyes."

"He's never had much family besides me," I said, joining her once again.

"What about your parents? Aren't you close?"

I grabbed a beer from the cooler at our feet and offered her one. I popped the top, and she took it.

"We are." I grabbed another beer and popped the top. "They adore Noah, but right around the time he was five, my dad was eligible for early retirement. They always dreamed of living somewhere different. So, after giving my blessing, they moved to Washington. They have a beautiful house, right on the beach, and my dad owns a boat. They're in heaven."

"Good for them," she commented.

"Yeah, I just wish we saw them more often. Washington is a long flight."

She was silent for a moment, her gaze set on the horizon, as the sun slowly faded away, giving in to the impending night.

"Noah talked about his mother, too," she finally said.

At the mere mention of her, I stiffened instantly, a knee-jerk reaction even now after all these years.

"What did he say?" I asked hesitantly.

"Not much. Just that she left when he was a baby."

She paused, and I felt her eyes on me.

"Jackson, he thinks something is wrong with him."

"What? Why?" My head jerked up.

"He assumed something had to be wrong with him for her to leave," she said softly.

Shaking my head, I let out a shallow breath. "Jesus."

"I think I set him straight." She smiled warmly.

"It should have been me." My hands moved up to my face and through my hair as I leaned forward in my chair.

"Sometimes, kids need to hear these things from someone else."

"You're an amazing woman, Liv," I said, looking up at her.

Her smile widened. "You're not the first person to tell me that."

Edging closer, I reach out to tuck a loose strand of hair behind her ear. "But I'm the first man, right?"

Her lips were so close that I could feel her warm breath against my own.

"Would it make you feel better if I said yes?" Her tone was light and flirty.

"Sweetheart, please keep joking. It's water off my back because soon, every other man who has had the pleasure of paying you a compliment, touching this skin, or kissing these lips will be nothing more than a distant memory."

Just as my lips touched hers, finally doing the one thing I'd been dying to do all night, the screen door creaked behind us as Noah pushed through it.

We broke apart, and I looked up to catch the end of his eye roll. His attention quickly turned toward the grill, and he took in a quick sniff as his mouth curved upward.

"Are we having the steaks well done tonight, Dad?"

"What? Why?" I asked, leaping out of my chair to check on my precious dinner.

Moving swiftly, I lifted the lid, and I was met with smoke. Noah's laughter filled the air just as quickly as the dark plume engulfed the backyard. Noah and I began moving our hands back and forth in an attempt to clear the air.

I cut the gas and got my first look at the steaks. They were blackened beyond repair.

"So, pizza?" Noah suggested.

Liv joined in on the laughter.

"Pizza it is," I said.

Chapter Twelve

~Liv~

"You're dating your hot jerk of a neighbor?" Clare asked as we all gathered around her kitchen island, waiting for dinner to cook.

"Yes," I answered with a coy smile.

"So, your assessment of him has…changed?" Leah guessed, her back to us, as she cut a large baguette.

"Oh, he's still a hot jerk, and he definitely drives me crazy, but in a good way."

"Details!" Leah called out over her shoulder.

"Husband coming through!" Declan announced as he appeared at the doorway. "No more sexy-neighbor talk. I can only handle so much. Besides, he can't be that good-looking. I mean, come on!" He looked down at his own body and back up.

We all burst out in laughter.

He really was a cocky asshole.

"No one is as studly as you, baby," Leah crooned, her voice soft and sultry.

He wandered over to where she was standing, tucking himself behind her, and he scattered kisses across her neck.

"That's right," he purred in her ear.

"Okay, seriously. I'm not sure if I'm going to gag or spontaneously combust from watching the two of them," I said, turning away from the spectacle they were making in the kitchen.

"Join the club," Clare said.

"Speaking of club, where is Logan?" I asked, looking around for our missing member.

Everyone knew where Garrett was. We could all hear him in the living room while masses of children pounced on and attacked him. His laughter mixed with theirs was enough to turn any cold heart into a puddle of mush.

"Logan is on the phone in our bedroom," Clare said.

"Hospital?" Mia asked as she snuck a piece of bread from the pile Leah had been making.

"No, thankfully. Otherwise, he wouldn't be here," Clare explained. "His sister."

My eyebrows furrowed in confusion. "Logan has a sister?"

I'd been around this extended family for years, and I thought that I'd met every member, including Logan's mother. I knew he didn't speak with his father, but I didn't know he had a sister.

Logan came from a wealthy family. I had been brought up in an affluent family as well, but I had a feeling it was pennies compared to the bank account Logan's family was sitting on.

His parents had divorced when he was young, and from what I understood, it hadn't been a pleasant split. While growing up, Logan had barely seen his mother, and he'd spent most of his childhood resenting her. After he'd met Clare, Logan had reconciled with his mother, and she'd been slowly earning back his trust ever since.

"Yeah, his sister has been absent from his life for a while. When his mother, Cece, got married and traded her lavish lifestyle for something a bit simpler, Eva…well, let's just say she disagreed. Logan's been trying to get in touch with her ever since."

"Wow," I said. "I had no idea. What is Eva like?"

"She's exactly what you would expect a girl who had everything and anything she wanted to be like. She's spoiled and spontaneous. She has no sense of ownership or work ethic. I'm not sure she's changed one bit since the day she learned to swipe her daddy's credit card."

We all looked around.

Finally, it was Mia who asked, "What does Logan hope to accomplish?"

"He thinks he can save her from herself," Clare answered.

"What do you think?" Leah asked. The bread now buttered and in the oven, Leah turned and faced us with Declan's arms wrapped around her waist.

"I don't know," Clare admitted, shaking her head.

"Hey, guys," Logan said.

We all turned and saw him entering the room. He looked tired. His hair was a mess, probably from his worried hands moving through it, and faint lines appeared around his eyes. Those weren't normally there unless he'd pulled a double at the hospital.

"How did it go?" Clare asked, immediately moving to his side.

He wrapped his large body around her and held on like she was a lifeline.

"Not as well as I'd hoped. She wouldn't even tell me where she is."

"But she's okay?" I asked, concern echoing in each word.

"I guess. I mean, moneywise, yeah. She's got plenty of that, thanks to our father. He gave up on her a long time ago, and he just funnels it to her without even bothering to ask what she is spending it on."

"She'll come around," I said, hoping my words came true.

I knew how important family was to Logan, how important it was to everyone—even me.

~**Jackson**~

"Now, you're sure you know what you are doing?" I asked.

Liv looked up at me with slight hesitation. She was on her knees. It was quite a lovely sight actually.

"Yes," she answered.

I couldn't help but grin. "You're sure? Because once you start, there's no going back."

"You're making me nervous, Jackson!" she yelled, throwing a piece of sandpaper up at my face.

I ducked as my deep laughter filled the backyard.

"I'm just fucking with you, Liv."

Her gaze fell back on the wicker chair that was flipped over on its side in front of her.

After a few days of walking back and forth past my patio door, I'd decided against buying new patio furniture. Instead, I'd asked Liv to help me revamp the existing pieces. I'd seen what she'd done with some of the chairs and tables in her own house, so I knew she was experienced in salvaging old furniture. Plus, it was time alone with her.

When I'd asked Noah if he wanted to help tonight, he'd looked at me like I was clinically insane. He was happily inside where it was cool and air-conditioned, probably blowing up aliens or cop cars on the PlayStation.

For the next hour or two, I had Liv all to myself.

Dating a single father was an imperfect science—especially when the single father happened to be new in town, had a brand-new, highly demanding job, and had little babysitting contacts.

Adding in Liv and her own responsibilities, I had the biggest case of blue balls known to man.

I wasn't complaining.

Okay, I was—slightly. But I knew it would be worth the wait. Liv was worth a thousand dates that ended at the door rather than in a bed. The longer I knew her, the more I realized that Liv was the one woman I intended to keep. So, I could deal with the blue balls and dates that weren't really dates since we were never truly alone. I was in it for the long haul.

I just hoped she was, too.

"So, where do we start, boss?" I asked, kneeling down beside her.

"We need to scrape and sand off as much of the old paint as possible. It's not going to be fun," she warned.

"Guess we'll have to find something fun to talk about then," I replied.

"Like what?"

She handed me a gritty piece of sandpaper, and I watched as she began moving her own piece along the wicker, creating a plume of dust.

"Hmm…" I mimicked her movements with my own sandpaper. "Let's play Truth or Dare," I challenged.

Her smile turned mischievous, setting down the sandpaper to grab a large metal tool to scrape off a large patch of paint that had begun to chip away.

"Okay, but how exactly are we going to do dares when we are supposed to be working, genius?"

"Just truths then?"

"So, basically, you just want to know all my darkest, deepest secrets?"

"Yep," I admitted.

"Fine." She laughed. "But I get to go first," she said, her eyebrow angling up in amusement.

"Deal," I agreed.

"How old were you when you lost your virginity?" she asked, a gleam of wickedness cascading across her face.

"No holding back, huh?"

"Nope. Spill it."

"Okay, okay, but no laughing." I sighed. "I was nineteen."

"Nineteen!" she squeaked. "I would never have guessed."

"Yeah, well, I was a tenderhearted youth, and I had it in my head that I was going to wait until the right girl came along."

"And did she?" she asked hesitantly.

"Nope," I answered bluntly. "But I got Noah out of the deal, so I think that counts as a win."

I tried to cover up the bitterness with a smile, but I could tell I wasn't doing a great job.

"Her name was Natalie," I finally said. "We met in college. Coming from my middle-class, Southern upbringing, Nat was completely foreign to me. She was from Arizona, and she had lived on an Indian reservation for part of her life. She was exotic and looked like Pocahontas, and she was totally out there in the way she lived her life. To a wide-eyed boy like me, she was completely dangerous."

"Dangerous how?" Liv asked. Her sanding had stopped, and she was now focused solely on me.

"Everyone told me to stay away from her. They said she was bad news and that she'd bring me nothing but misery, but I was young and naive. She'd come from a questionable past, and she had broken a dozen hearts by the time we found each other. The attention she gave me was hypnotizing and addictive, and I swore she was the one I was meant to be with forever.

"I thought I was the special one because she'd stayed. We dated through college and lived together. Shortly after graduation, she told me she was pregnant. I was ecstatic, but she was less than thrilled. It wasn't great timing, but I knew we'd figure it out. I bought her a tiny diamond ring and promised to marry her after our son was born. When I saw the hesitation in her eyes, I told her that my father had given me a large sum of money. I thought she would be happy."

"Oh, please tell me she didn't—"

"She did," I said. "Being the trustworthy dumb fuck that I was, I gave her access to the account. She was my fiancée, and she was carrying my child. I wanted her to know that I would take care of her. Weeks after Noah was born, she was gone—along with the money."

Liv's hand touched mine, and I felt her warmth seeping into me.

"Were there any clues? Or were you completely blindsided?"

I shook my head. "I knew something was amiss. She hadn't been happy for months—basically since she'd found out she was pregnant. Toward the end, she was on the phone a lot. I tried to tell myself that she was just adjusting, but now, I don't know. There was probably someone else."

"Amazing," was all Liv said.

"Yeah," I answered. "An amazing bitch."

"No—I mean, yes, I guess. But I was referring to you. Think about what you just told me, Jackson, but fast-forward eleven years to now and include everything you've accomplished. That one event could have crushed you, but instead, you became stronger."

"I had to. Noah needed me to."

"There are always going to be people in our lives who will ruin us and pull us down into our own personal hell, but then there are the ones who will build us back up and help restore us to what we are meant to be."

"You're very wise, Miss Prescott." I smiled.

"I know. Lots of education." She winked. "We suck at this game. Quick, ask me something embarrassing. Better yet, give me a dare and even the playing field."

"I thought we weren't doing dares," I said, feeling my mood improving.

"Didn't anyone teach you that it's okay to break the rules every once in a while?"

"Okay, but don't say I didn't warn you." I grinned.

"Lay it on me, counselor."

"I dare you…to strip down…right here and let me take a picture of you."

She laughed, her eyes immediately darting to the warm glow within my house, knowing Noah was inside.

"He's glued to the TV. Don't use him as an excuse," I challenged.

"Need something for your spank bank, Mr. Reid?" she asked, her fingers moving down to the hem of her tank top.

"Something like that."

With a quick whoosh, her top was on the grass next to us. Black lace covered her beautiful round breasts, displaying a deep valley where I wanted to dive in and never come back.

"Now, the shorts, Liv," I instructed.

She stood up as I watched from below. She slowly unbuttoned them and slid her fingers underneath the denim before sliding them over her hips. When they fell to the ground, she kicked them aside. Thin lace panties barely covered her most intimate parts, making my mouth water as I yearned for a glimpse of what was hidden beneath.

She sank back onto her knees, spreading her legs as wide as they would go and leaned forward on her palms. "Well, are you going to take your shot or not?" she asked with a smirk.

"Right!" I nearly barked, shoving my hand into my pocket to grab my phone.

The pose she was in—covered in a few scraps of lace, her breasts jutting forward, as mountains of ebony dark hair cascaded down all around her—was enough to make any man forget his own name.

At that moment, I'd forgotten everything, except for the woman in front of me.

I clicked as many photos as I could get in quick succession, and then I dropped the phone to the ground.

I needed to touch her.

"Dear God, you're gorgeous," I whispered, moving closer until I was kneeling before her. My hand found the curve of her ass, as I pulled her heated body against me. "I can't wait to be inside you, Liv. I want you so bad."

"I'm right here." She nearly moaned in my ear. "Unfortunately, you didn't include that in the bet."

Wait—what?

I pulled back to find her smiling. Then, that smile led to a devilish giggle.

"Pictures only, remember?" she teased. "That means the clothes have to go back on."

She made a pouty face as she grabbed her tank top and shorts. Not bothering to put on either, she stood in front of me. I still couldn't move. I was in complete shock from this crazy woman.

Liv skipped across the yard without a care in the world even though she was half naked. She unlocked the gates separating our yards. "Good night, Jackson."

"What about the furniture?" I asked, nearly whimpering.

"I'm sure you can handle it. Have a good night." She winked. "Think of me."

My eyes followed her as she took her time making her way to her back door with her perky little ass swinging behind her. I heard the door lock behind her as I sat there on my knees, sporting the biggest boner in history.

I looked down, picked up my phone, and scrolled through the pictures I'd taken. "This woman is going to kill me," I muttered as I attempted to stand.

I had a feeling though that there would be no better way to go.

~Jackson~

A knock came to my office door late Tuesday afternoon as I was finishing up some notes on a case. I gave the okay to enter, and my boss Mark, one of the senior partners of the firm, greeted me. For a cutthroat lawyer, he was a pretty stand-up guy, and with each passing week, I had grown to like him more and more.

"Hey, Mark. How's it going?"

"Not too bad. How about you? Things okay over here?" he asked as a sly smirk spread across his face.

Many people had let Mark's young appearance sway them in the courtroom, assuming his lack of experience would hurt him in the long run. Those who doubted him were always the first to discover just how quickly he could crush them. He was a shark with a keen eye for detail and model good looks that could influence any juror in his favor.

"Yeah. Why?" I asked.

"Well, when I came over and said hi to Kate, I asked if you could spare a few minutes. She mumbled something and then said, 'It wouldn't do any good to call him. He won't answer anyway.' Then, she just shooed me in here."

I shook my head, cradling it in my hands. It was all I could do to keep myself from banging it against the hard wood of my desk.

"So, not okay then?" he guessed, as I looked up to see him taking a seat in one of the plush leather chairs in front of me.

"Things could be better," I admitted.

"You've been here barely a month, man. How did you piss off your secretary so badly?"

"I took her out on a date, maybe two," I confessed.

He laughed before saying the words I'd repeated to myself over and over, "You're a dumbass."

"I know."

"What were you thinking? You don't shit where you eat."

My face twisted in horror. "That is a terrible, terrible analogy."

He shrugged. "I'm not the one who fucked my secretary."

"I didn't fuck her!" I countered. "I barely even touched her," I added quietly.

"So, why is she so upset?" He leaned back, swinging his feet up onto my desk.

My eyebrow rose as he made himself comfortable.

"Oh, she wanted you to fuck her," he guessed. "And you brushed her off. You really are a dumbass."

"I just wasn't interested."

"Then, why did you take her out in the first place?" he challenged.

"Because I thought if I dated her, I'd stop thinking about someone else."

"That never works, my friend."

"Obviously."

"So, you left your sexy secretary hanging. What happened with the girl you were trying to forget?"

The small grin that spread across my face seemed to answer his question.

"Nice. Does Kate know about her?" he asked.

"She just called," I said, grimacing slightly.

"Oh, hence the crazy talk I was confronted with out there."

"Yep."

"Dude, you've got to find a new secretary."

"I can't fire her because I'm an idiot! That's just wrong, and… well, highly illegal," I replied, my head finding the comforting cradle of my hands once again.

"No, you can't, but Brayden needs a new secretary. His just left to be a full-time mom. Might be a good change of scenery for her."

It wasn't a terrible idea. "She'd probably be relieved to get rid of me," I admitted.

"And in the meantime," he said, "we'll work on getting you someone new. Maybe a gay guy or a nice old lady."

"Jackass." I laughed.

The rest of our talk was boring and mostly work-related, ending with Mark telling me the news buzzing around the entire office.

"We got a call this morning," he announced, his body nearly vibrating.

"Okay?"

"Senator Prescott is coming out of retirement. He's apparently putting together a team."

"What kind of team?"

"The word on the street is, he's going to make a bid for the presidency."

"Holy shit," I whispered.

This was huge. Senator Douglas Prescott was well loved in Virginia and beyond. Coming from South Carolina where we had our own political superstars, I hadn't followed his career closely, but I knew the bare facts. A conservative superstar, he'd gone from state politics all the way to US Senator, and he'd served for years before retiring during a time people believed to be the height of his career. Maybe it had just been a well-timed hiatus, so he could prepare for bigger and better things.

If he were indeed hoping to enter the race for the White House, it could be huge for the state.

"So, how does this affect us?" I asked.

"He wants legal representation on hand, and he's keeping everything local."

"This would be great for us."

He agreed, "It would be an amazing honor."

"A bit of a soft spot for the Senator?" I laughed.

"More like a giant hard-on if we manage to land this account."

I shook my head in wonder. This guy had a crude comeback for everything.

"So, tell me about your woman," he said.

"You say hard-on, and the next thing that comes out of your mouth is about my girlfriend?"

As he chuckled, the word *girlfriend* bobbed around in my head. I'd never said it before. Liv and I hadn't discussed it. I didn't even know if she would be okay with the term, but damn, the word had felt good leaving the tip of my tongue.

"Seriously though, what's she like?"

"The exact opposite of me," I replied. "She drives me insane. She's a vegetarian, and she wears a million pieces of silver jewelry all at once. She yells at me about my truck, and she has a huge tattoo that runs down her shoulder."

For once, Mark was silent—for a moment at least.

"The sex must be amazing."

"Dude!"

"Oh, come on, Jackson. I've been married for a hundred years. Throw me a bone."

"That's none of your goddamn business," I replied, chucking my pen at his head.

He ducked and came back up, laughing.

"Okay, I get it," he answered, his feet hitting the floor. He rose from the chair and walked to the door, pausing just before turning the knob. "If you need help with those blue balls you are obviously sporting, I've got an awesome lake house. Just ask, and it's yours to use whenever."

He'd made it halfway out the door before I made him turn around.

I ignored the rolling laughter that accompanied him back into my office.

~Liv~

I had just put my keys down on the counter, contemplating whether or not to grab a snack before starting dinner, when the doorbell rang. I looked over at the microwave and double-checked the time.

Jackson and Noah weren't supposed to be here for an hour.

Since I had walked away in the middle of the night, nearly naked, we'd been nearly inseparable. Meals were almost always shared in the evenings, and weekends were already being planned in advance.

I'd never thought long-term when dating someone. Honestly, I normally never thought past the meal I was ordering or the outfit I was picking out of my closet. Dating was casual and fun, but that was always the gist of it—nothing more, nothing less.

Had Mia been right? Had I really been dating all the wrong men on purpose?

I was guessing dating was different for the majority of others. The rest of the world surely felt something a bit deeper when becoming romantically involved with someone they were attracted to.

I didn't consider myself a shallow person—quite the opposite in fact.

Could I really have been self-sabotaging my love life—intentionally dating men I knew I'd never want to keep so that I'd never settle down?

How did I miss that?

My master's degree had definitely not prepared me for how to evaluate my own problems.

Moving swiftly, I headed for the door to greet my mystery visitor.

I came face-to-face with Victor.

What the hell?

"Hi, Victor. What are you doing here?" I asked, not even attempting to mask the rudeness in my tone.

"We need to talk, Olivia," he demanded, his clipped tone nearly slapping me in the face.

Why did I date this guy?

"It's Liv, remember? And I thought we already discussed everything."

He pushed past me, not bothering to wait for an invitation. The strong stench of alcohol accompanied him, and I felt unease starting to take root in my gut.

"You talked, Liv, and I listened. It's my turn now." His accent was thicker, hinting at just how angry he was with me.

"Look," I said, turning to face him, "I had a good time with you, Victor, but it was time to move on."

He laughed, cold and hollow. "Move on with whom?"

"I don't really see how any of that is your business."

His eyes flared with ire as he stalked forward. I took several steps backward until I felt the doorknob wedging deep into my back. He continued, his focus locked on me, until I was pressed against the door by his immovable hard body.

During the few weeks I'd dated Victor, I'd never feared him. He'd been intense and possessive, but I'd chalked those specific personality traits up to his nationality. Having been raised in a completely opposite part of the world, I couldn't fault him for being different. But this new Victor was beyond basic cultural variations.

In that moment, I was scared beyond reason.

"Victor, please," I whimpered, not knowing what I was asking for but knowing I needed to do something, anything.

"Please what?" His voice was deep and boiling with rage.

"Please stop," I begged. "You said you wanted to talk, so let's talk."

"No," he growled. "I like this position much better. Why are you so frightened, Olivia? It's not like we haven't done this before." His hand curved around my waist and gripped it hard. "Or are you afraid your boyfriend might find out?"

"Her boyfriend might kick your ass and toss it in jail," a familiar voice said.

I looked up to find Jackson grabbing Victor by the neck before pulling him off me and throwing him to the floor. I felt air rush into my lungs for the first time in minutes as I watched Jackson knock Victor out with one blow.

It's over.

My knees gave way, and my body hit the floor, trembling everywhere.

"Liv, sweetheart," Jackson called out.

His safe warm arms wrapped around me, and I was lifted into his embrace.

"I'm going to move you to the living room and call the police." His hand smoothed over my face, through my hair down my shoulder. "Did he hurt you?" he asked softly.

"No," I managed to say.

He gently laid me down onto the sofa and ever so carefully kissed my forehead before wrapping me in a throw blanket. Keeping one eye on the entryway where Victor was sprawled out on the floor and the other on me, he pulled out his phone and called the police.

Five minutes later, uniformed men roused Victor back into consciousness and threw him in the back of a cop car. Jackson and I each gave statements before the police officers left, and after what seemed like forever, the house was once again silent.

Jackson returned to the couch after locking the door. "I don't want you to stay here tonight," he said gently.

"Okay," I agreed.

I really didn't want to be alone.

He disappeared for a few minutes and returned with a bag. "I didn't know quite what you needed, so I guessed. If you need anything else, I can run back over and get it," he offered.

"I just need you," I confessed.

"That I can do."

With the throw still firmly attached to my shoulders, I walked next door with Jackson. He kept his arm wrapped around my waist until we entered the living room, and he helped me ease on to the sofa.

"Hey, Liv," Noah said quietly. He'd walked in from the kitchen, and he was standing behind his father.

"Hi, Noah," was all I could manage to say.

"I made dinner for everyone."

I glanced up at him, seeing his sweet and shy disposition. That was why the dam broke, and I lost it. "Thank you, Noah," I said through the tears.

Two sets of arms circled around me and held me as I cried. It was exactly what I needed—both of them.

~Jackson~

It had taken every ounce of control I had not to kill that man when I saw his hands on Liv. Seeing her now, so frail and weak in my arms made me seriously reconsider my levelheaded decision to see him behind bars instead of ripping him apart.

For a split second, I'd assumed the worst when I had pulled up to the curb and found that familiar car parked outside her house. Watching her leave in it before, I hadn't forgotten what it looked like.

I thought I would never see it again, but arriving home from work that night, I killed the engine to my truck, looked up, and found the bastard's car right in front of her house.

My first gut reaction was utter betrayal.

What an amazing dumbass I was to go down this path again. Hadn't I learned anything from my experience with Natalie?

My knuckles went white at the sight of his car sitting there, and my imagination ran wild with the images of what could be going on in that house.

A hint of rationale decided to make an appearance in my train of thought, and I suddenly wondered why Liv would invite him over at the exact time she knew I would be getting home from work.

What had I done to deserve such treatment?

Nothing.

One thing I'd learned about Liv along the way was, she would never do something so callous.

So, what piece of the puzzle was I missing?

I jumped out of my truck and took a step forward toward her house, hating myself for it.

What if I was wrong, and she really was in there with him, doing the very things I'd imagined?

Did I need the visual?

No, but I'd still pressed on.

Something about the entire situation bothered me, which was why I found myself at her door. Just as I was ready to knock, I heard her voice and stopped.

"Victor, please," Liv said, her voice sounding weak and fright-

ened.

"Please what?" a male voice answered back..

"Please stop," she begged, fear and terror seeping through the door.

Panic took over, as I ran towards the back of her house, knowing she kept a key hidden in a flowerpot for emergencies.

A week ago, after we'd gone jogging, she'd found that she locked herself out, and I'd watched as she snuck back here to dig the key out. I had told her that it was a terrible place to put a key.

She'd just rolled her eyes and said, "Maybe I should just give it to you. That way, you'll have an easier time with the balloons next go-around."

I'd just hoped she hadn't listened to me.

Making my way into the backyard, I raced up to the patio. My hands dug into the dirt and found the shiny metal key. With shaky fingers, I unlocked the door and silently walked in, trying to give myself the advantage I knew I needed. I couldn't allow this bastard to hurt her.

Knocking him out had been the least I could do. Knowing anything further would land me in a jail cell right next to him had prevented me from doing more.

Seeing Liv, usually so fierce and strong, reduced to a timid, scared mess had made me angry and brought out a protective side I didn't know I possessed for anyone other than Noah.

She'd been asleep for about an hour, curled up in my arms, as we lounged on the couch in the living room. Watching her fall apart in Noah's and my arms had been difficult, but I'd never been more proud of my boy for being so strong. When I'd called him while waiting for the cops to come to Liv's, I'd only said that Liv was attacked. He hadn't needed to know anything more.

He'd obviously been worried, but his chief concern had been what he could do to help. He'd volunteered to make dinner, grab a blanket, and do anything else to make our new guest comfortable. When Liv had started crying, I'd thought he might shy away from the immense emotions, but instead, he'd moved forward and held her. After Liv had calmed down a bit, Noah had gone to his room for the night, leaving just the two of us.

My little boy was growing up, and for once, the thought didn't scare me.

Shifting slightly, I tucked my arms under Liv's legs and lifted her from the couch. She stirred slightly but stayed asleep as I carried her upstairs to my bedroom. I wanted to make sure Liv felt cared for this evening. Therefore, she got the bed.

Laying her down on the soft mattress, I pulled the covers around her and bent down to kiss her cheek.

"Jackson, don't leave me," she murmured.

"Are you sure? I was going to sleep on the sofa."

Considering she had just had a traumatic event, I didn't know how much intimacy she would be able to handle, so I had decided earlier to let her have the room to herself.

"Please, just hold me."

I tugged off my pants, leaving my boxers and T-shirt in place, and I slid under the covers next to her. She was dressed in one of my old shirts and a pair of her own shorts. I pulled her closer to me until her back touched my torso.

"I should have been braver," she said softly.

I lifted my head and gently rolled her toward me. "What do you mean?"

"When he came at me, I froze. I didn't do anything. I'd just always thought that if I were ever in a situation like that, I would be braver, stronger."

"Listen to me, Liv. You are not weak. What happened today is a testament to that. I heard you. You did everything you could. You tried to talk him down. That was the smartest thing you could have done. Anything else could have gotten you hurt."

She rolled over, fitting her body into mine, as I wrapped my arm around her waist.

"Thank you for being there for me today," she whispered.

"I'll always be there for you," I vowed before sleep claimed us both.

Chapter Fourteen

~Liv~

For the first time since going into business on my own, I called my assistant the next morning, shortly after waking up in Jackson's arms, and I had her cancel all my patients for the day.

She didn't ask questions, but I knew she must have realized it was huge. I pushed End on my phone and set it down on the bedside table. Pulling my knees up to my chest, I gazed out the window toward my house.

"You okay?"

I turned back to find Jackson awake, his head propped up on his hand as the other reached out for me. I met his hand halfway and watched as our fingers wove together, realizing I'd never once craved someone as deeply as I did with Jackson. It was as if my body and soul recognized him as someone safe and special, long before any other part of me had.

"I canceled on my patients," I answered.

"You can't be everything to everyone all the time, Liv. Some-times, you have to take a moment for yourself."

He tugged at my hand until I snuggled down next to him. The tips of our noses touched and I could feel his warm breath on the nape of my neck,

"I just feel like I've failed them," I admitted.

His arms wrapped around me, and I felt the heat from his body soak into my pores.

"They'll understand," he urged. "Besides, you're evading the question. I asked if you were okay. I wasn't asking about your pa-tients."

It was a simple question. Was I okay?

Shouldn't it be a simple answer?

"Honestly, I don't know. I think back to yesterday, and I feel noth-ing and everything, all at the same time. It could have been so much worse," I said, my voice starting to quiver.

"But it wasn't."

"No, because you came." I looked up at him, staring into those silvery gray eyes I'd grown so fond of, and I saw a future I'd never known I would ever want. The possibility scared me. Feeling sudden-ly overwhelmed, I turned away, turning toward the alarm clock sitting on the bedside table.

"Shouldn't you be getting ready for work soon?" I asked, know-ing he usually left for work around this time.

"Actually"—he smiled,—"I was just about to call in sick myself."

"Jackson, you can't! You just started this job!" I nearly screeched.

Not moving an inch, his grin widened. "Watch me."

He leaned forward, grabbing his cell phone off the nightstand. I stared in awed silence as he punched a few buttons and pulled the phone up to his ear.

"You really shouldn't do—" I was cut off as he held up a finger and proceeded to greet the person on the other end.

He rose from the bed and motioned to me that he was headed downstairs. His phone conversation continued as he made his way down the stairs, the sound of his voice disappearing as he moved through the house.

I looked around briefly—for what, I wasn't sure—and I finally decided to get up. I'd never spent the night at a man's house without dying to vacate the premises as soon as the sun broke over the horizon.

Mia was right. I really was kind of like a dude.

Over the years, I'd convinced myself that it was because I was a solitary person who enjoyed my alone time. I'd hated staying over at a man's house because it was foreign to me—different bed, strange sheets, and unhealthy food options in the morning. But really, it had nothing to do with any of that.

The majority of my adult life, I had been living with a genuine fear of intimacy when it came to members of the opposite sex. I thrived on exploring emotions in other areas of my life—both professionally and personally—but when it came to my love life, I would close myself off.

Until now.

Jackson's mattress felt different, and his sheets were definitely new, but none of that mattered anymore because of him. If I went downstairs and all he had to serve me was Pop-Tarts and Frosted Flakes, I'd happily take it.

Because it was Jackson.

I wasn't ready to walk down the aisle or buy a minivan quite yet, but at least I could get out of this bed, walk down the stairs, and know that I was where I was supposed to be.

For once in my life, I wasn't closing myself off to the possibility of more.

~Jackson~

After setting the coffee maker to brew, I headed to my desk and flipped open my laptop.

I might have called in sick, but I still had a few things to accomplish remotely.

I logged in and waited for everything to boot up, my eyes shifting toward the window where I could see Liv's house next door.

I'd felt raw fear only a handful of times in my life.

When I'd awoken to find Natalie and every shred of her existence gone from my life, the dread of being a single father had hit me hard.

She'd left nothing but a note—a single sentence.

I'm not meant for either of you.

After walking into the tiny room we had converted into a nursery, I'd looked down at my newborn son and wept. I'd barely figured out how to be a father. How could I ever replace a mother?

But somehow, I had been enough.

Other times in my life, like when Noah fell or was injured, I'd experience that heart-stopping sensation because life had suddenly changed and things would always be different.

I'd felt it again last night as I walked up to Liv's door and heard her fragile voice begging for mercy.

Anger had welled up in my veins, and I'd surged ahead to take down the intruder who dared to lay a hand on her, but behind the all-consuming rage had been raw fear.

What if I had been too late? What if she had already been hurt?

Even after finding her untouched and unharmed, my anxiety hadn't lessened. The fluttering feeling in my gut had still twisted and turned me into knots.

But now, everything was over, and she was here, safe and sound, yet I still worried.

Would she pull away now?

I realized I had been gazing out the window for probably eons as my mind went on endlessly without reason.

Focusing back on the task at hand, I turned to my computer and pulled up the Internet browser.

Right now, I needed to focus—at least for a couple of minutes.

Taking the day off wasn't a problem. Normally, I wouldn't be asked to do much of anything, but a potential high-profile client would be visiting the firm tomorrow, so Mark wanted me prepped and ready for when the Senator walked through the door, which meant I had to do research. I was expected to know as much as possible by tomorrow morning. If I wanted to spend today with Liv, then I needed to start cramming.

Most of the information I found, I'd already learned from watching the news and reading the paper. Senator Prescott was the son of a local farmer. He was the top in his high school class, and he'd gone on to study political science at the University of Virginia. He'd received his law degree from Princeton, passed the bar, and taken his first position as a junior associate back in his home state of Virginia. He was married with one daughter—

"What are you doing?"

I turned around to see Liv frozen behind me with a mix of shock and horror written all over her face.

"Oh, sorry," I said. "Bit of research for work."

"You're researching Senator Prescott?" She folded her arms across her chest.

I nodded, motioning toward the article on the screen. She stepped forward to take a closer look at the photo towards the bottom. It was an older one from when he'd first run for state senate. It showed him up on stage, much younger-looking, waving to the crowd with his proud wife and child behind him.

Glancing up at Liv, I was about to explain the firm's opportunity, but I was halted by the look of pure devastation spread across her features.

"I loved that dress," she said softly.

"What?"

"The way it shimmered under the lights on that stage. It made me feel like a princess. He always said I was, you know? His princess. But after that moment, I wasn't. Work was. It became his wife, his mistress, and the very reason for his existence."

I jerked my head back to the picture on the screen, narrowing my focus on the little girl standing in the background. Dark curls framed her tiny face—a face I'd seen before.

"You're his daughter," I said, turning back to Liv.

She simply nodded.

"Why didn't you tell me?"

She shrugged. "I never tell anyone."

Since I'd met Liv, she'd never mentioned family, and when she had, all she'd ever said was, there was none. Sure, they had the same last name but so did a lot of people. Plus, Liv didn't exactly look like a senator's daughter. I'd never even considered her elusive family could in fact be state royalty.

"What happened?"

"It's a long story," she replied.

"Well, why don't I make us some coffee, and you can tell me

about it?"

"Okay."

She sat down at the small kitchen table, the one I'd sat at years before when I was small and came to visit for the summer. Nana would make pancakes and sing songs she'd learned from church while I'd color pictures or play with Legos on that worn, old oak tabletop.

Liv's fingers slid across the grooves and dents that age had brought to the table as she gathered her thoughts. I poured us each a cup of coffee and grabbed the cream from the fridge. I sat down beside her and handed her a cup.

"My father was my world when I was growing up. He was the best kind of dad," she said, smiling. "But then, he became Senator Prescott, and everything shifted—his focus, priorities and even me. His entire world revolved about his image, the next campaign, and what the voters thought. He was swept up in this whirlwind, and my mother and I were left by the sidelines to watch."

"You grew apart," I guessed.

She took a sip of her coffee, not bothering to add anything to it. I, on the other hand, poured in a hefty amount of cream and dumped in three spoonfuls of sugar before bringing the cup to my lips.

"It was more than that. I was always a little different. I never fit in with any of my parents' friends' kids—until Mia. Mia was like me, different and special. We got into our fair share of trouble, me especially." She grinned.

"But soon after graduation, Mia left, and it was just me. I went off to college, and for the first time, I was on my own. It should have been liberating. I should have felt free, but I had this sudden realization that none of that would actually happen. I had always lived with the understanding that my parents would take care of me, so I wasn't free or on my own, and I never would be until I learned to take care of myself. For the first time, I wanted to see what the world would be like without a safety net. So, I changed my major from business to sociology, and I told my parents I wanted to change the world."

"Your parents didn't approve?"

She shook her head as her hands wrapped around the warm cup. "No, not at all. My father was very upset. He gave me an ultimatum, thinking I would never be brave enough to defy him. But I did, and

I've been on my own ever since."

"They really let you walk away?"

"Not at first. My mother begged me to reconsider, but I knew what I wanted to do with my life. At this point, I think the press caught wind of some sort of family crisis, and that's when the lines of communication severed completely. Two weeks later, I received a check in the mail with a note that said they loved me—a parting gift, I guess. That was how I paid for my house."

"So, they helped you start over anyway?"

"Yeah"—she chuckled under her breath—"I guess they did."

"Do you ever think about contacting them?"

"All the time," she admitted.

"Why don't you?"

She looked out the window and sighed. "Perhaps I'm hoping they'll love me enough to make the first move."

"What if that never happens, Liv?"

"Then, I guess I have my answer."

~Jackson~

Liv looked up at me, her lips curved into a flirtatious grin that held mischief and humor. The serene water of the lake sparkled behind her. Boats zoomed by the windows on occasion, making white trails in the dark blue waves.

"Do you…have any eights?" she asked.

I shook my head, unable to keep from smiling back at her. "Go fish."

"Damn it. I have half the deck already!"

"Guess I should have warned you that the Reid men are supreme masters of Go Fish." I laughed.

"I should have given up after Noah kicked my butt the first time."

She threw a piece of popcorn at Noah, and he chuckled.

"It's not my fault you suck at this game."

"Hey, be nice to your elders."

"You're not my elder. You're just Liv."

She didn't respond, but the way she bit her lip, trying to cover the shy smile spreading across her face, told me Noah's response meant a lot to her.

Since that evening when I'd found Liv against her front door, frightened and scared, as a man she'd once trusted tried to take advantage of her, I'd watched her slowly coming back to life.

It had only been a few days, but I'd started to recognize the fiery woman I'd grown to know. Every day that pushed us further from that moment, she would come out of her shell more. The first day had been the worst. We had spent the majority of the day wrapped around each other, watching old '80s movies while eating popcorn and candy. I'd known it was bad when she ate an entire box of Milk Duds.

The following day, she'd seemed to find peace, going back to her patients and becoming immersed in their lives once more. It wasn't until she'd come home and remembered I'd met with her father that I saw her falter.

"I didn't tell him about you," I assured her.
"How was he?" she asked quietly.
"In charge, commanding, and captivating."
She nodded and fell into my arms. "I miss him."
"I know."

The instant her father had walked into the building, my fists had tightened, and the need to defend Liv had overwhelmed me. This man had hurt her.

The last man who had hurt her ended up with a broken nose and a trip to jail.

Yet, her father had stood in front of me, and I couldn't do a damn thing.

It had been excruciating to shake his hand and talk to him as if he were just another potential client and not the man who had crushed her heart.

I had wanted to ask him so many things.

Why?

How could he have forgotten about her? How could anyone forget about someone as amazing as Liv?

But I had Noah and bills and a life of responsibilities that I couldn't forget.

So, I had let reason win that day. I'd managed to keep my job and land the client my boss wanted so badly.

It looked like I'd be spending a lot more time with Senator Prescott.

"All right, I give up. I forfeit!" Liv threw her massive pile of cards down on the coffee table we were gathered around.

The *quaint* cabin Mark owned was light years from the definition of the word. It was massive, extravagant, and luxurious in every sense of the word. But Mark came from wealth, and he was a founding partner in one of the top firms in the city, so I guessed it made sense.

My romantic weekend hadn't turned out to be exactly what I originally planned, but considering the events of the past week, I wanted to play it safe and go for a family-fun theme rather than a couples retreat.

I knew she was recovering, and I had decided that pressure—in any form at this point—was the last thing she needed.

"I'm going to go upstairs and play on the Xbox," Noah announced, placing his cards on the table before stretching his arms above his head. He yawned loudly and then hopped up onto his feet.

I almost called him out on the fact that he hadn't bothered asking for permission, but realizing he was leaving Liv and me alone for the first time all day, I gladly let him go.

"What do you want to do now?" I asked, turning toward her.

The sun was disappearing into the lake, sending shards of orange and yellow light in every direction.

"I've been dying to go into that hot tub ever since we arrived," she said, her eyes meeting mine as she finished collecting the playing cards scattered in front of her.

My stomach knotted together as she spoke, and my dick twitched at the mere mention of us in a hot tub—alone.

"Sounds good." The words tumbled out of my mouth before my brain could even register what was happening.

This was supposed to be a safe and low-key weekend. Nothing was supposed to happen.

I would never survive seeing her in a bikini, wet and nearly naked beside me.

It was too bad my body hadn't realized that fact because I was already racing upstairs to change.

~Liv~

While Jackson changed in the guest bedroom, I pulled out my suit and began undressing. I let the fabric of my dress pool to the floor, and then I slowly removed my undergarments. As I put on my bikini in front of the large mirror, I stopped for a moment and just stared at the reflection in front of me.

I still looked like me, but I felt completely different.

If someone had told me a week ago that I would cower in front of an intruder, beg for mercy, and stand there completely motionless rather than fight back, I wouldn't have believed it.

Since I'd walked away from my family, I'd been fighting and surviving each day on my own. It hadn't been easy—at least, not in comparison to the life I once had. I had worked for everything I now had.

I was strong.

But in that moment, when I had seen the look in Victor's eyes, I'd felt nothing but weakness.

Mia and everyone else had assured me it was a completely normal reaction. It had nothing to do with strength.

"I would have done the same thing," she'd assured me.

Would she have though—with a family to protect at home? Wouldn't she have fought back to protect those she loved rather than curl into a ball and do nothing?

I should have done something, anything.

Since those first few days out on my own, I'd never felt so helpless—until my eyes had collided with Jackson's.

He'd made me feel safe and secure, and part of me had hated that. The independent and self-reliant part of me hadn't wanted to depend on anyone—much less a man.

But the rest of me—the empty void that had missed so much while I was busy convincing myself I didn't need love in my life—had wanted to cling to him desperately.

I let my arms wrap around the naked skin of my torso as I looked into my familiar brown eyes and wondered how anyone really knew who was *the one*.

I guessed that was what taking a leap of faith was—risking oneself in hopes of gaining something better.

I turned toward the door and headed downstairs.

I was ready for Jackson.

I was ready to leap.

"Are you okay, Jackson?" I watched him from across the bubbling hot water.

We'd been in the hot tub for a few minutes, and an eerie silence had settled between us. He'd seemed up to the idea of relaxing together and watching the moonlight shining over the lake but ever since I'd walked through the double doors and sunk into the water, he'd been on edge and almost twitchy.

"What?" he asked, his attention snapping up to me. "I'm good."

"Then why do you feel so distant?"

"I'm not distant. Just quiet." His eyes darted away again, and he focused on the lake, now nearly invisible under the dark sky.

Jackson nervously wrung his hands together, and I watched as he let out a deep breath that he must have been holding for far too long.

Why was he so nervous?

Moving forward, I rose from the water and took a few careful steps toward him, stealing his attention once again.

"What are you doing?" he asked.

"Bringing me here with Noah wasn't your original plan, was it?"

"What do you mean?"

"Go Fish, roasting marshmallows—that wasn't how this weekend was supposed to start?" I closed the remaining distance between us until my legs brushed up against the inside of his thighs.

The tender touch of his fingers trailed my thigh, curving toward the back to cup my ass.

"No," he simply answered.

I swung my legs around to straddle his trim waist. His arms

wrapped tightly around me and pulled me closer, every scorching inch seemingly bringing as much pain as pleasure. It was as if he were at war with himself, struggling to remain in control.

"Why? Why did you change your plans?"

His cupped hand dropped to the water, collecting a steamy palmful within as he brought it to my shoulder and let the contents slid down my back. His fingers followed the trail the water left behind, kneading sore muscles as he spoke.

"I thought you might need time," he confessed softly.

"Why?"

His gaze met mine, and I saw tenderness in his features.

"I don't expect to know everything you're going through, Liv, but I do know that to anticipate anything from you right now is out of the question. The only thing I'm sure of is, I'm here for you—in whatever way you need me."

My hands joined his that returned to my shoulders, and his warm fingers intertwined with mine.

"What if all I need right now is for you to touch me?"

"Liv—" he said hesitantly.

"Please listen to me before you say anything."

He nodded.

I continued, "In some ways, I feel like nothing happened. It was a near miss, you know? I should be happy for that fact. I'd trusted the wrong person, and that mistrust almost cost me something precious. Had you not been there, had you not saved me from him—I honestly don't know where I would be mentally right now."

"You doubt yourself," he said, not bothering to ask but rather forming it as a statement.

"Yes. It's something I'm still struggling with and working through. Even though the rational side of me knows I did everything right and that I shouldn't hold anything against myself for the way I handled that afternoon, I still feel weakness. I still feel a loss of the woman I once was."

I could see his lips about to move, his words forming. He wanted to rebuff my words, console me, and heal me, but I needed only one type of healing tonight.

"Victor was the last man I was intimate with," I said slowly as I slid our joined hands down the bare skin at my sides. "Help me forget, Jackson."

His fingers dug into my waist as I was pulled even closer to him. The water lurched forward and splashed, and I suddenly found myself flush against every part of him. My legs instinctively tightened around him as his lips met mine.

Every movement and every single touch felt deliberate and full of purpose. Nothing was hurried or clumsy. This wasn't another rushed late-night encounter that I had grown accustomed to over the years. This was a man showing me exactly what it felt like to be worshipped.

When his lips touched mine, I felt passion and tenderness along with deep longing unlike anything I'd ever experienced.

I wanted this man and not just for one night. The longer I spent wrapped up in Jackson's arms, the less intimidating the idea of finding someone permanent became.

Our kiss deepened, my mouth opening for him, and our tongues moved together like long-lost lovers. I felt him grow harder beneath me, heightening my desire. I moved, grinding my body against him, as my lips tasted his.

"Liv," he groaned.

"Please, don't stop."

My pleading words pushed him further, and his hands dipped under the edge of my bathing suit bottom to grip my bare ass. His skin against mine felt exhilarating. My heart raced inside my chest, beating and skipping in a staccato rhythm that seemed to match the butterfly sensation blossoming in my belly.

I wanted him with every ounce of my being, every fiber of my soul.

That thought was dashed as Victor's cruel face rushed to the forefront of my mind for one brief moment, shattering my Zen-like state.

Why?

Why would the memory of Victor come back now when I felt safe and secure in Jackson's arms?

Wanting to leave him and everything that went with him in the past, my movements became rushed, panicked almost, as our kiss intensified.

"Liv," he whispered, pulling back slightly.

I watched his chest heave, knowing mine was doing the same, as I tried to catch my breath.

"Sweet Liv," he said, smoothing his fingers down my cheek. "You have no idea how badly I want you in this moment, how badly I've wanted you since I first met you, but I can't allow myself to do it like this."

I frowned, suddenly averting my eyes from his gaze. Warmth touched my chin as he tugged my focus upward once again.

"Please, let me explain before you retreat."

I nodded, giving him the signal to go ahead.

"I know you probably think I'm going to feed you a line about how I think you aren't ready, how you couldn't possibly be mentally capable to move on after a traumatic event like that."

"Isn't that what you think?" I asked.

"No," he answered. "You might not be the greatest when it comes to psychoanalyzing your own feelings or hang-ups, but I know you well enough to know there is probably more going on here than you're willing to admit to. I can't allow our first time to simply be an eraser for all things Victor."

I opened my mouth to argue with Jackson.

"I know that wasn't your intention, but if we did sleep together to-night, it would always be this reminder of him and what he did. When we come together for the first time, it will be just the two of us—no one else up here"—he lifted his hand and tapped at my temple—"and no threat of an interrupting child," he said with a small grin.

I must admit, while I had been dry-humping Jackson, I'd completely forgotten about Noah being upstairs.

"And no terrible memories to erase. Give yourself some time to heal. You don't need to rush with me. I'll be here whenever you're ready."

I shook my head in astonishment. "You must be the first man in history to say no to sex after a make-out session like that."

"I never said I didn't want to. It damn near killed me to pull away from you, but I had to. When that day does come and we don't stop, I want it to feel like there is only you and me and no one else left on the planet."

"Like Adam and Eve?" I quipped, a mischievous grin spreading across my face.

He laughed, obviously grateful for the break. We'd been serious for far too long.

"They were the first two people on earth. I said, the last. It would be more like a bad sci-fi film…but with really amazing sex."

"So, a sci-fi porn?"

We both broke into hysterics.

"I'll rock your sci-fi world." He grinned.

"I can't wait for that. I'll go home and raid my secret stash of Star Trek costumes I saved for instances just like this."

"Awesome. It's a date."

~**Jackson**~

"I'm fairly certain I could lie here for the rest of my life," Liv said, stretching out languidly on the towel she'd laid across the boat bench. Her eyes were closed as she basked in a barely there bikini under the warm glow of the hot summer sun. It was a beautiful sight.

I'd suggested going boating early Sunday morning, and everyone had answered with an enthusiastic yes.

When staying at a multimillion-dollar lake house with a boat that would make most people weep in envy, how could we not take that baby out for a spin?

"I'm fairly certain I could do nothing but watch you lie there in that bikini for the rest of my life," I answered back with a devilish smile.

Her eyes peeked opened as her hands cupped her face to block the sun. "No, you'd eventually cave and fall prey to my beguiling beauty."

I rose from my spot across from her and knelt down before her.

The smells of coconut and the tropics assailed my senses, making my mouth water, as my eyes took in Liv's nearly naked form in front of me. Bikinis really were an amazing creation.

"Definitely beguiling," I agreed before placing a tender kiss on her shoulder.

"Gross," Noah said, announcing his arrival from down below where he'd gone to forage for snacks and drinks.

Mark couldn't have just bought a regular speedboat. He practically had a yacht with a cabin below that was big enough to sleep an entire family and decked out with a gourmet mini kitchen and full bathroom.

Who needed a hotel when we had one that could float?

"You're just jealous," I answered.

He tossed me the soda I'd requested. Being the gentleman I'd taught him to be, he politely handed Liv her bottle of water. She thanked him, and he quietly replied as he took a seat next to her. She sat up and twisted off the top of her water bottle.

"Who's ready for some fun?" I asked as I stood and settled back into the seat across from them.

Both looked at me with blank faces.

"I thought we were already having fun?" Liv challenged.

"Okay, let me rephrase. Who's ready for more fun?"

Liv turned sideways to meet Noah's gaze. They both lifted their eyebrows and broke into laughter. I watched in complete bafflement as the two continued to laugh, and then they finally turned toward me and raised their hands like kindergartners. Both hands shook in the air as if they were children begging for restroom passes. Soon, pleading followed.

"Me, me, me! Fun!" Noah yelled at the same time Liv said, "So excited!"

"Okay, stop placating me. Jerks."

The laughter continued, and I just shook my head, pretending to be slightly annoyed. In reality, I was overjoyed at the relationship Liv and Noah had created. It wasn't just the fact that he had grown close to the woman I was dating, even though that was an added bonus. It was simply that he had connected with someone—period. Since my parents had moved, I'd watched him retreat, almost refusing to allow himself to become overly attached to anyone—adults in particular.

I knew my parents had done what was best for them, and I loved knowing they were happy in their retirement, but Noah really missed his grandparents. Being with Liv slightly helped to ease the strain.

"So, what are we doing, Master of Fun?" Liv asked.

The laughter had died down a bit, but I could tell she was desperately trying to hold it in.

"I thought we could take turns on the inner tube."

"Oh, man!" Noah yelled out in enthusiasm.

"See? Your old man really is the Master of Fun."

"Hell yeah," he answered.

When I gave him the death stare, he immediately amended it to, "I mean, heck yeah!"

"So, who wants to go first?" I asked.

"Me!" Noah called out, nearly bouncing up from his spot on the bench.

"Anyone?" I asked, pretending not to see my son wildly flailing his arms in front of me.

"Me, me, Dad! Please!"

"So, no one then?"

"Seriously, Dad?" he shouted.

He grabbed my waist in a bear hug and nearly tackled me to the ground.

I chuckled. "Okay, okay! All you had to do was ask!"

Although brief, that bear hug was the closest thing to a hug I'd had in weeks. When his arms left me, I nearly groaned out from the loss.

When Noah was born, everyone had warned me how quickly he would grow.

Enjoy each and every moment, people would say.

But no one had ever told me how much it would hurt, how much my chest would ache when he took his first step or finally wiggled his first tooth loose. Watching him grow up was a balancing act. I would feel immense joy, seeing someone I'd created and raised transforming into a young man. Yet, at the same time, I would mourn the child who was leaving me behind—the little boy who had jumped into bed with me when a thunderstorm rolled through, or the infant who only had eyes for his daddy because I was his entire world.

Right now, I was mourning hugs—good-night hugs, the hugs that came from nowhere, the just-because hugs, and those hugs that he sometimes seemed to need to settle in at night.

I really missed hugs.

"Come on, Dad, help me set it up," he insisted, bringing me back to the present.

"Absolutely!" I answered, remembering that even though I'd mostly lost hugs, I still had Noah.

I'd blown up the inner tube before we left, and Noah and I carried it up from below the deck.

"You are seriously going to put me on that thing in the middle of the lake and drag me behind the boat?" Liv asked, looking at the tube as we dropped it into the water.

"Yep."

"That's insane."

"No, it's fun," I corrected.

"You'll be gentle?" She stood to glance over the edge of the boat.

"Of course," I lied.

"Okay."

Noah crawled over the side and made his way on top of the tube, moving around to situate himself. I knelt down, pretending to help him as I whispered in his ear. He looked up at me, nodding quickly, and added a grin.

"Oh. Well, that doesn't look too bad. He didn't even get wet," Liv said.

She watched me as I stood, none the wiser to my little chat with Noah.

"Nope. See? Totally easy. You ready, buddy?"

"Yes!" Noah answered, giving two thumbs-up. Lying belly down across the tube with his feet hanging off the edge, he wrapped his fingers around the handles. He looked like he was prepared for anything.

"Give me a thumbs-up if you want to go faster and thumbs-down to slow down. Got it?"

"Got it!" he replied excitedly.

I pushed us forward, slowly at first, and I steered straight, making sure to keep Noah and the inner tube aligned with the boat. This would most likely keep him from tipping over. I turned around to check on him, and he gave the signal to speed up. I accelerated, the engine roaring to life, and I heard Liv's laughter.

"That actually looks fun!"

Oh, just wait, neighbor.

~Liv~

"Okay, Liv, you're up," Jackson said.

Noah climbed back in the boat, almost as dry as the moment he'd climbed onto the inner tube ten minutes earlier. His hair was blown back and wet from the spray of the tube hitting the water, but he hadn't fallen into the water. He'd stayed on that little raft-looking thing the entire time, which was what I intended to do as well. That water looked cold, and I was way too warm to plunge headfirst into frigid water.

"Tell me what to do." I nervously walked toward the edge of the boat as Jackson handed me a life jacket.

My family had never been much into boating. I remembered a few elegant parties held on yachts, but that had been the extent of my boating experience until this morning. I much preferred lying out and being gently rocked back and forth by the waves than attending a stuffy party on a yacht circling the city.

However, the decision to be tugged behind a boat in an inflatable tube was still up in the air. Looping my arms into the vest and securing it into place, I was as ready as I'd ever be.

"One foot at a time," he instructed, taking my hand and helping me over the side of the boat where there was a large ledge. I could see the propeller below, currently stationary and quiet.

"Good. Now, the other foot. Okay. Carefully climb onto the raft like Noah did and grab the handles. Same directions—thumbs-up for more speed, thumbs-down for less. Oh, and do this if you want to stop." He made the universal cut signal, slicing his hand quickly across his throat. "Got it?"

"Yes." I nodded.

"Okay!" He slapped my ass, pushed the tube away from the propeller, and jumped back into the boat.

It was just me for a moment, floating across the serene water. It was peaceful—until the motor kicked on, and I started to fly.

"Holy shit!" I screamed, gripping my fingers tightly around the handles.

I couldn't hear them, but even from this distance, I could see Jackson and Noah laughing, loving the sounds of my shrill screams. I forgot everything Jackson had just told me—the thumbs, the signal to stop. I just screamed and laughed. It was thrilling, and I allowed myself to get completely lost in the moment.

The straight path suddenly curved, and my breath hitched as the tube grew closer to the white wake caused by the boat. I was jostled and bumped as my poor inner tube tried to stay steady until it finally gave up and flipped.

"Oh crap!" I managed to say right before everything turned upside down.

I saw the world spin once, maybe twice, before the water consumed me.

I was right. The water was freezing. If I could have gasped under water, I would have. I swam back to the surface and looked around for the boat. Jackson was already circling around to come get me.

His lopsided grin greeted me as the boat came alongside me.

"Did you do that on purpose?" I asked.

"You looked hot," he stated.

"You big jerk!"

I swam the remaining distance to the ladder and crawled back up to the boat's ledge where he greeted me with a towel.

"Your bathing suit got a little out of place." His eyes were full of fire as he covered me quickly before Noah had a chance to see me.

I looked underneath the towel and saw my left breast popping out of my vest and top.

Oops.

I reached down and stuffed my girl back into my bikini top, blushing. Then we climbed back over the ledge and sat down.

"So, feeling a little feisty today?" I asked, noticing the mop on my shoulders that had once been my hair.

"Just wanted to remind you of that feisty guy you met all those weeks ago."

"Hmm…" I answered. "Just remember, payback is a bitch."

"What the hell kind of s'mores are you going to make with this stuff?" Jackson asked, peeking into the grocery bag I'd asked him to carry outside.

"The best s'mores you've ever eaten," I answered over my shoulder with a wink.

He looked doubtful, but by the end of the night, I would prove him wrong after watching him cram at least four of these in his mouth.

Not all s'mores were created equal.

We'd decided to end our perfect weekend by making dinner on the grill and finishing with dessert outside. Among its endless amenities, this house also came equipped with a fire pit, which was perfect for roasting marshmallows.

After Jackson set down the bag of groceries I'd gone out and purchased hours earlier, I began pulling out the various ingredients, including homemade graham crackers from a local bakery down the street along with a selection of chocolate I'd found at a candy store. The owner of the candy store and I had chatted for nearly fifteen minutes on the importance of fresh and basic ingredients, and it really showed in her products.

The only thing I'd had to settle on were the marshmallows. I couldn't find those locally made anywhere, so I'd gone for the regular store brand for those.

We all began sticking our puffy white marshmallows on our metal sticks.

"Black or brown?" Jackson asked.

"Pardon?"

"Do you like your marshmallows roasted a lot or a little? I personally like mine black."

"I do, too. Charred on the outside, gooey on the inside. Perfect. How about you, Noah?"

"I like them light brown."

"He's a bit of a snob. It can't be too overdone, or he'll give it to me. When he was little, I ended up with a lot of his rejects."

"I'm sure that was hard for you." I laughed.

"Terrible," he agreed. "He's got it down to a science now though."

Jackson and I worked on turning our marshmallows into charcoal while Noah became a boy of precision. He placed it above the fire, not too close and not too far, and he would time how many seconds each side was exposed.

"Wow, that's fascinating," I commented as I watched him.

"He could be here all night." Jackson grinned.

We each took out two graham crackers and a hunk of chocolate, and we assembled our s'mores, placing our thoroughly cooked marshmallows in between the two crackers. I waited for Jackson to take his first bite.

He brought the s'more to his mouth and bit down, and then a groan escaped his lips. "Mmm…that's good."

That groan froze me in place. I was mesmerized and intoxicated by it.

Is that what he sounds like in bed? I really wanted to know.

"Liv? You still there?"

I realized my eyes had glazed over while transfixed on his mouth. "I'm good," I answered, remembering our present company.

He grinned, obviously knowing he'd had an effect on me.

This morning, I'd been flipped on my ass, and I'd found myself submerged in lake water.

Tonight, I wanted to flip him on his ass, and yeah, I was still the one who was wet.

~Liv~

Ever since little Asher had come into our lives, Mia's need to nurture had grown tenfold. When she'd heard the news of my unfortunate incident with Victor the week before, trying to keep her from freaking out and practically moving in with me had been a challenge.

After I'd talked her out of bringing me dinners, I had finally settled on allowing her to bring me lunch. I hadn't lost a family member, so casseroles were unnecessary. But when occasionally running late in the mornings, I'd forget to pack a lunch. If bringing me food would help ease her mind, then she could certainly help with my rushed mornings.

Right on time, like every day since I'd come back to work, Mia waltzed into my office at noon, carrying a bag of food in one hand and Asher in the other. Garrett was following close behind with a look on his face that made me laugh out loud.

"You look lost, Garrett," I said, commenting on his bewildered expression.

"I'm just wondering why she always insists on carrying every-thing when I'm standing right here." He raised his hands in mock frustration and shook his head.

Mia turned around and placed a chaste kiss on his nose. He re-turned the endearment with one of his own—a lingering kiss on the forehead. Asher watched the entire interaction between his parents with immense fascination as bubbles sprung from his tiny pink lips.

"I'm sorry, Garrett. I didn't mean to insult your manhood. Here. Would you like to carry the lunch bag?" she asked, grinning from ear to ear.

He took the bag from her outstretched hand and moved past her, swatting her ass as he did so. She yelped and giggled in response.

He approached me while I leaned against the doorframe of my office. "We brought burritos from that place you like down the street. Hope that's okay."

"Did you get extra veggies?" I asked, raising my eyebrow in question.

"Yep, sure did."

"Then, we're good. Hand it over," I answered with a grin.

He handed me a wrapped burrito marked with a *V*, and we all settled on the empty couches in my lobby area. I'd purposely leave the noon hour open, so I could take a lunch break. Sometimes, appoint-ments might go late, but for the most part, it usually worked out. The afternoons were my busiest times anyway. Everyone wanted to sched-ule appointments after school or at least toward the end of the day.

"So, Mia tells me you had a hot overnight date this weekend?" Garrett said through a mouthful of burrito.

"Jackson took me to his boss's lake house for the weekend," I replied before adding, "with his son."

"Oh, so not hot?" Mia asked as she picked around her taco salad.

"Well, we had our moments, but it definitely wasn't a romantic getaway, if that was what you were picturing."

"I'm trying not to picture anything," Garrett chimed in.

"Were you ready for that?" Mia asked. "Considering—"

"We didn't sleep together."

"Oh, I just assumed when you said—"

I smiled, remembering Jackson's sweet words. "We got close, but he put the brakes on."

"Hold up," Garrett said mid-bite. "He said no? To sex?"

I looked down, staring at my half-eaten burrito, as I recalled our evening in the hot tub. "He said he wanted to wait…until I was ready."

There was silence for a moment.

When I looked up, I saw tears in Mia's eyes.

"That's the sweetest thing I've ever heard, Liv."

"Am I missing something? Ready for what?" Garrett said, his eyes darting between the two of us.

"Dork." Mia just rolled her eyes.

We returned to our meals, letting the laughter eventually die down. I made googly eyes at my godson and watched as Mia fed him tiny handfuls of cheerios.

While Asher was busy eating, Mia looked up at me. "Are you okay? I mean, after last week. You haven't talked much about it." A serious tone replaced the jovial one she'd used earlier.

I knew she would ask after I'd mentioned Jackson. "I'm almost there. I'm nearing the realm of okay," I said with a small smile.

"I just don't feel like I've done anything. I feel like I should be helping you in some way."

I leaned forward, placing my hand on hers. "This, right here, having a nice, normal lunch with me—that's all I want. I know I can't expect to forget it, but I don't want to dwell on it either."

"Well then, good. I'm glad I'm helping you do that. Is he?" she asked, speaking of Jackson.

I grinned. "Yeah, he is."

~Jackson~

The Senator and his crew had been at the firm all afternoon, and it was well past closing time. I looked at the clock again and saw the minute hand tick one minute further past five. My lip twitched in annoyance.

Four agonizing long hours of brown-nosing and kissing ass had nearly sent me over the edge, and now, I was late in getting out of here.

My phone buzzed in my pocket, and I snuck a look.

Liv: I've got Noah. We're on our way.

Realizing I might have nights like these, I'd given the summer camp Noah was attending permission to release him to Liv. Thank God I'd thought of that. Otherwise, I'd be in sheer panic at this moment, wondering if my son was being hauled off to child protective services because I hadn't arrived to pick him up.

"Everything all right?" Senator Prescott asked from across the table.

I looked up and saw genuine concern in his expression. A career in politics was never good to the body. Over the years, the once good-looking and fit man, Douglas Prescott, had faded, and he now looked years older than his actual age. Stress had a way of doing that to a person.

"Yes," I answered. "Just making sure my son had a ride home from camp."

Raising his wrist, he glanced at his watch, and his eyes widened. "Look at the time, gentlemen! Someone should have said something. We can finish this up later."

Quiet chatter began as people around the table shuffled papers together and packed up their laptops. I began the same process, eager to meet Liv downstairs when she arrived.

"How old is your boy?" Senator Prescott asked me.

"Eleven," I answered.

"Ah, quite the age if I remember correctly. Although, I have a daughter, so things could be completely different."

I paused, amazed that he was openly talking about Liv, considering the man was about to launch a presidential campaign. I figured he would do everything he could to downplay his estranged daughter as much as possible.

"How old is your daughter?" I asked, intrigued to see just how much the old man would divulge.

"Late twenties now. She works as a family counselor, helping children mostly," he answered quietly, his eyes full of some deep-seated emotion. "Kids grow up way too fast. Remember that, and cherish every second."

"I'm trying," I answered.

"Good, good." He seemed to immediately shake out of the dark mood he'd put himself in, and he turned from me to speak to Mark about setting up another meeting.

Our little conversation was forgotten, but I was still sitting at the table, completely bewildered by him.

Had he checked up on Liv? Did he miss her? If so, why hadn't he just reached out and apologized?

The large gaping hole in her heart that could only be filled by him and her mother grew each and every day they stayed away. Didn't they realize that?

Promising myself that I wouldn't interfere, I rose from my chair and headed for my office to drop off my laptop and notebook. Once again, my phone chirped in my pants pocket, and I was greeted by another text from Liv.

Liv: Coming up! Is that okay?

Shit. I had told her I would meet her downstairs to avoid this very situation. I'd come to the conclusion that when it came to working with Liv's father, being vague with her was the key. She didn't need to know when he'd come to the office or how many times we'd had lunch. It worked better for her to stay clueless. Every mention of him was like a jab to her side, and I preferred not to be the one giving them.

So, rather than mentioning the reason, I'd just suggested that I would meet her in the parking garage.

Too late for that.

I raced to the elevator just in time to hear it beep and see the double doors open. I swiftly stepped in front of Liv and Noah and shoved them back inside before pressing the button to close the door.

"What the heck?" Noah said. "I wanted to see your office, Dad! We were just going to peek and wait until you finished your meeting."

I exhaled, hating myself for even having to be in this position. "Your dad's here," I said, turning to Liv.

Her eyes widened, and something in her features suddenly reminded me so much of her father in that moment.

It was her eyes.

They were her father's.

"Oh," she simply stated.

"I didn't think you'd want a reunion today."

"No."

I expected a flurry of questions to spring from Noah's mouth.

146

Kids were always so inquisitive, especially in sticky situations when parents would rather not answer any. But, in that moment, he showed me just how much he had matured. He remained quiet, and instead of unintentionally embarrassing Liv by quizzing her, he simply sidestepped past me to grab hold of her hand.

She didn't bother asking me about her father. She hadn't since that day she found out how I'd met him, which was when I'd instated the don't-ask-don't-tell policy regarding Senator Prescott.

"I heard someone doesn't know what cool clothes are," Liv said, a smile trying to work its way across her face.

I glanced sideways in her direction.

"Who me?" I asked, grateful she was starting to return to me.

Noah had done that. He might not be the little boy who gave me hugs anymore, but if he could manage to lift Liv's spirits with a single hand, I was okay with the loss.

The elevator dinged, and all three of us exited out the double doors toward my car.

"Noah said when he asked you to take him school shopping, your suggestions were terrible. Ralph Lauren? Really, Jackson?"

"What? I buy stuff there!" I scoffed, unlocking the truck so both of them could climb inside.

I'd won a game of rock-paper-scissors last night so the gas guzzling ozone killer was our ride of choice tonight.

We'd come back later to pick up Liv's tiny circus car.

"Suits and clothes for work, Jackson! You don't buy school clothes there!"

"Okay," I relented. "Point taken."

We all took our seats in the truck, and I revved up the engine. I drove out of the parking lot and stopped at the light just outside the gate.

"So, where are we headed?" I asked.

"Where else do tweens and teenagers go to get cool clothes?" she asked.

"Obviously not Ralph Lauren."

"The mall, silly."

This was going to be a long night.

147

~Jackson~

Who knew shopping could be that exhausting?

Besides the brief stop at the food court, we'd hit every major retailer that sold clothes in Noah's size. I could barely see beyond the four-thousand bags in my hands on the way out. I'd thought we would be in and out, an hour tops, considering I'd spent a fortune to enroll Noah in a prestigious school that had uniforms four days a week.

Who knew shopping for that one free day would be so time-consuming?

Wasn't this a chick thing—worrying about clothes and what other kids thought? Being the father of a boy, I always figured I wouldn't have to worry about such things, but I was quickly realizing that middle school was an exception to the rule. It made everyone nervous, gender be damned.

After we got home and Noah raced upstairs to most likely play video games, I shuffled into the living room, still brimming with my grandmother's antiques and handmade doilies, and I tried to remember what it was like to be Noah's age. Taking a peek out the window where I'd watched Liv disappear into her own house minutes earlier, I recalled that eager, nervous feeling I'd had when starting a new school and settling into a completely different way of life.

Middle school was the big leagues as far as any kid was concerned. It was when a kid would put away dolls or action figures and grow up. It was a hard middle road, one that I still recalled living. Even though I couldn't remember making my mother buy me clothes or worrying about my haircut for the first day of school, I did remember coming home and racing up the stairs to play with my favorite toy and realizing I couldn't—or shouldn't.

What if the other kids found out? Would they call me a baby?

Sadly, I had packed everything up and stuffed it under my bed, saying good-bye to the little boy I'd been the day before.

I guessed Noah had been doing the same thing all summer.

The familiar sound reminding me of wild elephants alerted me that my son was flying down those ancient wooden steps once again. No matter how many times I'd reminded him, he'd always take them two at a time and race down as if he were being hunted by an ax murderer.

"Hey, Dad! Bye, Dad!" he announced before running to the door. A stuffed backpack was slung over his shoulder.

"Hold on!" I called out, halting him mid-step.

He turned just before he reached the front entrance, and a smug grin was on his face.

"Where do you think you're going?" I asked, wrapping my arms across my chest.

This was my fierce, imposing dad pose. It was supposed to cause fear and rampant obedience. It wasn't working. He didn't look threatened.

"I'm spending the night at Leah and Declan's house. They have a son around my age. His name is Connor. He likes soccer, too, and baseball and Xbox."

My head hurt. Too many words were coming out of his mouth at once.

"You mean Liv's friend Leah—the one I've never met?" I asked.

149

"Yep." He shrugged.

So damn confused.

"And you're spending the night?"

"Yeah, Liv called and said Leah and Declan had a son named Connor, and he really wanted to meet me, so they invited me over to spend the night. Pretty cool, huh?"

"Uh…"

"So, I'm gonna go. Leah is picking me up, and she just texted to say she's outside. I sent you the number. It's on your phone. See you tomorrow! Bye!"

Then, he was gone, just like that.

What the hell?

I stood there in a daze. I turned back to the window and watched as a beautiful blonde woman around Liv's age greeted my son. A young boy got out of the car, and he waved at Noah. Minutes later, they were gone.

I'd been dragged through the mall for hours with nothing more than a crappy hot dog to keep me going. I'd spent hundreds of dollars on clothes my son apparently needed to feel grounded and better about this life-altering shift in his existence.

Now, Liv had taken it upon herself to send him away for a bros' sleepover—without my permission.

I was not in a good mood.

Stalking forward, I yanked the door by the handle and stomped forward. That woman was about to get a piece of my mind. We might be close, but there were lines, and this was one of them.

I didn't bother knocking on her door. Knowing she would have locked it, I fished out the key she'd given me after last week, and I slipped it in before turning the knob and stepping inside.

The house was quiet. There was no sign of Liv anywhere.

"Liv!" I shouted. "Where are you?"

"Upstairs," she responded, seeming unfazed by my abrupt appearance.

Grumbling, I headed for the stairs, practicing my speech as I went. I would tell her how much I appreciated her help, how I understood her love for Noah, but I was the parent, so I made the decisions.

She would understand.

As I took the last step onto the top floor, I noticed an amber glow reflecting off the oak hardwood just outside Liv's bedroom. It flickered and danced along the floorboards, creating a pattern all its own. Walking farther, I noticed the origin of the lights. Candles lined the entire entryway of her bedroom and beyond. Treading softly, I entered, seeing the same flickering pattern from the hallway dancing up the walls and across the bed—where I found her.

Covered in satin and lace, she looked like a divine virgin sacrifice ready to give up her mortal soul.

"Sweet Jesus," I cursed.

Bad mood gone.

The only thoughts running through my mind were Liv, lace, and *mine*.

"You're drooling," she said, her lips curving into a smug grin.

"You're nearly naked," I replied.

"Did everything go okay with Noah?" she asked, sitting up slightly. It pushed the swatch of fabric passing as a bra tonight up and forward, accentuating her breasts even more.

I sucked back a bit more drool.

"If you mean, I stood there, completely confused, while my son disappeared for the evening, then yes."

She smiled, a hint of amusement crossing her features.

My hand twitched as if the sheer torture of not touching her was driving it insane. I stayed where I was, knowing if I took even one step farther, there would be no going back. Every muscle in my body physically ached for the smooth touch of her skin and warm feel of her body beneath me.

"I'm ready," she uttered, shattering the last remnant of control I had left.

My eyes wandered over every inch of her exposed skin as my heart raced into a gallop.

"How can you be sure?" I edged forward, only to halt myself.

"I know."

"I need to know, Liv. I need to know that you're ready for this, for me, because this is anything but casual for me."

"I know you have to think about Noah—"

I cut her off, stepping closer, the adrenaline pumping in my veins so hard that I felt like Superman.

"No. Tonight has nothing to do with Noah. This has to do with me wanting you and only ever you. When I take you, I want to bury myself so deep that you'll never forget. So, you might think you're ready to give yourself over to me, but are you prepared for what will come when I give myself to you?"

"Yes."

Thank God I wasn't an adolescent teenager anymore because that one word from her lips would have ended me. As it were, I was rock hard, the need to take her consuming my every thought.

Moving swiftly, my legs hit the bed, and my hands found hers as she tumbled backward. A low growl reverberated from my throat as my lips found hers. My tongue traced the corner of her mouth, and I felt her teeth gently bit down on my bottom lip, causing my dick to twitch.

I needed all of her, naked—immediately.

Slipping my hands beneath her, I unhooked her bra with ease and watched the straps fall to the sides, giving me a glimpse of the tender flesh underneath.

Our eyes met briefly, and I recognized the same emotions that I was feeling in her gaze—desire, longing…maybe something more.

My fingers wandered up the path of her left arm, and I grabbed the bra strap to slowly begin its downward journey, exposing her body to me.

Exquisite.

Taut and pink, her nipple was begging for my mouth. I pulled it between my lips and sucked. Her body bucked beneath me, and she cried out.

"That's it, Liv." I soothed her, swiveling my tongue around her swollen bud.

I made fast work of the rest of her bra and moved on to her right breast, loving her body's reaction to my touch. As I sucked up and down on that rosy tip, my hand meandered to the edge of her panties. Dipping lower, I found her already wet and ready for me. Smiling against her chest, I sucked harder on her nipple while my hand found her clit, swollen and tender.

"Shit!" she screamed, pushing hard against my hand.

So fucking hot.

Still working her with my hand, I kissed a path down her chest and across her belly button until I reached her panties. "It's time for these to go," I said.

My hand moved up to shed the lace from her body, and I heard her whimper from the loss of my hand. I watched in fascination as I moved the fabric over her hips and down her long legs before it finally fell on the floor next to us.

What was left was nothing but Liv.

She was breathtaking.

"I planned on making you scream out my name with my tongue alone, but seeing you like this is driving me insane."

"Please, Jackson," she begged.

Kneeling before her, I watched as she propped herself up on her elbows and spread her legs farther apart, giving me the most beautiful view in the world.

With hooded, hungry eyes, she watched as I yanked my T-shirt up and over my head before dropping it to the side of the bed without a single glance.

"Keep looking at me like that," I said.

"Like what?" She bit into her bottom lip with a grin.

"Like I'm the most fascinating thing you've ever seen."

"Maybe you are," she purred.

As I flashed her a wicked grin, my hands traveled down to my belt buckle. "I haven't even taken off my pants yet, sweetheart."

She watched intently, her eyes never wavering, as I made quick work of my jeans and boxers before dropping them onto the growing pile of forgotten clothes on the floor.

"Even better than I imagined," she said softly.

I crawled back onto the bed. My body brushed against her heated skin, sending shivers down my spine.

"You mean, bigger—bigger than you expected." I grinned against her shoulder as I scattered kisses along her collarbone and neck.

"I always knew you were well-endowed, Jackson. You tend to be very alert when I'm around. Plus, there was that night in the hot tub." She laughed.

Memories of her sexy little body grinding against mine suddenly clouded my vision. I'd wanted her more in that moment than my next breath—much like right now.

"No more talking. I need you—now," I demanded before slamming my mouth on hers without mercy.

She took everything I gave while arching into me with enthusiasm and such passion.

Our lips molded together, and my hands gripped her hips, pulling her tight against me. It would never be enough. I wanted to crawl inside her and brand my name on her heart, making a permanent reminder that I'd been here and I was never leaving.

Jesus Christ, I loved this woman.

It was so much different than the love I'd thought I had for Natalie where I felt the need to prove it to the world, to her, and even to myself. This love for Liv had crept up slowly, making itself known with a whisper rather than a roar. It didn't need to be justified or backed up with a fancy job or any of the other ways in which I'd tried to prove myself to Natalie. It just was.

I loved Liv.

It was so easy, so simple.

The tricky part would be convincing Liv how much she already loved me.

~Liv~

Every inch of my body was on fire.

Any second, I was going to combust and burst into flames.

I'd had several lovers in my life, but Jackson had erased every memory of them the moment he walked into my bedroom. Even before he'd even touched me, I'd known I would never be the same again.

His eyes stared straight into my soul, like he was searching for the missing half of himself.

Had he found it?

I'd never believed I could have a perfect partner, that missing puzzle piece people always talked about, until I'd met Jackson—well, maybe a few weeks after I'd met Jackson. That first week, I had been sure he was sent by Satan himself to punish me for some unknown crime against humanity.

But now, I saw him for what he could be—in the life I thought had been so perfectly planned out.

It scared me.

It thrilled me.

It made me feel alive.

His fingers slid down my hip and anchored to the back of my knee, pulling my leg around his body. I felt him everywhere, as I pushed against his hard length.

"I want you inside me," I begged.

"God, yes," he answered before pausing. "I don't have any condoms."

"I'm on birth control, and I was tested after—" I didn't bother finishing.

He nodded. "I'm clean, and it's been—well, it's been a really long time."

Our eyes met as he slowly guided himself into my slick core. Every inch was like a shock wave to my system, stirring deep moans from my lungs.

"I love that sound," he groaned.

Our hip bones met briefly before he pulled out slowly, letting our bodies grow accustomed to each other.

"Fuck," he cursed. "You feel so good."

In and out, he set a slow, sensual rhythm at first, rocking his hips so that his body would hit my clit at just the right angle. I cried out in pleasure, completely lost in my passion.

Hands gripped my hips, and I was pulled upward until my body was seated on his lap. With his legs folded underneath him, he moved me up and down on his throbbing cock.

The friction, the heat, the rawness was too much. My hands wrapped around him, and I dug my nails into his back, crying out as my body quaked with release. His movements sped up as I continued to orgasm, my body tightening around him like a vise.

"Shit!" he cried out as he slammed into me from below.

Harder, faster, deeper—it was all I felt, and it was divine. My head fell into the crook of his shoulder as I matched each power thrust with enthusiasm. Suddenly, he tensed as a low masculine moan escaped his lips. His arms encircled my waist, and he held me close as he came, long and hard. My fingers wove into his sandy colored hair, and I smiled as he rested his head on my chest.

"Still think cookies are better than orgasms?" he asked.

I felt his lips curl into a grin against my damp skin.

"Cookies suck," I answered.

"Good answer."

~Jackson~

I'd been awake for hours, watching the way her skin looked under the moonlight and the rising sun. I'd studied the curve of her hips and the tiny freckle on her right shoulder. My fingers ached to trace the delicate pattern of her tattoo as it disappeared down her back. I'd memorized the exact color of her hair and the way it looked while fanned across her naked chest.

When I'd realized my infatuation with Liv had more to do with attraction and less to do with wanting to duel with my annoying new neighbor, the thought had scared me. It'd shocked me actually.

Falling for a neighbor had many risks. What if it didn't work? Would one of us have to move? Or would we have to build a giant fence or schedule outside time so that we didn't have to see each other on a regular basis?

But falling for the neighbor when my child seemed to be doing the same was even riskier. I'd walked into this knowing that it wasn't just me who could end up hurt and alone.

My son, the most important person in my life, was falling for Liv just as hard as I was. Having never had a mother, the role always fascinated him. He'd spend time at friends' houses and come home to tell me stories, like how Brian's mom had baked him a cake or built forts with them in the living room. He never made me feel like I wasn't enough, but I knew there were certain things I'd never be able to replace.

A mom's hug just felt different, and no matter how hard I tried, I could never duplicate that.

It was only natural that he'd be curious about the first woman I'd shown genuine interest in.

I'd allowed their relationship to blossom and develop naturally, without interference, hoping that ours would do the same.

As I'd walked into Liv's bedroom last night, I'd found a woman who was ready to take the next step.

She might still have reservations or need time to come to the same inevitable conclusion I'd already reached, but there was one thing I knew for certain.

Olivia Prescott was mine—forever.

Convincing my free-spirited hippie girl that she was taken for good might be challenging.

I grinned as my fingers wove through her raven hair, thinking of how much fun I was going to have convincing her.

"Good morning," a sleepy voice said, her eyes peeking up at me.

"Hi."

"Have you been awake long?"

"Yeah, just watching you sleep."

"Normally, I would find that creepy, but on you…it's kind of hot."

"Everything is hot on me," I replied with a wink.

"I know," she purred, rising up onto her knees. The sheet and blanket fell away from her waist, exposing her beautiful tanned skin.

"You're so damn gorgeous."

"So are you," she answered, crawling into my lap to straddle me.

My hands skimmed up her back and down to grip her ass.

She lifted her body, and I positioned myself at her slick entrance just as a cell phone went off.

"Ignore it," I commanded.

"I can't. It could be Leah calling about Noah," she said.

"They have my number."

"And where is your cell phone?"

I looked around the room to the pile of clothes, and I honestly couldn't remember whether my phone was in there or not.

"Exactly. It will only be a second. Let me just check who it is."

She reached over my shoulder and grabbed her phone, giving me a momentary nice view of her breasts before they were pushed against my face. I stuck out my tongue and licked the tip of her nipple, causing her to yelp.

The yelp quickly turned into a gasp.

"Liv?" I said, looking up to find her turning white with panic. "Liv, what is it? Who is it?"

She held out the phone. "It's my dad."

Chapter Nineteen

~Liv~

The phone went silent as I stared down at it, wondering if it had all been a mistake. My sexy time with Jackson now interrupted, I climbed off of him, and instead, I cuddled up next to him. He pulled the covers around us, and his arms enveloped me, making me feel safe and secure even though my heart was racing and my mind was panicked.

"Do you think he meant to call me?"

"You think it was an accident?" he asked.

"Well, it's been eight years."

My phone chirped, and I nearly jumped off the bed. Jackson's warm touch calmed me as I held the phone in front of me once more.

I had one new voice mail.

My heart went into double-time.

"Are you going to listen to it?" he asked softly.

"I don't know," I answered honestly, staring blankly at the screen.

I felt his eyes on me, watching and waiting. Pulling my head closer, he kissed my forehead and smoothed down my hair. He cupped my chin, and his gaze met mine.

"I'm going to go take a shower and give you some time to think. I'll be here if you need me."

I nodded. "Thank you."

Without asking, he always seemed to know the difference between when I needed him and the times I just needed a bit of space.

Right now was one of those moments when I needed space.

I stared back at the phone while the sound of his footsteps against the wood floor filled the quiet room. The shower kicked on, and I heard the old pipes groan to life.

One new voice mail.

I looked at the words on the screen again, still unable to believe that with a quick press of a button, I would be able to hear my dad's voice again. I'd heard it over the years on the news and radio as he'd conducted campaign speeches and live interviews, but it never sounded the same. He always sounded so formal and professional. This time, when I heard him, he'd be talking to me.

What would he say? Was he sorry? Did he regret the choices he'd made? Or maybe my parents just needed something? After all this time, perhaps they just needed an organ donor or wanted to write me out of the will.

I huffed out a large breath of air, trying to find the courage to listen to that fateful message. I knew one thing. Once I did, things would somehow never be the same.

Perhaps my life was better not knowing. *What if it were bad news?* Surely, not knowing was better than the truth.

Finally making a decision, I hit the button and held the phone up to my ear. Tears stung my eyes when his familiar deep voice came across the airwaves.

"Hey, Livvy," he greeted, taking a deep breath before continuing. He sounded older and tired maybe, but it was him. Not the politician or the great man of Virginia, it was my dad.

I blinked away more tears as I listened to what he had to say.

"I know it's been a long time, and I know we have a lot to make up for, but your mother and I would like to extend that olive branch we've been too stubborn to give until now. I know what has happened between us can't be fixed in a day or even months, but give us one dinner. Just one to start, and we'll go from there. You know how to reach us. I love you, Livvy Lou."

I listened to the message two more times, feeling my heart tighten in my chest when he referred to me by my childhood nickname. Much like Jackson's grandma calling him Jax, my father was the only one who had ever referred to me as Livvy Lou. I hadn't heard anyone call me by that name since I was in college before I'd left home for the last time.

This phone call was everything I'd ever hoped for. Hearing his voice, those words, was exactly what I'd been thinking of since the moment I realized how lonely and scary a world without my parents could be. While living a life of privilege, I'd dreamed of being on my own and fending for myself. I'd had aspirations that didn't include the chosen path my parents had set forth. But sometimes, looking at the world through the rose-colored glasses of a charmed life didn't give an accurate description of what the real world would actually be like.

I'd spent months adjusting and acclimating myself to what others would describe as a normal existence. I'd never been grocery shopping or done my own laundry, and I most certainly had never lived on my own. By the end of the first month, crying myself to sleep had become routine. There had even been a low period when I considered crawling back home and begging for forgiveness.

But I'd slowly realized that I was doing it—living the life I'd always wanted. It might not have been perfection, but it was mine. The student loans, shoestring budget, and years of barely making it—it was all mine. And wasn't that what growing up was all about?

It just would have been nice for my parents to see what I'd accomplished all on my own.

I guessed now was my chance.

~Jackson~

Turning the faucet off, I stood in the shower and let the water drip slowly from my body. Silence echoed through the room as I reached for the towel I'd slung over the side.

Had she called him back already? Or was she still staring at that phone?

Leaving her like that had been difficult. I'd had to physically fight myself on it.

But I had begun to learn the many sides of Liv, and her need for independence was one of them. She was courageous, fierce, and strong-willed. The last thing she needed was a clingy, overly dominant partner who barked orders and made her feel inferior. I wanted us to be equals, and that meant giving her the space she needed even when I wanted to do the opposite.

Drying off quickly, I wrapped the towel around my waist and ran my hands through my unruly tawny brown hair, not bothering to brush it. It tended to do its own thing when it got too long, and I was desperately in need of a haircut.

I stepped back into the bedroom and found Liv in the same position I'd left her in. The blankets were pulled up to her chin, and she was curled into a tight ball in the center of the bed. She looked small and fragile, such a contrast to her usual self.

"They want to have dinner with me," she simply stated, her eyes still trained on the ceiling.

I stepped forward and joined her, sitting on the side of the bed. "Did they say why?"

"Olive branch."

"What?" I asked in confusion.

"They're offering an olive branch. I guess they want to start over," she said with a shrug, her gaze finally meeting mine.

"What are you going to do?" I asked hesitantly.

"I think I'm going to call them back and say yes," she answered.

"Are you sure?"

Her eyes rounded slightly, and she sat up, snugly pulling the sheet around her body. "You don't think it's a good idea?"

"I just don't want you to get hurt, Liv."

"I won't," she said adamantly.

"You're already hurting. You have been for eight years. I wouldn't be able to stand to see them drive that sword in further."

Her eyebrows furrowed together in frustration. Standing now, she began to pace across the floor. "It's not your decision," she snapped.

"Sweetheart," I said softly, moving to stand behind her. I kissed her left shoulder, just over the spot where the bright orange floral design started. "I will support whatever decision you make. Please don't take this the wrong way. I just want you to be cautious, that's all. He's running for president. Try to lead with your head, not your heart, okay?"

She leaned back into me, and I felt her body relax.

"Okay," she agreed.

"Now, where are we going to dinner?" I asked.

She turned around, a surprised and amused expression on her face. "We?"

"Well, yeah. I think your old man should meet your boyfriend."

"Boyfriend? I don't remember ever calling you that." She smiled.

"Well, the next-door neighbor you like to fuck is a mouthful—literally—so I paraphrased."

Her mouth dropped before laughter filled the air. I pulled her into my arms and softly kissed her lips.

"He'll recognize you," she warned, stating the obvious.

"Yes," I answered. "It will be fine. Olive branch, remember?"

"I guess I have a phone call to make," she said, nodding.

I agreed and followed her back to the bed as she picked up her cell phone and dialed her father's number. A few seconds later, I heard her name being said quietly on the other end.

"Hi, Dad," she replied. Her breathing was deep and slow as if she intentionally had to do so. "Look," she replied, apparently cutting him off, "we can catch up soon. I just wanted to call and say yes to dinner. Anytime this week is fine." She looked up at me for confirmation, and I nodded. "Text me the location, and make the reservation for four. I'm bringing someone."

She ended the call and turned to me, letting out a deep breath that she must have been holding for far too long.

"Want a milkshake?" I remembered that night in the diner when I'd sworn I'd always be there to remind her of happy days when the rough ones came along. I thought today was one of those days.

"Can we get Noah first?" she asked.

Smiling, I nodded. "Of course. You just have to tell me where he is first."

"Deal."

Chapter Twenty

~Liv~

What did one wear to a dinner like this?

What outfit said, *I'm all grown up, and I did it without any of your money or help*?

I looked at my closet, full of vibrant hues and rich tones, and my shoulders slumped in defeat.

Right now, I felt anything but grown up. I felt much more like the twenty-year-old college girl I'd left behind—the one who sat on bare floors because she was too scared to spend any money on furniture, fearing she might never get a job, and the one who spent weeks and months hoping to see her father on her doorstep, begging her to come home. But he never did, and that young girl had eventually stopped looking out the window for a man who wasn't coming. She'd found a job and carved out a tiny piece of the world for herself—without anyone else to help her.

It was amazing how one call could reduce eight years to nothing.

My phone buzzed on the nightstand near my bed, pulling me from my spiraling thoughts. Moving quickly, I nabbed the phone, saw Jackson's name, and smiled.

"Hello?" I answered.

"Let me guess. You're standing in front of your closet, trying to decide what to wear?" His baritone voice made my mood instantly lighten.

"How did you know that?" I asked.

"Did you know," he started, his voice growing deeper, "that our rooms are directly across from each other? And right now, your curtains are wide open. Nice bra by the way."

I laughed, looking immediately out the window, and I saw him standing there in nothing but a pair of tight boxer briefs. With one arm above him, he leaned against the window frame, holding his phone against his ear with his free hand. It was a good look, and I couldn't help but step closer.

"I forgot the master bedrooms in these houses faced each other. Mrs. Reid always kept her curtains shut. She liked her afternoon naps," I commented with a grin.

"I'm much more partial to the view."

"It's not so bad from this side either."

"Take off your bra," he commanded, "and grab that chair you have in the corner. You're going to give me a show."

My stomach clenched in anticipation. I normally hated being ordered around in the bedroom, but with Jackson, it was thrilling.

Grabbing the chair in front of my antique vanity, I positioned it in front of the window and took a seat. Ever so slowly, I made a show of unhooking my bra and letting the black lace fall down, revealing my full breasts.

"Now, the panties, Liv," he growled.

Still holding the phone to my ear, I stood and pulled one side of my thong down and then the other until they fell to the floor.

"Good. Now, sit back down. I want to watch you touch yourself, over and over, until you're screaming out my name."

"So bossy," I teased.

"I like to think of it as assertive and sexy. Besides, it doesn't take a window for me to figure you out. You need this distraction right now just as badly as I do. I know you more than you realize."

He did. I didn't know how, but in the short amount of time we'd known each other, he'd managed to weasel his way in and learn the many sides of me.

Right now, he knew the one thing I needed most of all was a distraction from the evening we were about to begin. I was quite fond of his choice of distractions.

My hand slipped down my body toward the juncture of my thighs.

"That's it, sweetheart—nice and slow."

Parting my slick folds, I stroked myself once, moving up toward my clit. I circled the sensitive nub, involuntarily moaning from each tantalizing caress.

"Spread your legs. I want to see all of you."

My legs shifted farther apart, giving a clear view of my most intimate parts and the way I was touching them.

"God, you're beautiful," he breathed into the speaker.

Syllables, words, and sentences escaped me. So focused on my own pleasure, I could only respond with a deep moan as I sunk two fingers deep inside my core.

"Faster. Work those fingers faster, Liv," he dictated.

I listened. Placing my thumb on my clit, I fucked myself, moving my fingers in and out, as I rocked my body against them.

"Jackson," I managed to say.

There was no answer.

"Jackson!" I yelled as I felt myself growing close.

Suddenly, a loud noise from downstairs startled me, and hurried feet rushed up the stairs.

Before I had a second to cover myself, he appeared, standing in my doorway. He'd barely pulled down his jeans over his boxers briefs, which were now straining against the ridge of his hard cock.

With his hand pointed toward the bed, he ordered, "Hands and knees—now."

His eyes were wild with desire, and I knew he was probably hanging on by a string. I didn't waste any time. I stood from my chair in front of the window. As I walked past him, my hands brushed his bare chest, and his breath hissed out in response.

Crawling onto the bed and baring my ass in all its glory, I went on all fours. The bed dipped behind me as strong hands slid up my thighs and wrapped firmly around my hip.

His body bent forward, and his warm breath caressed my ear as he whispered, "Seeing you touch yourself like that, knowing you were thinking of me while you did it...I couldn't stay away. I don't think I'll ever be able to stay away Liv."

His words halted as his body slammed into mine.

"Oh fuck!" I cried out, pushing back against him.

Over and over, he plunged into my slick body, sending me deeper into ecstasy. My legs shook, and my arms trembled as sweat dripped down my face. It was primal, dirty, and downright beautiful.

My body started to spasm as he let out a guttural moan while moving faster and harder. We came together, our bodies detonating like two exploding stars. Unable to stay upright a second longer, we both collapsed onto the bed, curled in each other's arms. I could hear the rapid rhythm of his heart beating against my back as he kissed my shoulder.

"Stress level better?" he asked softly.

"Much."

"Good, 'cause we're running late now."

I looked over at the clock and saw it was now twenty minutes from the time we were supposed to be at the restaurant.

"Shit!" I jumped out of bed, stark-naked, with my just-fucked hair sticking out in every direction.

"If it helps at all, you should wear the purple dress right there," he said, pointing to a simple wrap dress. "I always like you in purple," he confessed sweetly.

His naked body was draped across my bed, doing all sorts of crazy things to my frazzled brain.

"You, out," I commanded, pointing to the door.

He laughed, standing proudly, without an ounce of shame.

With a body like that, who needs shame?

Focus, Liv.

"I can't think with all that yummy nakedness around. Go get dressed, and be back here in ten minutes!"

"Yes, ma'am," he answered, playing up his Carolina boy accent.

He peeked out the window as he was pulling up his jeans. "Looks like Leah is here to pick up Noah. I'd better run out and say good-bye to him. Wish I had a shirt." He shrugged and then quickly kissed me on the cheek. "Oh, and if it ever comes up, you're afraid of spiders."

I raised an eyebrow at him. "Spiders?"

"I might have mentioned something to Noah about you being afraid of spiders and needing someone to kill one for you before I ran out of the house as if a fire were chasing me."

Before I had a chance to answer, he slapped my bare ass and gave me a parting wink.

I shook my head, covering a giggle, as I moved to the closet to get dressed.

I stopped as it all came back—dinner, parents…olive branch.

My phone rang, and it was Jackson again.

I glanced up at the window across from me, but he wasn't there. "Hello?"

"Purple dress, remember?"

"How did you—" I began to ask.

"I just did. Take a deep breath. It's going to be okay."

Nodding, I let in a long gulp of air and allowed it to fill my lungs.

No matter what happened tonight, I knew that everything would be just fine as long as Jackson was there to hold my hand.

~Jackson~

The restaurant was exactly the type of place I'd expected a Senator and his wife to dine. Upscale and refined, it was known for its exclusive menu and world-class chef. It was also impossibly hard to get into—unless, of course, one had money.

It was rumored that Douglas Prescott's wealth was grossly exaggerated. Having been in several confidential meetings with him now, I knew this to be fairly inaccurate. The man was loaded. But wealthy politicians didn't go over well in an economy where jobs were scarce and prices were sky-high. Even a rich Republican had to do his best to connect with the regular folk, and that was exactly what the good old Senator from Virginia was trying to do.

My opinion on the man was still on the fence, and most of it hinged on how he behaved tonight.

He could wine and dine the American people until he was blue in the face. What he did with his campaign was his business.

What he did with Liv, however, was my business.

I didn't care that his account meant more to my boss than life itself. I would do whatever was necessary to protect what was mine—even if it meant leaving the position I'd come here for.

I had no idea what to expect as Liv's hand slipped in mine, and we walked through the double doors of the restaurant.

Would her father be rigid and formal? Or would he break down at the mere sight of his little girl? Would he feel betrayed at the sight of me by her side wondering if I'd known who he was this entire time and never told him anything about Liv?

Honestly, I didn't give a fuck what he thought of me, but I did care how he treated Liv, and I didn't want my professional involvement to affect that.

After quickly checking in with the maître d', we were escorted to a cozy table near the back of the restaurant.

So, the old man had requested privacy for this little reunion?

I wasn't exactly sure how I felt about that.

I squeezed Liv's hand, quickly grabbing her attention. "You ready for this? We could still turn around." I winked.

She smiled hesitantly and rubbed my knuckle with her thumb. "Nervous, counselor?" she joked.

"No way. I'm pumped."

"Liar."

When we reached the booth, the maître d' formally announced us, "Sir, here is the rest of your party. Shall I bring the bottle of wine you selected?"

"Yes, that would be lovely," the Senator replied.

I couldn't see him yet. My view was blocked by several plants and lavish floral decorations placed between each booth, obviously creating a feeling of intimacy.

"Olivia," he greeted, his voice growing noticeably choked. "My Livvy Lou."

"Hi, Daddy," she replied.

I'd never heard that nickname, but I instantly loved it. It was endearing and sweet, and it gave me visions of a little girl with long braids climbing trees and piggybacking on her father.

A petite woman with dark chestnut hair and bright blue eyes, brimming with tears stood to greet us. She pulled Liv into her arms and held her tightly.

As they embraced, I got my first glimpse of the Senator outside of the conference walls of my office building. He looked up at the sight of his daughter and wife with satisfaction and obvious emotion. It wasn't until Liv stepped back to take my hand once more that he seemed to notice anyone else.

"Mom, Dad, I'd like you to meet my boyfriend," Liv said formally. She snuck a smirk in my direction, no doubt a response to her choice of title for me.

Her father rose from the table, outstretching his hand toward me. "Jackson Reid," he stated.

"Yes, sir. Pleasure to meet you—again," I added.

"I hadn't realized," he said, gesturing for us to join them at the table.

Liv went first, taking the seat closest to her father, and I slid in next to her.

"I apologize for blindsiding you, sir," I began.

"Please, call me Doug," he requested.

Nodding, I continued, "I didn't want my relationship with Liv to appear as me trying in any way to get the upper hand with you in our day jobs. Considering the situation, I also wanted to protect Liv. I hope you understand my decision."

Moments passed as he stared at me from across the table. I knew what he was doing. He was sizing me up. I didn't back down or look away. Although I could really give a rat's ass about what Liv's absentee father thought of me, I would not appear weak in front of the woman I cared about so deeply.

"I appreciate your honesty, Jackson. I know being in the middle couldn't have been easy for you, and quite frankly, most people would have taken advantage of a situation like that. Thank you for being a decent human being. I see why my daughter keeps you around. I would never have expected to see her with a lawyer." He smiled.

"Well, she wasn't too keen on the idea to begin with, but I wore her down." I grinned, giving Liv a slight nudge with my shoulder.

"He's still working on it," she joked.

Wine was poured, and orders were soon placed. The conversation was kept light as Liv's parents asked about her life. Liv told them all about the counseling center. Both sets of eyes were focused directly on her. Her parents listened to every word she said with rapt attention even though I got the feeling they already knew most of the information she was telling them.

"Sounds like you've done well for yourself," her mother replied.

The way Doug had spoken about her the other day in the office sounded much like a father who had kept at least some tabs on his daughter over the years.

Perhaps I'd underestimated the man, and Liv hadn't been as alone as she thought.

For her sake, I hoped so.

Chapter Twenty-One

~Liv~

The sun was barely over the horizon as I parked my car in front of the old studio and stepped out into the humid heat. Late August always brought record-breaking temperatures to Virginia. Looking around for Leah's car, I realized I was a few minutes early, so I decided to take a seat on one of the wicker chairs in front of the studio and enjoy the quiet early morning.

After eight long years, I'd seen my parents, hugged them, and held them in my arms.

They'd spoken the words I'd been longing to hear. It was like a dream come true, yet part of me couldn't accept that it was real.

Why now? Why, after all this time, did they suddenly have a change of heart?

The little girl inside of me had wanted to run into the shelter of their arms, uncaring of their reasons behind the long-awaited decision.

The adult in me—the woman who had spent so many years alone—couldn't help but worry about what else might have been lurking to ruin my perfect homecoming.

A car door slammed, bringing my attention upward. Coming toward me in tight black yoga pants and a barely there hot pink sports bra was Leah. She was the type of friend who everyone wanted to hate because she was tall, lean, and freaking perfect. Adding in the ridiculously hot, completely faithful ex-movie star husband to the equation, she was lucky that women even spoke to her.

But after we'd become close friends and I'd begun regularly attending yoga and Pilates classes with her a few times a week, I'd quickly figured out one thing. Leah worked hard to keep her body looking so damn good.

I'd always considered myself in shape and physically fit. I'd run several times a week, and I had taken a few classes at the gym. I had never truly felt out of shape until I'd walked into a Pilates class with Leah and spent the next forty-five minutes wondering what in the holy hell I'd done to this instructor to deserve such torture. It had hurt to walk, sit, and pretty much move for the next two solid days. Pilates had taught me a different way to move, and my muscles had hated me for even attempting it.

But Leah had convinced me to give it another try until the pain eventually lessened, and I'd even added in yoga to my weekly routine as well. Now, it had become a sort of weekly ritual for us. On yoga days, Clare would join us, but today, it was just Leah and me.

"Hey, hippie girl," Leah greeted, sitting next to me on one of the chairs outside the studio.

"What's up, crazy?" I replied with a grin.

"Oh, you know, the usual. Just doing my best to stay out of trouble."

The lock on the studio door flipped, and the lights inside suddenly turned on, announcing the instructor's arrival.

"Yeah? How's that working out for you?" I laughed as we rose from our chairs and headed toward the entrance along with another woman who had just walked up.

"Well, it's only six thirty in the morning, but so far, so good." She winked.

"Does this mean you are going to refrain from getting us kicked out of class again?" I gave her a meaningful look.

Playing innocent, she held up her hands. "I have no idea what you're referring to. I'm always a model participant in this class."

"Who never stops talking," the woman next to us added with a smirk.

I burst out laughing and covered my mouth to muffle the sound, but it didn't help. "Oh my God, she's got you pegged, Leah! It's true. You run your mouth from the time class starts until it ends. I have no idea how you can hold your legs at a forty-five degree angle and still maintain speech. It's inhuman."

She shrugged. "I'm good at it I guess."

"Talking or Pilates?" I laughed.

"Both, bitch! Now, tell me about this sexy man and the dinner with your parents while I attempt to annoy the shit out of everyone in class."

"Oh God, I should just leave now and save myself some money," I huffed.

"Now, what fun would that be?"

We set up our mats on the floor and took our seats as we waited for the instructor to begin.

"Jackson is just…well—"

"He's what?"

"Amazing."

"Amazing?" she echoed.

"Yeah. What's wrong with that?"

"Nothing. It's just that I don't think I've ever heard you describe a member of the male species as amazing. You even said it in a dreamy tone. Usually, they're hot or sexy or good in bed…but never amazing. Well, there was that one guy who was amazing—in bed. Is that what you meant? If so, ignore everything I just said and carry on."

"I think my head just exploded," I said, shaking it to make sure I was still in one piece.

Spending a day with Leah was sometimes very exhausting.

"Well, which one is it?"

"Amazing. He's just amazing. I mean, he's fantastic in bed— okay, better than fantastic. He deserves a blue ribbon for best lay, but he's more than that."

"Whoa, you're gushing—over a guy."

"I know." I giggled.

"And you're not even denying it! Was that a giggle?"

I just smiled.

"I want to meet this guy."

"You have," I pointed out.

"For a minute doesn't count. Also, he didn't have a shirt on. By the way, that was weird, considering he came from your house."

I chose not to reply, and she just laughed.

"We should throw a dinner party. Clare has been dying to have one for ages."

"Don't we have dinner together all the time?"

The instructor, a perky young redhead, tried to gather everyone's attention toward the front of the room.

Who knew this many women actually enjoyed waking up this early?

"Clare thinks a dinner party sounds fancy. She loves to watch HGTV when Maddie is at dance class. She is constantly calling me with crazy ideas about dinner parties and new festive holiday decorations. The other day, she blew up my phone all afternoon with ideas for Christmas. Seriously, Liv, it's August."

Cupping my hand over my mouth, I leaned over and whispered, "Could it have anything to do with all the baby hormones running rampant through her system?"

"Oh, definitely, but try to tell her no. Go ahead. I dare you."

I held out my hands in defense just as we were instructed to lie on our backs for some core exercises.

"Oh, no, I'm not stupid. Dinner party it is."

"Good," she whispered. "And bring the next-door hottie."

~Jackson~

When I was younger, my father had loved watching old TV shows. *The Andy Griffith Show*, *Lassie*, and *My Three Sons* were some of his favorites. He'd said it reminded him of a simpler time during his childhood—when life was easier and people were far less cryptic and cynical.

Long before I was old enough to think that hanging out with my father was lame, I'd sit and watch these black-and-white classics with him, thinking about how differently people treated each other in the television world.

But I'd soon realized that it wasn't just in TV shows. It was a way of life that had begun to die out. The simpler generation my father had so loved where people would help each other just for the sheer satisfaction of doing so seemed to be slipping through our fingers just like the old shows he used to watch.

Back before the world was a blur of cell phones and crunching data, people had moved at a slower pace, seeing the world and everything around them. Helping your neighbor had been a daily occurrence. It hadn't been a burden but just a natural a part of life.

The morning after the dinner with the Prescotts, I silently drove my son across town, passing the camp he regularly attended. Instead, we drove across town and pulled into the driveway of Noah's new best friend.

As we hopped out of my truck, I took a moment to look around. There was a mailbox in front with the last name *James* neatly printed in gold script. That morning when we came here to pick up Noah after he'd spent the night, I had no idea I was walking into a movie stars house. Apparently, a wealthy father wasn't the only interesting fact when it came to Olivia Prescott.

From the outside, it looked like a typical upperclass all-American family home—nothing outlandish or overdone. The lawn was a vibrant green and well kept. Pink and yellow flowers lined the walkway, and I couldn't help but look down to see what color mulch was hidden underneath the deep green leaves. Of course, it was regular brown mulch.

I shook my head and chuckled under my breath as we approached the door.

"You okay, Dad?" Noah asked as he pressed the doorbell.

"Yeah. You sure this is okay?"

"You spoke with them last night," he reminded me.

"Yeah, I know," I huffed.

Favors, a nice deed, helping out a friend—whatever it was referred to, I was having a hard time accepting it.

I guessed it was a product of my generation.

All last night, I'd agonized over taking Declan and Leah James up on their offer to watch Noah for the rest of the summer.

Who does that—offering to watch someone else's kid for two weeks for free?

The James family obviously.

Before I had another second to reconsider, the door swung open, and I was greeted by Declan carrying their daughter in his arms.

"Hey there, Noah!" Declan exclaimed. "I'd give you a high five, but I'm pretty sure I have jam or…. something all over me."—he pulled his hand closely to his face for inspection and Lily giggled. —"Anyway, I'll spare you the sticky fingers."

"Thanks. I mean, hi Mr. James. Thanks for having me over."

"You can call me Declan, Noah. Connor is upstairs if you want to head up there."

Seeing a clear escape route now, he said a quick good-bye over his shoulder as he ran through the door and up the stairs, disappearing immediately.

I chuckled, waving my clean hands at the little girl in his arms. She smiled shyly and snuggled into her father's chest.

"Hey, Jackson. Good to see you again. You got time for a cup of coffee?" Declan asked.

"You, too and sure, I could probably squeeze in a few minutes," I said, quickly looking down at my watch.

He invited me inside. Their house was impressive, but I hadn't expected anything less.

"Hey, thanks for doing this," I commented as we reached the kitchen. "You really don't have to. I feel like I'm taking advantage here," I rambled, watching as Lily squirmed out of his arms and ran off towards the living room we'd just passed through.

"No problem, man. We actually feel that way. You're doing us a huge favor by letting us borrow Noah during the day. Most of Connor's friends have been gone a lot this summer with vacation plans and what not. He's been going a little stir-crazy. Having Noah here the other night was great."

"Good. I'm glad to hear it. He's been pretty bummed since we moved. It's great to see him finally making a friend."

"Yeah, they've really hit it off."

He poured me a cup of coffee, and I watched him dump creamer and a heaping pile of sugar into his own cup.

He caught me grinning. "What?"

"Nothing." I laughed, taking the sugar bowl from him and repeating the same treatment to my own cup of coffee.

"Liv give you shit about how you drink your coffee too?" he asked, as I pulled the steaming cup to my mouth. It was so sweet, my teeth nearly fell out as I took my first sip.

Perfect.

"No," I answered.

"She will. I purposely try and sit next to her if we go out to breakfast just so she can watch me toss ten packets of sugar into my cup. The way her eyes bug out? Fucking hilarious."

"I've never met anyone quite like her, that's for sure," I commented, with a slight shake of my head.

"So, I've got to ask, what's the deal with the two of you? Is it serious?"

My expression hardened as I slowly placed my coffee cup down on the counter.

Where exactly was he going with this conversation?

He held out his hands in front of him. "Easy, Jackson. Don't misinterpret this as some sort of territorial thing. Leah is my fucking world, and everything that is part of her, I protect. That includes her friends. I just want to make sure you aren't going to hurt her."

I visibly relaxed. "I have no intentions of hurting Liv. I also protect what's mine."

He looked surprised but pleasantly pleased. "Good. Now, I can offer you doughnuts. Only friends get doughnuts."

Turning, he opened a large pantry and pulled out a small pink box from the highest shelf. "I have to hide them from the monsters," he whispered. "Damn kids eat everything in sight."

After opening the box, he extended it to me first. I picked out a doughnut and took a large bite. It was really fucking good.

"Apple doughnuts," Declan said before I even had the chance to ask what they were. "Leah's obsessed with them. They're from this little Christmas tree farm up in the mountains. We go there every year to pick out a tree. Years ago, she worked out an arrangement with the owners, and now, her habit is supplied monthly. I don't even want to know how much it costs me."

"I'd say these are worth it."

"No," he said. "She is."

We ate a few more doughnuts and polished off our coffees before I glanced at my watch. We headed for the door and went over when I'd be back to pick up Noah, but I felt myself lingering. Since last night, something had been bothering me, festering my mind from the moment it had happened, and I didn't have a soul to talk to about it—until now.

Finally, I said, "Declan, can I ask you a question?"

He shrugged. "Shoot."

"Last night, Liv and I had dinner with her parents. I'm not sure how much you know—"

"I know," he said.

"Okay." I nodded, grateful Liv had such great friends. "The evening went well…for the most part."

"Except?" he added, guessing where I was headed.

"Except for toward the end. We were finishing the evening with coffee, and just as we were about to say our good-byes, a man came to the table."

"Who was it?"

"Someone from the local paper," I said.

"What?"

"Now, I don't know much about the press, but the way it all went down seemed very shady to me."

"Tell me," he said, leaning against the doorframe.

"The man introduced himself and said he was from the paper and that he just happened to recognize Senator Prescott from across the room. He said he was sorry to interrupt our family dinner but wished to take a picture for the social section—the paper was considering doing an article on the restaurant we were dining at. The Senator was very gracious, and of course, he complied. Liv was nervous but didn't want to make a scene, so we all pulled in tight and smiled. Then, it was over."

"How did he know Liv was family?" he asked.

"I honestly don't know. Liv hasn't been seen in public with her family for years." Had the reporter assumed the Senator was out with family? Or had he been tipped off?

Declan shook his head. "I might be out of the game, but I know one thing. That kind of stuff doesn't happen by accident. Everything about that scenario was set up ahead of time. I've seen it happen more than once in the entertainment world, like staged outings to gain momentum for a movie or show. Nothing is ever as it seems."

"I thought so," I said, a wave of sadness tingeing my every word. I feared the worst.

After seeing Liv's father last night, I'd wanted so badly to believe he wanted her back in his life for no other reason than a father had missed his little girl.

But what other reason would there be for a politician to go through the trouble of setting up an elaborate photo opportunity other than to gain new voters?

I really hoped I was wrong.

Chapter
Twenty-Two

~Liv~

"Your friends do realize that just because I'm a lawyer doesn't mean I need fancy dinners and hand printed invitations, right?" Jackson said, holding up the ivory pearl card stock Clare had sent over.

She had invited all of us over for a black and white–themed dinner this evening.

"We could meet over pizza," he added. "Chuck E. Cheese would be fine."

Shaking my head, I grabbed my purse, and then I walked up to him and straightened his tie. "First thing, Chuck E. Cheese? Gross. That pizza is horrible. Secondly, Clare is pregnant, so we do whatever she says, including ridiculous dinners that require a new dress and shoes."

His eyes appreciatively traveled the length of my body as his hand slipped around my waist. The decision to spend a little extra on the black-and-white strapless lace dress was definitely paying off.

"On second thought, I really like this idea. I'll be sure to thank our hostess."

"Stop that thought right there, counselor. You're going to make us late—again."

His voice lowered as he said, "Come on, Liv. Just give me five minutes."

My insides tightened. Biting my lip, I looked over to check the time on the microwave.

He dropped to his knees and lifted my skirt before I even had a chance to say yes.

"We're so late," I said, trying to smooth down my hair for the tenth time since we'd left the house.

"You didn't seem to mind at the time." He chuckled, wrapping an arm around my waist. "Besides, isn't it good to be fashionably late to these sorts of things?"

"This is going to be a disaster," I huffed, shaking my head.

He stopped me in the middle of the walkway in front of Clare's house, and he cupped my chin. "Hey," he said in a soothing voice. "Why the sudden stress? I thought I took care of that."

A smug grin tugged at the corner of his lips as he looked down at me.

"I've never done this before."

"What?"

"Introduced a guy I'm dating to my friends."

His grin widened. "Really? Never?"

"No. You're the first."

"Well then, I'd better use my best Southern manners," he said, playing up his accent. "I'm going to be the last, too."

I laughed as he held out his arm in a ridiculously formal gesture. I took it, and we walked the rest of the way to the front steps. Just as I was about to press the doorbell, the door opened, and Clare, Leah, and Mia, greeted us.

"Took you long enough," Leah said, her black-and-white sequins dress shimmering under the lights. "We had a bet on whether or not you were going to run back to the car."

"Oh, yeah? Who won?" I asked, raising an eyebrow at my best friends.

"Clare," they all said.

"Figures."

Jackson and I followed everyone in, making our way toward the formal dining room. Clare had gone all out, decorating the entire house to create a look that was thematic yet not overdone. Black and white pearls hung from the chandelier. Black and white candles floated in tiny glass bowls, and hot pink roses were set in vases throughout the house for a pop of color.

I looked around the room and watched as everyone mingled and greeted Jackson.

Damn, I had good-looking friends.

Leah and Declan looked like Hollywood royalty. His black-on-black suit fit his body like a glove as he held his wife tightly by his side.

Clare was just beginning to show, her black dress rounding slightly where her third child was growing safely in her womb. Logan dressed in a pinstripe suite entered the room, carrying a glass of water for his wife.

Then, there was Mia and Garrett. Mia, always understated and demure, was wearing a black-and-white A-line dress and red Mary Jane heels.

Little rebel.

Everyone introduced themselves to Jackson. Each female gave me a little thumbs-up behind his back.

I'd spent years on my own until I found this group of friends. Their approval of Jackson meant more to me than I could put into words. I never thought I'd care for anyone enough to take this step. Seeing them meet was like watching two parts of myself intertwine and meld together.

"Clare, where are Colin and Ella?" Leah asked, taking a sip of wine as she nuzzled into Declan.

"They aren't ready to detach themselves from the new baby just yet," Clare answered.

"How old is she now?" I asked, trying to remember the last time I'd seen Logan's best friend Colin and his wife.

"Four months," she replied. "Their parents were busy and they didn't feel right asking my mom to watch a newborn on top of all the other kids she had tonight."

"Your mom probably could have handled it," I laughed.

"Garrett and Clare, you really must thank your mother for me. I can't believe she volunteered to watch all the kids tonight. Should we have someone deliver a bottle of wine later?" Jackson asked jokingly.

Clare waved her hand dismissively. "She loves having a houseful of children. Ever since our father passed away, it seems to be her favorite thing to do. I keep telling her that she can take them one at a time, but she insists on having all of them at once. And Noah was a welcome addition."

"Plus, my dad is there to help," Mia added.

Logan reappeared from the kitchen where he'd vanished to minutes earlier to uncork a bottle of wine, and he began giving out filled glasses. Jackson took two and handed one to me.

"So, I've been avoiding this for a while, but I can't any longer," I said before taking a sip of my merlot. "What the heck is going on between your parents?"

All eyes focused in on Mia and Garrett and then over to Clare. We were obviously all wondering the same thing.

"We think they're dating," Garrett said.

"You think?" Leah echoed.

"Well, neither one has outwardly said it. I'm guessing they're afraid of how we will react," Mia chimed in.

"And how will you react?" Leah asked, leaning back against her husband's large frame.

"Honestly, the thought of it bothered us at first, but as long as they're happy, we really don't care," Clare confessed.

"You should tell them," I suggested.

"Is that your clinical opinion?" Garrett asked, grinning.

"No, you'd have to pay for that. This is my opinion as a friend. All that hiding can't be easy on them. Give them your blessing."

"We will, but it has been fun watching them sneak around." Mia laughed. "Yesterday, I swung by to bring some cookies as a little treat for my dad, and I found Laura there. He told me she was dropping off some dry-cleaning for him."

"Maybe she was—along with sex," Leah quipped.

"Gross, Leah! That's my mom!" Garrett yelled.

"I might never sleep again," Mia uttered.

"Well, on that note, I think dinner might be ready. Anyone hungry?" Clare said, obviously trying to change the subject.

The room erupted into laughter.

Clare had wanted to serve everyone, but we quickly threw that idea out the window. Instead of the dining room, we all headed toward the kitchen.

"Did you really think we were going to sit around your dining table and allow you to serve us?" Mia asked.

Clare pouted. "Well, yes, I'm the hostess."

"The pregnant hostess," Leah added. "Come on, friends, let's get dinner on the table."

We all put on oven mitts and began plating food onto large platters and in serving bowls
before carrying our feast out to the table.

"It all looks amazing, Clare," I commented, giving her a squeeze.

"Thanks. Logan did most of the cooking."

"You didn't let him touch dessert, did you?" I asked as we made our way back to the dining room to take our seats.

"No." She laughed. "Dessert is safe."

Food and dishes were passed around until plates were piled high. Laughter filled the air.

"Oh, Liv! I almost forgot!" Clare said, jumping out of her seat. She rushed out of the room and returned seconds later with a newspaper clipping. She dropped it next to my plate. "You and Jackson made the news. You're celebrities now!"

"What?" I looked down at the black-and-white print. There, looking up at me, was the photo that had been taken of Jackson and myself at dinner with my parents.

Below the photo, the caption said, *Senator Prescott enjoying dinner with wife, Michelle; daughter, Olivia; and boyfriend, Richmond attorney, Jackson Reid.*

It had been ages since I saw a picture of my family and me together, and I spent a moment looking down at the grainy photo, memorizing the faces and happy smiles of my parents sitting with me.

I slowly looked up to see my friends staring at me with curiosity. I caught Jackson sneak a glance over at Declan, and the two men seemed to be exchanging something between themselves.

Jackson's gaze returned to me, and I found myself questioning him for the first time.

"What's going on?"

Taken aback, he asked, "What do you mean?"

"You and Declan—what's going on?"

"It's not important right now," he said with a wave of his hand.

"I want to know." My tone was clipped and to the point.

He let out a deep breath of air just as Declan spoke up, "It's not a big deal, Liv. Jackson's just worried about you. He told me about the newspaper journalist from the other night and—"

My temper began to rise, and my heart rate accelerated. "You were talking about me?"

The room went dead silent. No one was touching the food anymore, and I felt terrible for disrupting the meal Clare had put so much effort into, but I just couldn't stop pushing.

"I asked Declan what he thought of the situation because of his background with reporters. That's all," Jackson said.

"You think my father is using me, don't you?"

My eyes darted around the room and saw a sea of blank faces. *Did they all think that?*

"I just want to make sure you're safe."

The tiny room began to spin and my stomach churned with embarrassment. "I don't feel well all the sudden. Clare, do you mind if I leave early?" I tried to plaster on my best smile.

She gave me a weak smile as she began to rise from her chair.

"Don't bother, honey. I can show myself out."

There wasn't enough air in the room. I felt like everyone was staring at me, judging me.

I had to get out.

~Jackson~

We drove back home in silence.

The sheer fact that she was even in the same car with me right now was a miracle. I could feel the anger and hurt radiating off her body like an overworked furnace.

I spent every second between Clare's house and ours thinking, contemplating, and figuring out my plan of attack. With Liv, it was always about strategy.

Going into this relationship, I'd known that it wasn't going to be easy. Both Liv and I had been single for far too long, but her situation was vastly different than mine.

She'd basically been abandoned by the two people in her life who were supposed to be there for her. The results of this experience had made Liv's strong personality even more so. She had been fiercely determined to prove to the world just how capable she was on her own two feet.

Making a partnership with someone who'd spent years living on her own and asserting her independence was no easy battle, but it was one that I was willing to fight because she was worth it.

Together, we would always be worth it.

I pulled into my driveway, and she jumped out of the truck the second it came to a stop.

"Liv, wait," I hollered after her, once I'd shut off the ignition and pushed open the door. I raced after her.

"I'm done talking tonight, Jackson," she hissed as she walked across the grass between our houses.

"Well, I'm not."

"You don't want to know what I have to say, so drop it and go home. We can talk tomorrow," she said.

Somehow, I knew that if I let her walk away, there would be no talking tomorrow.

We reached the sidewalk, and her heels clacked against the concrete as she tried to outpace me to her front door. I sped up and cut her off, blocking the entrance.

"What the hell, Jackson?" Her eyes were narrowed into slits as she angrily folded her arms across her chest.

"I'll let you pass, but you have to talk to me," I said.

"Fine," she said.

"Inside," I added, remembering whom I was playing with. Liv was a sneaky little thing. If we stood out here to talk, I'd find a door slammed in my face in five seconds flat.

"Fine!" she yelled.

I pulled out my keys and unlocked her door.

"You know I could do that."

"Yeah, but then I'd probably end up with my ass on the doormat and you on the other side, sliding the chain in place to keep me out."

"Prick."

"Nice one." I grinned, letting her name-calling slide off my back. At least she was talking to me.

I opened the door and stepped inside before she had a chance to scoot past me. Once I was safely in, I ushered her to join me.

"Gee, thanks."

"Anytime."

She dropped her purse in its normal spot on the counter and turned back toward me, obviously not taking the time to sit and get comfortable. She thought this was going to be quick.

She was so wrong.

"So, talk," she snapped.

"I thought I should have the opportunity to explain myself."

There was no reply. She just waited.

"Look, Liv, I don't have a clue what's going on in that head of yours, but I think I have a pretty good idea. Those people you ran out on tonight love you. Not a single soul in that room wanted to cause you harm. If Declan and I were talking about your father, it was only because we wanted to make sure he doesn't hurt you."

"I can take—"

"I know. You can take care of yourself. Goddamn, woman, would you just let me speak?"

Her mouth snapped back shut.

"I don't know why you think me wanting to take care of you or protect you is in some way an insult to your independence. Haven't you already proven that enough already?"

"I just don't know if I'm cut out for this," she whispered.

"What do you mean?"

Motioning between the two of us, she took a step forward. "You…me…us. I just don't know if I'm meant to be in a relationship like this. It's too much, too soon. We're too much. I can't handle it."

Heart failure—that was what I felt in this moment.

"What are you saying, Liv?"

"Maybe we need a break."

"We've barely even started," I whispered.

"Then, perhaps we should just go back to being neighbors?" she suggested softly.

"You could never be just my neighbor, Liv."

My eyes fell to the floor as I tried to come up with something to say that would make her reconsider. What could I say or do if she'd already made up her mind?

"I think I'm done talking for the evening," I finally said, turning toward the door.

I couldn't make her love me. Every step felt like I was walking away from a future I'd hardly begun—a life of milkshakes and practical jokes. It was something worth fighting for, but I wasn't doing that. I was giving up.

"No," I said, stopping just before the door.

I turned around and found tear-stained eyes staring back at me.

"No?"

Closing the distance separating us, I grabbed the back of her neck and pulled her close.

"I'm not going anywhere, Liv. I know you're scared, and the easiest thing to do is push me away, but love is never easy. I love you, Liv, every part of you, even that fiercely independent, pain-in-the-ass side that is telling you to flee right now. You wouldn't be you without it. But you need to trust me. You need to trust us."

"I don't know how," she whispered, tears running down her cheeks.

"Trust this." I tenderly touched my lips to hers. "What do you feel?"

"Tenderness, warmth…desire," she answered.

"Go deeper," I instructed before kissing her again. I gave her everything in that kiss—my heart, soul, and future.

When I pulled back, she was smiling.

"Happiness…pink flamingos…love."

"That's my girl," I said gently. "Welcome to the other side."

We spent the rest of the night together discovering just how much love could be found in each other's arms.

~Jackson~

"I need a drink," I said, feeling defeated.

Liv sat down next to me on the couch. "It's not that bad, Jackson."

"Says you."

She rested her head on my shoulder, and I caressed her thigh as I listened to her breathe.

"You knew this day would eventually happen," she reminded me.

"Yeah, but I didn't think it would actually ever really happen. It was *someday* and always so far in the future that I didn't need to think about it."

"And this summer? What kept you from thinking about it over the summer?" she asked.

"Moving, new job…you."

"Don't blame this on me!" She laughed.

"Can't he be a kid just for a little longer?" I moaned.

"Jackson, he's still a kid."

"No, he's a tween. They're like mutant kids—pint-sized teenagers who listen to weird bands and talk funny. It's fucking scary."

She giggled, pulling my face toward hers.

God, I loved her.

Since the night, so many weeks ago that I had put everything on the line and fought to keep her, fought to stay in her life, I'd watched her blossom into the woman I knew I couldn't live without.

It wasn't that she'd changed really. By revealing her feelings for me, she was finally able to relax and be completely herself around me without any more walls or hesitation.

It was just her, me, and whatever came next.

"He's still your kid, Jackson, regardless of what school he's starting. So, let's put on our brave faces and go see how our little middle-schooler is fairing the eve before his big day."

"Yeah, okay," I grumbled.

She pulled me off the couch, and we climbed up the stairs to Noah's room. I gently knocked on the open door, giving him a heads-up of our arrival, and found him shoving a few pencils into his backpack.

"Almost ready?" I asked.

"Yeah, I think so," he answered quietly.

Liv took a seat on the bed next to him. "Did I ever tell you about my first day of middle school?" she asked.

He shook his head, placing the backpack on the floor beside his feet.

"My dad was up for re-election for state senate, and there was talk of him running for the US Senator seat. My parents decided it was no longer safe for me to continue attending the public school where I'd been going."

"You went to a private school, too?"

"I did," she answered. "Not the same one as you but very similar."

"Was it horrible—your first day?" he asked hesitantly.

"I thought it would be. I begged my mother to reconsider. I even told her I'd be okay with a bodyguard if she'd just let me go back to the public school. For the record, we were not cool enough to have bodyguards. I was just being melodramatic."

"Girls are like that," he added.

"Tell me about it." I laughed.

I got the evil eye for that remark, but she threw a wink in my direction as well.

"When I arrived, I got snide looks, and people were shy to come up to me. I was new and mysterious, and of course, I was the Senator's daughter. Eventually, as the day went on, people started to warm up to me, and I began to find my niche."

"I hope I can," he said quietly.

"You will. Just take it one day at a time. Besides, you always have Fridays to fall back on."

Both Noah and I looked at her in confusion.

"Dress-down days! Come on, do you guys not remember all those dope clothes we got you? When you're finally able to bust out of that uniform at the end of the week, those kids will be hanging on your every word. And you'll be thanking me because of it!"

"Ah, yes, because that's exactly how to make friends." I chuckled.

"Hey, whatever works. They're eleven." She shrugged.

We said good night, and I took one last look at my little boy before walking toward the door. Liv and I stepped over the threshold.

"Liv?" Noah said.

"Yeah?" she answered, swiveling back around.

"Do you think…you could maybe—"

"I'll be here in the morning. Don't worry." She smiled, reaching out for my hand.

"Thanks," he answered, a touch of obvious relief coming out in his slow exhale.

I followed her as she moved toward the stairs, our hands still tightly joined together. As she took the first step, I stopped. She turned around, grinning, and met my gaze.

"Stay," I said.

"Are you sure?" She looked over at Noah's room with unease.

"It wouldn't be the first time," I reminded her.

"Yes, but that was before—"

"Before what, Liv?"

"Before the sex," she said, whispering the last word so softly that it was barely audible.

I pulled her hand to my lips and slowly kissed each of her knuckles with care.

"Stay," I said again.

"Okay," she relented.

She trailed behind me as I led us to the bedroom. It wasn't late, but if she was going to sleep in my bed, I would take advantage of that situation right away.

Letting the door click in place behind us, she looked around and grinned. "You know your son is still very much awake down the hall, right?"

"I'm aware," I said, walking toward her.

"And you know these old houses have super thin walls, right?"

"Yep." My hands slipped around her waist, and I picked her up.

Like clockwork, her slender legs wrapped around my torso, and I felt her melt into me.

"What are we doing?" she whispered in my ear.

"We're going to read a book," I said in my most seductive voice possible.

Her head lifted, and her eyes met mine. "Come again?"

"Oh, I plan to, but give me an hour or so." I grinned. "For now, I wanted to show you one of the many perks of a relationship."

Over the last week or so, I'd been doing this quite frequently, constantly reminding her of the joys and certain extras one received when committed to another. Last week, I'd dropped off lunch for her at her office. Her secretary had been out for the day, so we'd also locked the door, and I'd shown her how much fun a desk could really be. On Monday, when she hadn't felt well and refused to go to a *quack* doctor, Noah and I had spent the evening taking care of her even though she wouldn't touch half the stuff I recommended. Instead, she'd stunk up the house with some crazy scented oils.

"Oh, yes, another perk. How is reading one of those? I can do that on my own," she argued.

I walked us to the bed, bent forward, and slowly let her body dip into the mattress.

"Yes, you can, but then you wouldn't get to listen to my sexy voice doing it."

"You're going to read to me?"

"We're both going to read out loud." I grinned.

"Like kindergarteners?"

"I'm fairly certain grade-school kids have never touched the book I picked out for us."

"Oh." Her eyes gleaned with interest. "Now, I'm intrigued. Is it sexy?"

Reaching into the drawer of my nightstand, I pulled out the book I'd ordered online after a particular late night of sexting with Liv. In an attempt to keep myself from running out the door to do a repeat of our window encounter, I'd come up with the perks idea.

It was no secret that Liv was experienced in the bedroom. How experienced? I didn't fucking want to know. For most of her adult life, she'd convinced herself that relationships weren't for her, and it was now my job to show her otherwise. Ever since lunch, I'd been showing her the many benefits of dating Jackson Reid.

Tonight, we would be reading in bed—with a twist.

"Erotic poetry?" Liv glanced at the title of the book I held in my hand.

"Were you expecting something with whips and chains?" I asked, flopping down on the bed with her.

"I never know what to expect from you," she answered, rolling to her side.

"Exactly. Now, who wants to go first?" I gave her a challenging look.

"Give me the damn book." She laughed.

Cracking the cover, she flipped through the first couple of pages, and she began searching the text of the poems, obviously trying to find the perfect one. Her eyes rounded and bugged as laughter tumbled from her mouth. Obviously, not all of them were great.

"Found it," she finally said. "It's an old one."

"Good. Now, wow me."

"'Enthralled,'" she said, "by Alfred Bryan."

"*Teach me to sin— / In love's forbidden ways,*" she recited, her voice almost a whisper. "*For you can make all passion pure; / The magic lure of your sweet eyes / Each shape of sin makes virtue praise.*"

My skin tingled with every sound she made, and my mouth watered in anticipation of what was to come.

"*Teach me to sin—*" she repeated.

Dear God I wanted to.

"Enslave me to your wanton charms, / Crush me in your velvet arms / And make me, make me love you."

My fingers inched toward her, reaching out to touch the exposed flesh where her shirt had crept up.

"Make me fire your blood with new desire, / And make me kiss you—lip and limb, / Till senses reel and pulses swim. / Aye! even if you hate me, / Teach me to sin."

By the time she finished, I was nearly panting. Our eyes locked, and I saw that she was just as affected as me. Every word she'd recited was literary foreplay. When she'd read those words of lust and passion, her voice had turned into liquid sex, and I was suddenly dying of thirst.

"I really hope Noah's asleep by now," I said, pulling the book from her hand and tossing it to the floor.

"Why?" she purred.

"Because I'm about to fuck you so hard that the walls are going to shake."

"A big fan of sexy poetry, Jackson?" she quipped.

I pulled my shirt up over my head. "Only when it's coming from that dirty mouth of yours. Now, lift your dress, and show me your wanton charms." I grinned.

She complied and slowly lifted the vibrant orange fabric up her thighs and over her stomach until she exposed her bare breasts, and then the dress fell to the floor.

That was one of the many things I loved about Liv. She wasn't a huge fan of bras, and she often went without on many occasions. She was like unwrapping a mystery gift each time I undressed her. I never knew what I'd find—sexy lingerie or nothing but Liv. Either way, it would be the sexiest damn present I'd ever had.

"So beautiful," I murmured before kissing a path along her neck.

I moved down her body and slid off the bed. I knelt beside it and tugged on her legs until her ass was resting on the edge. I reached for the silky panties around her waist and pulled until the last piece of clothing hit the floor, and she was bare. Like a desperate addict waiting for his next hit, my hands shook with need as I placed her legs around my shoulders and met her heated gaze.

"Never forget the way this feels, Liv, the way we feel together."

Parting her thighs, I bent down and buried myself in her sweet, intoxicating body. She tasted like fine wine and honey delivered straight from Olympus, and I was the lucky bastard who got to enjoy it over and over again.

I'd told Liv never to forget us and how we felt together because I never would. This woman—her body, heart, and mind—had permanently altered me, and I never wanted to go back to the man I had been before.

With the swirl of my tongue, I brought her close to climax and backed off, feeling her body tighten, as her fingers dug into the sheets above.

"Jackson!" she whimpered in frustration, feeling the loss of my mouth from her core.

Without answering, I shoved my hands under her ass and hoisted her onto my shoulders. A yelp of surprise followed.

"What are you doing?" she said in a hushed voice.

I answered by pushing her against the far wall and picking up where I'd left off. My tongue rubbed her clit, and I held her high up above me on the wall. Muffled cries came soon after as her body pressed and writhed against me until she finally broke apart.

Sliding her body down, I pinned her between me and the wall with one hand. Not wasting a second, I undid the button of my jeans.

"Teach me to sin, Jackson," she whispered, watching me with hooded eyes.

I grasped my hard length in my hands and slowly lowered her inch by glorious inch.

"Being with you could never be called a sin, sweetheart," I answered.

"Then, make me, make me love you," she cried out, ad-libbing the poem, as our bodies joined tightly together.

Her legs wrapped around my waist as my fingers dug into her backside. Every thrust was rough and merciless as I made good on my promise to shake and rattle the walls around us.

I would continue to make this woman love me until the last breath left my dying body. With my soul, my touch, and my heart, I would capture hers and hold on to it like the precious treasure it was.

My primal need to claim and make her mine raged on as I buried myself into my chosen mate, over and over, feeling like my soul was being branded by her just as strongly. As we both hurdled over the edge, my lips crashed into hers, and our muffled cries softened.

I knew only one thing.

Olivia Prescott owned me, body and soul.

I just hoped she understood what that meant.

~Liv~

"I'm going to beat you!" I nearly sang into my cell as I turned around the corner toward our houses.

Jackson and I had both scheduled short days, so we could be there when Noah arrived home from the bus on his first day. Every other following day, he'd come home by himself. Jackson had decided Noah was old enough to do a trial run.

But today was special, and we wanted to celebrate it—assuming Jackson ever made it through downtown traffic.

"Tell him I'll be there in five minutes, ten tops," he grumbled loudly.

"He'll be fine. I'll bring him over to my house and make him a snack. We'll see you in a few."

"Sounds good. And, Liv?"

"Yeah?"

"I love you."

The call ended before I could respond, but it didn't stop the multitude of butterflies from coming to life in my stomach. That man did an amazing job of making me feel like a giggly schoolgirl just by uttering three tiny words.

Hell, one lopsided grin could turn me into mush.

Turning onto our street, I parked in front of my manicured green lawn, trying to stop myself from smiling when I noticed the way Jackson had taken extra time to mow diagonally rather than straight across because he knew I liked it.

Now, I was getting crazy over grass.

I had become one of those women, the kind who went weak in the knees when her man was around and sighed like a lovesick puppy when he wasn't.

Love was weird.

Luckily, I didn't have much more time to find anything else to send my heart a flutter. With a high-pitched squeal of the tires, the bus came to a stop in front of Jackson's house, and I watched as the door was tossed opened.

Not wanting to ruin any cool points Noah might have earned during the day, I stayed back, and for a moment, I pretended to be highly interested in my flowers, all the while looking over my shoulder as he made his way off the giant yellow bus.

Head down, hands shoved in his pockets, he didn't make eye contact as he headed straight for his own house.

Did he not see me?

"Hey!" I said cheerfully as the bus pulled away. "How was your first day?"

He didn't answer. He pulled out the key from his backpack and began to unlock the door.

"Your dad is running a bit late. We're supposed to go to my house and wait for him."

With the key halfway home, he paused. Shifting slightly, he pulled the key back out of the lock, shoved it in his pocket, and turned back around toward my front door.

Still, there was no peep.

"So, what's up with the silent treatment?" I asked. I'd been given it more than once in my career. It didn't really faze me, but it hurt a great deal more coming from Noah.

We made our way through the front door, and he continued saying nothing. He dropped his backpack on the floor next to the couch and followed me into the kitchen.

"Want something to eat?"

He shrugged.

Well, that was something I guessed.

Riffling through the pantry, I pulled out a box of organic cookies he always seemed to love, and dumped a handful out on a napkin. I turned toward the fridge to grab the almond milk—something else he had grown to like since meeting me.

I'd thought I was on that list of likes as well, but now, I was starting to doubt myself.

He begrudgingly sat down at the counter and silently stuffed a cookie into his mouth.

"Okay, Noah. I can handle this with my patients, but this is driving me nuts. Please tell me what's going on."

His eyes met mine, and I was nearly slapped in the face by the sheer volume of his anger.

"You lied to me," he said slowly.

"I've never lied to you."

"You said I would have a great day. You said everything would be okay." There were tears in his eyes that he quickly brushed away with the sleeve of his shirt.

I took a step forward, wanting to comfort him, but stopped as I watched him move away.

"No one was nice, Liv. No one was kind. They all laughed at me and called me Hillbilly Jack because of the way I speak."

"Noah, I—"

"Don't."

He turned and walked away, collapsing into the couch in the living where he tried to make himself invisible by curling into a tiny ball.

I took a few hesitant steps forward before walking toward the living room. I chose a seat across from him, hoping the small amount of distance would give him some breathing room.

"You don't need to baby me, Liv, or pretend like you care."

"But I do care," I fought back.

"Why? You're not my mom!" he said, the hurt in his voice bleeding through.

"No, I'm not your mother," I answered calmly. "But I am someone who loves you, Noah, and that's all that matters right now."

Nothing but silence was awaiting me, so I pressed on, "You're right, Noah. I did lie to you."

His head popped up, and I was met with more tears and red-rimmed eyes.

"When I said I found my niche, I led you to believe it was the first day. I guess I wanted you to have the courage and belief that if I could do it, so could you. I see now, that was wrong."

"So, you didn't have a great first day like you said?" he asked.

With my head lowered, I answered, "No, it was the worst."

"Tell me about it."

"I ate my lunch in the restroom. All the girls were mean and catty, commenting on the way I wore my hair and how quiet I was. I was shy, but to them, shyness just meant stuck-up."

"You're not shy now," he said.

"No, I learned to overcome it. Or rather, I learned senators' daughters couldn't be shy."

"Did it ever get better?" he asked quietly.

"Yes, eventually. Being the new kid is never easy. It's not like the movies. You can't just stumble in and suddenly become the popular kid. Find one friend, Noah. That's all you need for now."

"There was this one kid who seemed nice," he said, sitting up a bit straighter. "He had the same Redskins patch on his backpack as me."

"See?"

He shrugged.

"It will get better, I promise. Just take it one day at a time. Your dad and I are here for you, no matter what."

He nodded, and even though he thought he was all grown-up and tough-as-nails, that boy sprang off that couch and catapulted into my arms in less than a second.

Now, there were two people crying in the room. Even though I'd solved a million problems like this over the years, feeling his arms wrapped around me in gratitude and love felt a hundred times better.

"And don't worry about your accent," I added. "They're just jealous because they don't sound like a younger version of Matthew McConaughey."

He looked up at me in confusion. "Who's that?"

I giggled. "Never mind. Come on, let's get some more cookies."

We walked back over to the kitchen just as Jackson was stepping inside.

"Well, damn, I was hoping to surprise you by coming in this way!" he announced. He walked over to Noah and ruffled his sandy hair, looking completely surprised when small arms wrapped around his waist.

"Hey, buddy. Good day?" Jackson asked, his eyes meeting mine.

His expression softened for just a second, and it was then I realized that he'd heard everything.

I love you, he mouthed. Smiling, he shoved a cookie in his mouth.

I love you, too, I answered back.

"It was okay. Tomorrow will be better," Noah replied.

"It always is," Jackson said.

~Jackson~

"Noah?" I yelled from the bathroom. I quickly finished brushing my teeth.

"I'm right here, Dad. You don't have to yell."

A small chuckle escaped my lips, hearing him harp on me for yelling.

"Hey," I said, walking into the room, "did you give our home number to any of your friends at camp?"

"Why would I have done that?" He tugged at his tie, made a face and then tugged at it again.

"We keep getting calls from numbers I don't recognize, and when I answer, the person hangs up. Just thought it might be a girl trying to get a hold of you."

He looked at me through the reflection of the mirror as he readjusted his tie one more time.

"No one does that anymore, Dad," he said, rolling his eyes.

"Really? That's a shame. I still remember calling Mindy Sims for the first time in sixth grade. My palms were sweaty, and my knees shook. I nearly pissed myself when her dad answered the phone."

"Yeah, that sounds fun."

"I know. You're way too cool for that."

It was now my turn to roll my eyes.

"Why do I have to wear a jacket when it's still ninety degrees out-side?" he whined, studying his appearance with a woeful expression, as he straightened out the lapels of his jacket.

I walked up behind him, admiring how grown-up he looked in his tweed blazer and khaki pants. Liv had taken him shopping, and with a bit of guidance, he'd managed to pick everything out himself. I was amazed by how a few pieces of clothing could age him so drastically. Even though he tried to act years beyond his age, when he dressed in bright-colored skater shoes and shorts, he still looked like an eleven-year-old boy. Today, in clothes fit for a young gentleman, he appeared years older.

"It's eighty-five out today, and you have to wear the jacket be-cause the invitation says so. Besides, you look good," I said, smiling, as I adjusted my own tie behind him.

"Now, I do," he grumbled. "But I will be pretty dumb looking when my clothes start to melt off, and you have to explain why a half-naked kid is running around the lawn."

"Well, that was vivid. At least we know you haven't lost your imagination with age."

I saw his eyes roll in the reflection, and I laughed.

"When is Liv coming over?" he asked.

I moved across the room to gather my shoes. "She's not. We're picking her up."

I sat down on my bed and began lacing up my shoes as silence blanketed the room. I looked up and saw Noah staring at me through the mirror, his expression blank as though he were in deep thought.

Finally, he cocked his head to one side and asked, "Dad, are you going to marry Liv?"

I sat up erect as he turned around to meet my surprised face.

"Yes, eventually—I mean, if she wants me—us," I answered, stumbling over my words. My heart was suddenly racing, and my pulse quickened. The thought of marriage didn't scare me. At least, the thought of marrying Liv didn't scare me.

But the idea that she might not say yes frightened me beyond belief.

As far back as I could remember, I knew I'd be married one day. Two souls could never fully become one until vows were taken, and promises were made. That was how I had been raised and what I believed. It was probably why I'd so easily given my heart to Natalie when she told me about the pregnancy. It was only a natural progression for me.

Love equaled marriage, right?

But what if it didn't for everyone?

Would a woman like Liv ever settle down? Did the idea of marriage seem old-fashioned and outdated to someone as free-spirited and modern as Liv?

"Dad, you look like you're going to pass out. Are you sure you tied that thing right?" Noah asked, suddenly pulling me out of my mini panic attack.

"What? Oh, yeah, it's fine." I pulled at the fabric around my neck, which now felt like a vise.

I just needed to take things slow.

Slow and steady wins the race I tried to convince myself

I'd managed to do the impossible. The woman who had never believed she'd fall in love had fallen straight into my arms, and I wasn't about to lose her.

I'd make Liv my wife—or I'd die trying—even if I had to use a cane to walk myself down that damn aisle.

~Liv~

"So, you're going back to the mothership, huh?" Mia laughed into the phone.

"Cute. That's really cute," I said as half my body was nearly eaten by my closet.

"Why do you sound so muffled?"

"I can't find my other beige high heel," I grumbled.

"Well, I can't imagine why. They're your favorite pair," she answered sarcastically.

I managed half an eye roll before I found the other one, hanging out near the back of the closet. It was coated in probably five years' worth of dust.

"I know, but I didn't know what else to wear. It's not like I have a wardrobe for political fundraisers anymore. Just what my father needs, is for me to show up in a sundress and turquoise wedges."

"At least you would be showing up as yourself," she said.

"Hush, you."

"Are you sure about this? I mean, after the dinner party and the newspaper article—"

"I'm sorry about that. I really am. I called Clare the morning after to apologize and I told her that I didn't mean to make the evening awkward."

"Liv, stop. You know I didn't mean it like that, and you don't have to explain family drama to me. We grew up together, remember? Drama is my middle name. I just meant, you've been stressed since the minute he called. Is it worth it?"

"Is having your dad back in your life worth it?" I knew the answer before she even uttered it.

"Point taken. Carry on. But please at least find a different pair of shoes. I don't even need to see those things to know they are hideous."

I was still laughing when we hung up. She was right. The beige pumps were awful.

Knowing how much Jackson loved purple, I'd selected a similar shade, going with a deep burgundy. The gauzy fabric was still light enough for the weather but provided the elegance needed for the occasion. Plus it had the added bonus of being incredibly comfortable. Searching around further into the recesses of my closet, I found a gold pair of high-heeled sandals that worked perfectly with my dress.

I added a delicate pair of earrings to finish the look when the doorbell rang. I spritzed a bit of perfume and grabbed a beaded handbag. Then, I made my way downstairs to greet my men.

Pulling the door open, I smiled at the two faces awaiting me.

"Feeling awfully formal today, aren't we?" I said, commenting on the fact that they'd rung the door rather than just marching in as they usually did.

"Well, it is a special occasion…and damn, you look mighty fine." Jackson stepped forward to kiss me sweetly.

"Did you know that whenever you get cheeky, your accent deepens?" I smiled.

"Or maybe you just bring it out of me."

His thick Southern drawl melted me like butter.

"Does he sound like Michael McConaughey?" Noah asked.

My hand flew up to my mouth in an attempt to hide the giggles.

"It's Matthew, and oh, yes, he does—better actually," I answered smoothly after I recovered from my snickering.

Jackson's eyebrow lifted as he gave me a cocky grin. "You ready to go fraternize with the rich people for an afternoon?"

"So excited," I answered.

He held out an arm, and I took it. We headed for the car, and it felt like we were making our way to the other side of the world. I was going back to a place I hadn't been to in years—my parents' house.

Everything looked the same, yet it didn't.

The same weathered fence still stood proud and tall, surrounding the old house from intruders. As we got the go-ahead and were let inside the iron gate, I still felt that tiny flutter of awe as we approached the house I used to live in as a child.

It really was breathtaking. Built in the 1800s, it had been completely renovated and remodeled to its former glory, still maintaining the historical integrity without looking worn-out or tired. Walking through this house was like talking a step back in time, minus all the Jags and Mercedes parked out in front.

We pulled up behind another car, and I laughed as Jackson nearly jumped out of his seat when an attendant opened his door.

"I thought you were a fancy lawyer." I watched him drop his keys into the other man's hand.

He walked around to take my hand. "A fancy lawyer who parks his own car," he corrected.

"Sexy."

Noah joined us from the backseat, and the three of us approached the front door. As I lifted the heavy brass knocker, I suddenly felt like Dorothy with her band of misfits, approaching Emerald City's gates. Would we be turned away or welcomed with opened arms?

A bearded man did indeed answer the door, but he was not covered in green, and no color-changing horses were in sight as we stepped through the double doors.

I looked around at the house where I'd grown up, taking in the slight changes and upgrades. The floors had recently been polished, no longer carrying the heavy grooves and dents of the years. A couple of new pieces of furniture sat in the formal living room next to a grand piano I remembered from my youth.

A few people milled around the interior of the house, pointing at various pieces of sculptures or paintings, but the majority of the guests had made their way outside, which was where we were also headed.

Jackson said nothing as we made our way to the back garden. He just clutched my hand as he rubbed my thumb with his own, silently supporting me, while I tried to keep the ghosts of the past at bay. I knew my parents were making an effort to make up for all the heartache and pain, but that didn't keep the hurt from surfacing. The sudden reappearance of my parents' affection couldn't erase eight years of loneliness in an instant, and as I wandered through the house that had once brought me so much joy, those truths became abundantly clear.

Jackson leaned over with a small smile. "One day at a time, remember?" he whispered in my ear.

"Is that your milkshake wisdom of the day?" I grinned back.

"Something like that. Did it work? Or do I need to run out and grab the Oreos and ice cream?"

We reached the double doors leading to the grand garden my mother was so proud of when I paused. I kissed his cheek fondly. "It was perfect. Let's go fraternize."

"Do I have to hold my pinkie up when I drink?" Noah asked, somehow managing to make me giggle at just the right time.

"Be a rebel," I answered, looking over at him with a smirk. "Pinkies down."

He gave me a sheepish grin as Jackson opened the massive glass door, and we stepped out onto the patio. Everything was exquisitely decorated down to the twinkling lights and the floral arrangements that probably cost more than my car.

All of this—the lavish party and huge expense was just an elaborate effort to raise money, so my father's team could spend it on additional campaign functions to collect even more cash. My head started to spin from just thinking about it.

"Olivia!" my father's exuberant voice called out through the crowd.

Dressed in a tailored jacket and slacks, he looked exactly as I remembered him standing on that stage all those years ago while watching him deliver his victory speech. A man of the people, he was dressed for business and ready for action.

Before, he used to come home and shed the monkey suit, as he'd called it. He'd trade the stiff slacks for a pair of worn jeans, so he could chase me and play with me in the backyard among my mother's flower and herbs garden. Those were the days when he had still been mine.

After becoming a man of the people, he wouldn't take off the suit much, not even when he'd returned home late at night. He'd disappear into his office, shutting the door to take conference calls. I'd see him loosen his tie and shed his jacket, but the jeans had been forgotten, like many things—including me.

My mother would be more sympathetic to it or perhaps she'd learned to adjust better than I ever had. I was young and in need of a father, and I'd lacked the maturity to understand what was happening.

I shook my head, trying to clear out the sad memories, and I focused on the man who was coming toward me. This man was attempting to make amends, and I should at least give him the opportunity to do so. He was my father after all. A little bit of that man who had worn the jeans and told me fairy tales at night must be in there somewhere.

"I'm so glad you made it," he said, pulling me into his arms for a tight hug. He pulled back and gazed at me as if he were studying my face. "You've grown into such a beautiful young woman, Livvy Lou."

"Livvy Lou?" Noah said from behind me, giggling at my nickname.

"Shut it," I grumbled.

"And who might this be?" my father inquired, a large welcoming smile on his face as he turned his attention to Noah.

"This is my son, Noah, Senator."

"Now, what did I say about calling me that, Jackson? Please, call me Doug."

"I shall try," Jackson replied, squeezing my hand when he saw me smirk.

"The boyfriend has a son?" a man next to my father interjected.

I'd been so focused on my dad meeting Noah that I hadn't noticed anyone else joining our small group, but indeed, there he was—a stubby old man who had a snarl for a smile. He reminded me of Mr. Burns from *The Simpsons*.

"Is there a problem?" I asked pointedly.

"No, we'll figure out a way to spin it," he mumbled to himself before quickly walking away from our little circle.

I looked up at my father for answers.

He seemed embarrassed and promptly apologized, "Sorry, that is Ned. He's one of my campaign managers, and he's a bit quirky."

Quirky wasn't exactly the word I would choose to describe him.

"Is there something I should know?"

"No, darling. Please don't think anything of it."

"Okay," I answered.

A quick glance over toward Jackson told me he was anything but okay with it.

In an attempt to defuse the tension, I suggested we grab some food. Food always seemed to make everything better, and if I knew one thing, my mother had spared no expense in that area.

"Holy—" Noah began to say. He quickly stopped when Jackson's eyes darted over and gave him a death stare.

"This looks good," Noah amended.

I tried not to laugh at his obvious language blunder.

Oh, to be young and impressionable again.

I didn't think Jackson found it nearly as funny as I did.

We found an empty table under the shade and spent the next thirty minutes enjoying the expensive food, people watching, and talking among ourselves. Noah casually announced that he'd made a friend at school named Sam, who liked Xbox and played the guitar. Jackson and I looked up at each other, our eyes widening in excitement, but we tried to keep our cool.

"That's great, buddy," Jackson answered as he stole a canapé from Noah's plate.

Watching the two of them, I couldn't help but smile. Opening myself up to Jackson and Noah had made life a hundred times scarier.

What if I ended up hurt? What if I hurt them?

In retrospect, it had also made life a million times more exciting. My smile wasn't just a smile anymore. It was a window into my soul because they made me feel completely alive.

"Where's your mother? We haven't had a chance to say hello yet," Jackson commented. Sitting back in his chair, he sipped on his beer.

"She's usually incredibly busy at these types of events. She sees to every detail. I guess it makes her feel like a part of the team."

"Well, we should go find her and thank her for including us," he suggested.

"Sounds like a great idea," I agreed.

Leaving our happy spot, we all stood and wandered around, looking for my mother. She was nowhere in sight, so I suggested we head inside to continue our search for her.

Walking back into the air-conditioned house was like stepping inside a freezer. The cool air hit my body like a wall of ice, and my skin prickle everywhere.

"Here, take my jacket," Jackson offered, sliding the dark gray blazer off his shoulders to hang on mine.

"Thanks. Why don't we try my dad's office? Maybe she's paying one of the caterers or something."

We rounded the corner, walking down the long hallway, and we stopped just outside the office. I held up my hand to knock when I heard my father's voice, and I stopped.

"I can't do anything about the fact that her boyfriend has a son. You figure it out. This was your idea."

"Well, she wasn't dating anyone when I suggested it, but we'll work something out. Right now, we need your family intact. When your bid for presidency is officially announced, those reporters will start digging. An estranged, crazy daughter is exactly what we don't need. Fix it, Doug. Fix it now."

Tears stung my eyes, and wetness spilled down my cheeks. Jackson's hard chest engulfed me, and my body buried itself into him. I barely remember moving. Everything felt slow and out of sync. As the hallway blurred past us, the last thing I saw was a family portrait. My own eyes stared back at me—warning me, cautioning me that one day this would all be over because every fairy tale must end eventually.

~Liv~

The phone rang for the tenth time that morning, and I threw it across the room. After the ninth unanswered call, shouldn't people start to understand that I didn't want to talk—ever?

I was the therapist, not them.

I'd sort through my own shit—eventually.

It just wouldn't be today or tomorrow…perhaps not even this millennium.

Someday, I'd muddle through it all. I'd be fine.

I was a survivor.

I didn't remember much of what had happened after my dad shattered my heart with that single conversation I'd overheard.

I vaguely recalled Jackson escorting us away and helping me into the car. After arriving at his house, he'd tucked me into his bed and held me until we had both fallen asleep. When I'd woken up and tip-toed out, I'd hated myself a little more every time a floorboard creaked beneath my feet. I'd run across the lawns separating our houses, back to my own house, and I hadn't been back since. That had been nearly two days ago.

Why was I shutting him out?

I had no idea. *Why do any of us do the stupid things we do when we are angry and upset?* All I knew was, I was devastated.

Therefore, my entire life must be devastating, right?

It seemed logical to me.

While consuming the double fudge with nuts ice cream at nine o'clock in the morning, I tried not to think of the patients I was letting down once again by calling in sick. For two days now, I'd disrupted their days, messed with their schedules, and dishonored their trust.

I was a failure.

A loud bang sounded at my door, startling me so much that I almost dropped the nearly empty pint on the floor. I turned to find Jackson barging through it.

"Space—I've given it. Now, we talk."

"What?"

"The first rule I have is to always give you space when you seem to need it. I never want you to feel smothered, so when you disappear on me in the middle of the night, I take that as a cue. But it's been long enough, Liv. Twenty-four hours should be enough time for you to figure out some shit. If not, we'll do it together. I'm about to go apeshit from sitting over there, waiting for you to give the all-clear."

"You didn't go to work?" I set the ice cream container down on the coffee table.

"No. Of course, I didn't. Do you think I would just leave you and go to work?"

I shrugged.

"You do. Jesus, Liv. Why haven't you answered any phone calls?" He began pacing in front of me.

"I didn't feel like talking," I answered.

"What are you so damn afraid of?" he bellowed, his hands going through his sandy brown hair in frustration.

"Nothing!" I answered back. "I'm not afraid of anything."

"That's a damn lie."

I jutted out my chin and angrily crossed my arms over my chest as I tried to keep the tears at bay.

"Goddamn it, Liv! When are you going to realize that no matter what those two people do to you, it has no bearing on you or the life you've created here?"

"I know—"

"No, you don't. This place," he said, gesturing with his hands, "your friends, Noah...me—we are your home and your family, Liv. Nothing else matters. We love you—not for the person you could be, but for the person you are. Stop wishing for a family you don't have, and look around, sweetheart. We're right here."

A single tear escaped as I gazed up at him in wonder. How could one person manage to know me better than myself?

"You want to be my family?" I asked, tears racing down my cheeks.

He stepped forward, kneeling in front of me, and I caught a glimpse of his toothy grin.

"Try to stop me."

"I'm so sorry," I cried.

"Hey," he soothed. "Nothing else matters, okay? What happened the other day is behind us. I know they hurt you. I wish more than anything I could take back that afternoon and give you something better in its place, but I can't. All we can do is move forward and make the best of what we have together."

"Can we go get a milkshake?" I asked, my voice still hoarse from crying.

"Sure, sweetheart. But can I ask a favor?"

"Yeah." I smiled.

"Go take a shower. You smell."

I threw a pillow in his face for that one.

~Jackson~

The Reid house was quiet Tuesday morning as we prepared for the long day ahead. While I sat at the foot of my bed and stared at the wall, I listened to Noah as he stumbled around his room, his half-hearted, half asleep attempt at getting ready for another day of middle school.

Clunky footsteps grew louder until Noah was standing in my doorway. His mouth was full of toothpaste foam as he absently brushed back and forth, looking at me curiously.

"You going to work today?" he managed to say between the bubbles.

I nodded, rising from my spot on the bed. Taking a deep breath, I made my way to the closet and began the process of pulling out my clothes for the day. It was something I'd done for months, years actually, but today was different. Today, as I slipped my suit on, it felt liked a marked occasion for something big.

I heard Noah walking back to the hall bathroom as I pulled up my slacks and tucked in my shirt. The blue tie went around my neck like a noose, tight and snug, underneath the tailored black jacket.

Finishing up, I hurried down the stairs to prepare breakfast. Noah was already pulling out a bowl for cereal, and rummaging around in the pantry.

"Liv brought over that healthy crap you like," I commented, pointing to the left.

He immediately went and grabbed the tan-and-brown box with the weird name and pictures of wheat fields on the back,

"It's good. You should try it," he said, dumping a huge mound of the flaky stuff into a bowl.

"Not until she has a steak." I grinned.

"You're crazy."

"Yep."

Since no one else was enjoying them, I poured Froot Loops into a large bowl for myself and dug in. I felt like the worst kind of role model as I watched my son eat a bunch of fruit and grains while I stuffed children's cereal into my mouth.

I shrugged.

I didn't care. *Froot Loops were the bomb.*

Besides, I had a shitload of other things to worry about besides my breakfast choice at the moment.

I watched my son as I finished my cereal. For years, it had just been him and me against the world. Every action and every decision in my life had revolved around this little guy. When Liv had walked into our world, our circle had grown just a bit larger. Suddenly, those decisions that had seemed so easy to make before were ten times harder. Now, there were two people in my life who mattered.

How did I make the right choices when I had two lives to consider?

I stared at him, waiting for an answer that didn't come, and I hoped that what I was about to do today would be the right decision—for all of us.

"You can't do this to me, Jackson," Mark begged, rising from his desk. His eyes were wide with shock and surprise.

I'd just dropped the mother of bombs.

"It's already done," I said, holding up my resignation letter.

"If you want more pay, consider it done."

"It's not about my salary, Mark. I just need to move on," I tried to explain.

"You just fucking got here!" he yelled, his hands flying up in frustration. "You haven't even given us three months. What am I supposed to tell the Senator? He's going to think something is going on internally."

"You won't need to explain anything, Mark," I assured him.

"I seriously doubt that." He slumped back in his chair, every bit the defeated man he appeared to be.

Silence settled around us as I watched my boss from across the room.

"I'm in love with his daughter," I finally confessed.

"Say what now?" he asked, his eyes flying up to mine.

"Olivia Prescott is my girlfriend. We've been dating for months."

"You've got to be fucking kidding me."

I just stared at him.

"Holy shit. Why didn't you say anything? We could have probably bagged this account from the start!"

I cocked my head to the side, the unpleasant mood written all over my face.

"Right. That would have been wrong. Of course," he said, coughing slightly. "This still doesn't explain why you are resigning. I would think the old man would be happy to have his future son-in-law working for him. Or does he not like you? Did he catch you boning her? From behind?"

"What the fuck, Mark? Could you be serious and grown-up for two minutes? Fuck."

"Sorry. Please continue."

"Liv and her parents don't get along. Things between them are… not going well at the present moment. I can't put myself in the position of being in the middle."

"So, you're picking sides?"

"It's not a matter of choosing," I answered. "I will always choose her, no matter what."

"Do you have anything lined up, man?" he asked, his voice actually sounding concerned.

"No, not yet. But I'm sure I can find something. I've got enough in the bank to hold me for a while."

He nodded. "I'll put out some feelers and write you a killer letter of recommendation, if that helps."

"It does. Thanks."

He stood, stretching out his hand across the desk. "I know I act like a jackass some of the time—well, most of the time, but I get it. I do. There isn't anything I wouldn't do for my wife and kids. Despite how much I joke around, they are my fucking world."

"Thanks, Mark. Under all that asshat exterior, you're not a bad guy."

We shook, and I could see his grin appearing.

"Thanks, man. That means a lot."

We said our good-byes, and Mark wished me luck.

I needed all the luck I could get because when Liv found out I quit my job for her, I would be a dead man.

Chapter
Twenty-Six

~Jackson~

My foot bounced nervously as I stared out the window, counting down the seconds as they ticked by. The sleek lobby of the downtown law firm was well decorated and appointed just like all the others I'd sat in over the last two weeks while waiting to be called into interviews.

I tugged at my scarlet red tie, hating the way it felt tighter now that I'd gone a couple of weeks without them. It left me wondering if this little taste of freedom was a hint that I was supposed to be doing something bigger, something greater than sitting in an office every day for the rest of my life.

But if so, then what?

This was what I'd been trained to do, what I'd worked my ass off to accomplish. What else was there if I didn't do exactly this?

I adjusted my tie again and pondered just how long the folks at Turner and McCollum Law firm were going to make me wait and sweat it out here.

Performance under pressure—I guessed this was my first test.

The alarm buzzed on my watch, notifying me of the time. It always beeped at this exact moment so I wouldn't forget when the bus dropped off in front of our house. Noah always got off the bus at exactly a quarter past three every day, and he was expected to call me within five minutes without fail. This was our agreement, and so far, he'd adhered to it perfectly. I was amazed by his maturity and ability to handle himself. When I had been still working and would come home at night, I was surprised to find the house didn't look like a train wreck. The dishes would be neatly stacked in the sink, and his homework would already have been completed and put away. It was eerie how well behaved he was.

Three minutes had passed, and I was starting to get restless. He knew this was my one condition of his staying home alone, and even though I'd been home for a few weeks, I knew he wouldn't have forgotten.

Maybe the bus was late?

Another minute passed without a call.

I sent a quick text message to him, basically saying that he should call or he'd be grounded for life.

There was no reply.

I stared at my phone, willing it to ring, when the administrative assistant called for me.

Perfect.

I followed her back to the conference room, and several of the partners greeted me. They were all in their late forties with various shades of the same designer suit.

"Nice to finally meet you, Jackson. We've heard great things." A tall, lanky man in a dark blue suit stood to greet me. "I'm Cal Turner."

I nodded. "Thanks for taking the time. I appreciate it."

We all took our seats around the sleek wooden table, and I casually leaned back as the assistant floated around, serving everyone coffee and water.

"Let's get right to the point, Jackson. We like what we've heard, and we'd love to have you on our team," Mr. Turner said.

I had been fed this line in practically every interview I'd been in. At first, I had been shocked and a bit flattered. Then, I'd heard the whispers and rumors that the relationship between my former employer and Senator Prescott was rocky at best since my departure, and he was possibly looking for new representation. Everything after that had started to make sense, and now, I was just extremely annoyed.

"Where have you heard this exactly?" I casually took a sip of my coffee.

The guy who seemed to be in charge, an overweight man who reminded me of a younger version of my father, spoke up, "Around."

"Around where?" I pressed.

"Look"—he sighed—"you're young and come with an excellent letter of recommendation. What more could we ask for?"

Right, because finding a job in a place like this was so damn easy.

I looked at the clock on the wall. Ten minutes had passed, and Noah hadn't called.

I needed to wrap this up.

"You saw me in the paper?" I asked flatly.

"Perhaps, but that has little to do with our job offer," he answered quickly.

I was not convinced. "While I'm flattered, I'm going to have to decline. I've already left one job because of how it interfered with my personal life. I will not be hired because of it either."

"Jackson, please reconsider. Just take a look at our offer and sit on it. We'll chat in a day or two."

I was already rising from my chair. "I don't think we have anything further to discuss. For the record, my relationship with Olivia Prescott does not give me access to the Senator, nor would I want it. In fact, if you want someone to suck up to the old man, I'd say I'm the last person you want on your team."

I didn't even give them the chance to respond. I had hoped this interview would be different—that perhaps I might be judged on my own personal merit, rather than what my personal life might be able to offer them. Apparently, like all the others before them, Turner and McCollum were just like everyone else.

Letting the doors swing behind me, I moved swiftly toward the elevator. I called Noah's cell phone while I loosened the tie around my neck.

It rang and rang until his voice mail picked up, making my stomach churn in apprehension.

I called him once more, and again, he didn't answer.

God only knew how long it would take me to get through traffic and make it back home. Entering another number into my phone, I waited until someone answered.

"Hey, it's Jackson—is she busy?" I asked Liv's receptionist.

"No," she answered. "She just finished up with a client. Let me get her."

I tried not to call Liv's cell during office hours. She tended to leave the ringer on, and I wouldn't want to distract her if she were in the middle of a session.

I was unlocking my car by the time Liv picked up.

"Hey," she said, her voice coming through loud and clear.

"Hey," I answered. "Can you do me a favor?"

"Sure, what's up? You sound worried. Did your interview go bad?"

"Yes, but that's not why I'm calling."

"Oh God, did they offer you another job? Shame on them. How dare these people keep throwing all this money at you," she mocked.

"Liv," I stressed, my voice alerting her that something was wrong, "Noah's not answering his phone."

"How many times did you try it?"

"Twice, plus a text. He should have gotten off the bus almost half an hour ago."

She paused for a moment before answering, "I'm leaving now. I'll call you when I get there."

"Thanks, sweetheart."

"I'm sure he's fine," she said.

I thought she was trying to assure herself more than anything.

"Let me know when you get there."

"Okay."

Ten minutes later, as I was speeding down the road, I got the phone call.

"Hey, is he okay? How many weeks do you think I should ground him?" I said, a hint of nervous laughter following.

"Jackson," she said, her voice panicked and hoarse, "he's not here."

~Liv~

"What do you mean, he's not there?" Jackson's horrified voice echoed through the phone.

"The door was unlocked, Jackson. He was here at some point. I came in and called out for him—"

"Maybe he's upstairs," he interjected, his voice becoming more and more panicked by the second.

"I already checked."

"What about a note? Maybe he went for a walk?"

"There isn't a note. Jackson, his phone is here."

Silence.

"He left his phone?"

"Yes, and his backpack."

"I'll be home in a minute."

The phone went dead, and he was gone. I looked around the empty house. My heart pulsating and my ears roaring from the rush of adrenaline and absolute terror,

What should we do first? I asked myself, trying to remain calm when it was absolutely the last thing I wanted to do.

Check his phone.

I ran over to where his backpack and phone were lying on the kitchen table. It was as if he'd left in a hurry. I didn't know if that was good or bad, but I tried to stay focused.

I began searching through emails, contacts, and text messages. Nothing stuck out.

I saw random messages with friends and a bunch of emails about schoolwork, but nothing shouted, *Calm down. This is where I am right now!*

The door burst open, and I turned to find Jackson rushing toward me.

"I searched his phone." My last bit of resolve began to fade as tears dribbled down my cheeks. "Where is he, Jackson? Where did he go?"

"I don't know," he answered, pulling me into a tight hug.

"Let's go check with the neighbors," he suggested, squeezing me tightly.

Hand in hand, we walked next door to the other side of Jackson's house. A young family lived there, and the mother was usually home with two toddlers during the day—but not today. We saw her unpacking groceries from her car, and she waved at us.

She'd been out all day.

Most of the other neighbors worked during the day, so as far as we knew, Noah had disappeared.

There was only one thing left to do—call the police.

"I can't believe I'm doing this," Jackson said, holding the phone up to his ear. Shaky fingers ran through his hair as he waited for someone to pick up.

Everything moved quickly after that. Police officers were at the house within a matter of minutes. Statements were taken, and an AMBER Alert was issued.

When my phone went berserk, notifying me of the alert, I finally broke.

When I saw Noah's physical description and last known whereabouts flashing across my screen, not knowing if he was safe or hurt, I couldn't breathe.

The police officers kept the media at bay. After several hours, things settled, and we were told to try to get some rest.

I looked up at what was left of the man I loved, and I wondered, *Who could possibly rest when his entire world is crumbling?*

The house grew quiet, too quiet, once again.

I watched the sun set across the street, and I questioned where Noah could be. *Was he fed? Was he cold? Oh God, had he been hurt?*

Just then, Noah's phone rang.

Both Jackson and I looked at each other.

"Do you think it's maybe one of his friends?" I asked.

"I don't know, but I'm answering it."

Jackson pressed down the call button and held the phone to his ear.

His eyes went wide in shock and horror as he whispered one word, "Natalie."

Chapter
Twenty-Seven

~Jackson~

I recognized her voice in an instant, that cold, raspy resonance coiling around my eardrums like a snake. It was a sound I would never forget.

"Jackson," she purred, "it's been far too long."

"Where is he?" I demanded, feeling my fists tighten.

"He's gotten so big. My, how the years have flown by."

"Damn it, Natalie! Where the fuck is he?" I shouted, banging my fist down hard on the wooden table.

Liv's loving touch wrapped around me, her fingers clutching my bicep.

"Now, let's be civil, Jackson," Natalie said, laughter pulsating through every frustrating word.

"Civil? You kidnapped my child!"

"Ours," she hissed. "Or did your new girlfriend suddenly make you forget who gave birth to him?"

I turned, looking over my shoulder to find Liv. Her eyes were filled with agony. She'd heard every word. Changing it to speakerphone, I hissed, "He stopped being yours the day you walked out of our lives, remember?"

Her cold, heartless voice filled the room. "I remember you giving me a tiny-ass diamond ring while we lived in a shoebox of an apartment, only to find out you had a fortune sitting in the bank. You obviously didn't love me and Noah enough to provide for us the way we deserved."

"You mean, the way you expected? That money was for law school, for a down payment on a home, for our future. I told you that, but you could never see beyond your own immediate needs."

She laughed. It was a harsh sound filled with bitterness and contempt. "You're right about one thing. Back then, I thought that I was leaving because I wasn't ready to be a mother and that I was somehow doing both of you a favor. But I've grown since then. I've really come into my own skin, you could say, and there's one thing I've realized about myself along the way, Jackson."

"You're a coldhearted bitch?"

A breathy giggle filled the airwaves. "I will always come first."

As my nails continued to dig half moons into my palm, I decided I was done with reunions. I was done with listening to this woman talk about the past and her need for vengeance or whatever maniacal plan she'd set into motion.

I only wanted my son back.

"Natalie, where is Noah?" I asked, my voice eerily calm and determined.

"Don't you watch the movies, Jackson dear? I'm not just going to hand him back over without getting something in return. This is an exchange."

"Is he safe?" Liv spoke up, her voice desperate, as tears fell down her face.

"Oh, so the Senator's daughter is there with you?"

My eyes locked with Liv's, and I saw the moment it clicked, the moment Liv realized how Natalie had found us—the newspaper article.

"Really moving up in the world, aren't you, baby?" Natalie said.

I shook my head, holding Liv as she struggled not to fall apart.

None of this was her fault. If the blame belonged to anyone, it was mine. I'd fallen for the wrong woman. I hadn't known Natalie would someday pull something like this.

"Don't call me that," I hissed.

"When I saw your face plastered all over the newspapers, I was shocked. I didn't think it was possible, but you've gotten even more attractive over the years. Too bad I didn't stick around longer."

Blood dripped down my hand as I broke through the tender skin of my palm.

"Please just tell us he's safe," Liv begged.

"He's safe. He doesn't even really know what's going on. For all those years of telling him what a horrible person his mother was, he sure seemed eager to leave with me. I'd expected him to put up a fight, but he happily said yes to my proposal for ice cream. We've been hanging out ever since."

"I never told him you were a horrible person," I said softly, shaking my head back and forth, regretting every single instance I'd tried to paint her in a better light for the sake of my son. Pictures, stories and the few mementos I had left of her was all given to him in hopes he would at least have something of the woman who gave him life.

I'd tried to be the better person. And now, it had cost me everything.

"Well, I guess that was your ultimate mistake."

"What. Do. You. Want?" I asked again, punctuating every word.

"Two things actually. First, you're going to call off that pesky AMBER Alert. It makes getting out of the country a little difficult. Second, I want money—lots of it. Around a million should do it."

"Didn't get enough the first time around?" I seethed.

"Always room for improvement. Plus, with your new love interest, I figured it shouldn't be too hard for you now."

That was what this was really about.

She'd seen Liv and me with her father, the wealthy Senator, and immediately thought of money. The press was still under the impression that all was well with the Prescott family. His camp had managed to keep everything under wraps, and to the outside world, Liv and her father were riding unicorns and skating on rainbows together. So, naturally, Liv would have access to mounds of cash.

God, what a clusterfuck.

"I don't have that kind of cash," Liv said.

"I'm sure you'll figure something out, Miss Prescott. I'll call back in the morning, Jackson. Get rid of the AMBER alert. Otherwise, Noah and I might be going on an extended vacation. It's been so long since we've seen each other. A son really should know his mother, don't you think? Perhaps a little trip is exactly what we need."

"You fucking bitch!" I yelled.

The phone went dead.

I screamed out in frustration, every molecule in my body crying out in anger for my son. Falling to my knees, my cries turned into heaving sobs that tore through my entire body. I struggled to breathe from the sheer force of my internal torture.

Liv wrapped her arms around me and held me as we wept together, mourning the sudden loss of innocence we'd felt.

The world was not a safe place to us anymore.

It had taken the one thing that was pure and good.

And all that remained was despair.

~Liv~

Every time the phone rang, my heart leapt and firmly lodged in my throat.

I knew our friends and family meant well. I knew each and every one of them was calling because they cared, but I needed them to stop.

I needed it all to stop.

Nothing in my years of training and professional experience had ever prepared me for this. I didn't know how to mentally process this sort of loss.

In my mind, we'd already lost.

How could we get Noah back when I couldn't give Natalie the one thing she wanted?

I looked over at the phone, willing it to stop, begging it to end its constant reminder of my failure.

I didn't deserve anyone's empathy or love. Jackson's tight hold around me only furthered my belief that I should have stayed away. I should have kept them safe.

"You're spiraling." Jackson's quiet voice cut through the silence. "I can feel the guilt seeping through your pores." He pulled back, and our tired, wet eyes met. "I can see it wrapped up in your soul, Liv. You can't blame this on yourself," he said, grasping my hand in his.

"She would have stayed away if it weren't for me," I cried out.

"No." He shook his head. "She would have come back eventually. She was just waiting for an opportunity. If this were just about money, I'm sure she could have found a hundred ways to rip off some other lonely bastard far easier than hurting us. This was about revenge."

"I just don't understand why someone would do this," I whispered.

"And you never will. Don't try. Focus on getting him back. That's what we need to do."

A lone tear trickled down my cheek as I took a moment to study his features. He looked worn and haggard, nothing like the man I'd woken up beside a few days earlier, yet there was a fierce determination I recognized. I'd seen it the night of the dinner party when I told him we would never work and again the day I'd heard my father basically say that I was nothing more than a way to the White House.

Jackson's family had been threatened, and he was struggling to find a way to piece it back together again. He always said that I was a part of that sacred circle, but until now, I hadn't really believed it.

"How do we get our boy back?" I asked.

"I don't know, but we're not going to let her win."

"I was hoping I might be able to help with that," a deep voice said behind us.

We both turned around to find my father standing by the back door, dressed in jeans and a dark jacket with a baseball cap.

"Senator, how—"

"The back door was unlocked. A few police officers and media personnel are still outside, but I figured I'd try to slip in unnoticed."

"What are you doing here?" I asked.

"What I should have done a long time ago," he said. "The right thing. Let's get to work."

Chapter Twenty-Eight

~Jackson~

Natalie texted me the address an hour after we'd hung up.

It was an older hotel just outside the city.

I was to deliver the money in exchange for my son—alone.

I still couldn't believe this was happening.

I said good-bye to Liv. I kissed her softly, letting my thumb slowly rub across her cheek one last time. Then, I walked to the car and tried not to think about how fucked-up my life had become in the last twenty-four hours.

Two days ago, my biggest fear had been whether or not I had enough Froot Loops to last me through the week, or if anyone would ever take me seriously at another job interview.

Now, without Noah, everything else seemed completely trivial.

I drove in a daze. Streets, cars, and trees all passed by me in a blur until I reached my destination. The hotel had seen better days, but it wasn't the worst place I'd been to. It had a roof and a working sign.

Natalie had at least given Noah shelter during his captivity.

By now, he had to know something was going on. Hours had passed, and the morning sun was just peeking its head over the horizon. Noah must have realized his innocent afternoon reunion with his mother had been anything but.

Was he scared? God, had she fed him?

A million questions rolled through my mind as I parked the car. I entered the building while my brain tried to comprehend what I was about to do.

I easily found the room. Taking one final breath, I raised my hand to knock, ready to meet the demons of my past.

The door creaked open, and Natalie appeared. She was just as I remembered her. Tall and exotic with curves to spare, she smiled, but I saw the malevolence hiding behind her dark brown eyes. There, creeping beneath the charm, was the true Natalie—the one who would lie, cheat, and steal from those who trusted her, the woman who would kidnap her own child.

"Where is he?" I demanded, not bothering with a proper greeting.

"Safe." She smiled, pushing the door open wider.

I looked around from one double bed to the other, searching for him, but I found nothing.

He wasn't here.

"Where the hell is he?" I asked, pushing past her. I searched every corner, every inch of the room and adjoining bathroom, but Noah was nowhere to be found.

"So anxious." She sighed. "I told you, he's fine. He's in the lobby with a friend. I thought we might need a few minutes to catch up."

I turned around, furious, and met her gaze. "We have nothing to discuss. I've done everything you asked, Natalie. I made myself look like an absolute ass on TV last night, saying my son's disappearance was a huge mistake. Liv drained her trust fund. What more do you want?"

"You. I want you."

"What?" I said, completely blindsided.

She took a step forward, her low-cut tight jeans accentuating every step. "I want you, Jackson. I've decided I was a bit too rushed with my disappearance. I hadn't taken the time to properly say good-bye. I don't believe in making the same mistake twice."

My eyes went wide with shock as I backed away. "You're fucking insane."

"No. You want to know what's insane? During the years we spent together, you swore you loved me and that you'd take care of me, and then I found out you had done nothing but hide from me. When you love someone, you share, Jackson. Everything. You had us living like paupers when we could have been royalty. Why?" she yelled, backing me into a corner. "Why didn't you give me everything I deserved?"

Her eyes were manically darting back and forth. I saw wildness and that same deceptive need to control I'd been confronted with when I first arrived.

Beyond that, I saw the girl I'd fallen in love with all those years ago.

Somewhere along the way, Natalie had been broken or abused. I wasn't sure how much of it had occurred before I met her, but since leaving me, it had become irreparable. The woman now standing in front of me was nothing but the remnants and shards of the bubbly, vivacious girl I once knew. I'd never seen a greater tragedy.

"I tried," I said. "There was nothing more important to me than you and Noah."

"You lie."

"I know you think I was hiding the money from you for some sneaky, underhanded reason, but that couldn't be further from the truth. I had nothing but the greatest intentions for us. I had such plans for our future, Nat. We would have had that house you always wanted with the wraparound porch and a Dalmatian running around in the backyard. You could have continued your art while I practiced law. It would have been a great life," I said softly.

A tear trickled down her cheek. "Why can't we have it now, Jackson?"

"Sometimes, life doesn't give us second chances, but there is always time for healing."

She nodded her head and collapsed in my arms. For the first time since arriving, I didn't feel repugnant by the thought of her touch. Wrapping my arms around her, I held her as she wept—for her mistakes and grievances, the brokenness of her situation, and the life we would never have.

It was the closure we'd never been given and what she so desperately needed.

By the time her tears began to dry up, the room door was pushed open, and three officers made their way in.

Natalie's wide eyes met mine.

"I'm sorry, Natalie, but I had to." Turning to the police officer to my right, I said, "Noah's downstairs."

More tears flowed from her as she sobbed through the cuffing and reading of her rights. As the officers escorted her out of the room, she turned back toward me one last time.

"Tell him I'm sorry, Jackson. Tell him I'm so sorry."

I nodded. "I will. Good-bye, Natalie."

"Good-bye, Jackson."

Then, she was gone—for good.

Rather than feeling relieved or happy, I just felt nothing.

~Liv~

I'd been instructed by the burly redheaded cop to stay in the squad car until they gave the all-clear. I had fully intended on following his directions to the letter of the law. He looked scary, and I didn't want to screw up this plan we'd spent all night concocting.

After my father had arrived the night before, we'd made the hard decision to include the police. If Natalie got wind that we had double-crossed her, we would run the risk of possibly losing Noah forever, but it was one risk we had to take.

We were in over our heads.

Kidnapping wasn't something to take lightly, and luckily, my father had been able to contact the proper authorities discreetly and without media attention. His untraceable phone had helped as well.

I didn't even want to know how he'd gotten his hands on one of those.

The cops didn't think Natalie had the ability to run surveillance or had anyone working with her, but with a child involved, they were taking extra precautions.

Everything had been planned carefully and with precise calculation. Every last penny had been withdrawn from my father's bank account and placed in a briefcase for Jackson to use in the handoff. Even though we knew she'd never get farther than the hotel doorway, seeing him walk away from me with all that cash had still seemed like a dream—or rather a nightmare.

The plan was to wait ten minutes before following Jackson inside. We wanted Natalie completely occupied when the cops stormed the room.

When I'd been told to stay behind at the house, I had adamantly replied to the men in charge, "Hell no."

Reluctantly, they'd allowed me to ride along in the back of one of the unmarked squad cars—as long as I agreed to behave.

Three minutes had turned into five…then eight as we stood by. I stared at the run-down motel as I waited for a sign that something, anything was happening.

As my mind lit off a hundred different scenarios, the men in the front seat prepared to go upstairs.

"You stay here, Ms. Prescott." The burly cop said.

I nodded. "Please keep them safe."

"That's our job," he said with little emotion.

I'd never been much of a religious person, but in that moment, I nearly fell to my knees in that backseat, begging any deity within earshot to please hear my silent plea and protect my family.

Within minutes, two of the officers were racing back out of the building toward the entrance. My head darted back and forth as I searched for any sign of Noah or Jackson, but neither were visible.

My heart raced frantically as I watched them storm the lobby.

Minutes later, the redheaded cop walked back out with his arms wrapped around Noah.

I leaped from the car and raced across the parking lot toward him.

"Liv!" he cried, tears racing down his cheeks, as he flung himself into my arms.

"Oh, thank God!" I sobbed.

My hands went everywhere, searching every single hair on his head and up and down his body, just to be sure he wasn't injured.

"I'm okay. I'm okay," he kept chanting.

"I was so worried," I said, tucking him into my body. "Have you eaten? Were you scared?"

"Yes, and not all the time. I mean, yes, I was scared when it started to get late, and she wouldn't take me home. I knew then that I'd
made a bad decision going with her. But she was never mean to me.
When she'd first shown up, we talked about me and school. I could
kinda tell that she was distracted, you know?"

I nodded, urging him to continue.

"Then, when it got dark and we showed up here, she stopped
talking and just began to pace—back and forth, over and over. That
was a little scary. After a few hours, she calmed down and started
asking me about my teachers and stuff. I think she actually listened
then," he said.

"But this morning, when she woke me up, she looked agitated
and distracted again. She told me to go downstairs for the continental
breakfast, and she made me swear I wouldn't run off." He looked
frightened.

"You were brave," I assured him.

The police officer escorted us back to the squad car where I'd
promised to stay, but I obviously hadn't. As he opened the door, I
looked over and saw her.

Her hands were handcuffed behind her back while two uniformed
officers were on either side of her. They swiftly walked her to the opposite side of the parking lot where a police car was parked and ready
to take her away.

As she passed, our eyes met, and I saw the raw pain radiating
through them. Her gaze quickly darted to Noah, and then she looked
away as if it hurt too much to do so.

As I was pondering what the hell I'd just witnessed, Jackson appeared, and he was immediately covered by two sets of arms. Noah
hugged his waist while I wrapped myself around his shoulders as I
softly kissed him.

It was over.

"Let's go home." He breathed out a sigh of relief as he bent down
and kissed Noah's forehead.

"I've never agreed with you more."

Chapter Twenty-Nine

~Jackson~

"I should have known," I said. "I should have done more—helped her."

Liv's hands trailed down my naked chest as we lay in bed, watching the moonlight dance around the room. Hours had passed since we sat outside of Noah's room, waiting for him to fall asleep. We'd spent almost the entire day on the phone, assuring everyone that we were all fine and safe, and all I'd wanted to do was sit there and listen to him breathe.

Walking away had been difficult, but I knew now that he was safe. Natalie would most likely be serving time well into his geriatric years. The thought should have given me relief, but I felt little.

Could I forgive the woman who had kidnapped my son? *No.*

I couldn't help but question if I hadn't played a slight part in everything that happened.

Had I really known the woman I claimed to be in love with? Or had I not cared enough to learn?

Looking back, there was so much about her I didn't know—chunks of her life I'd never bothered asking about. Had she purposely kept them from me or did I not care enough? I could blame it on youth, but deep down, part of me wondered if I just hadn't wanted to know the real Natalie.

"You can't help someone who doesn't want it, Jackson," Liv urged.

"I just can't stop thinking that if I'd taken the time early on to be more…caring or attentive, maybe she would have found the help she so desperately needed, and none of this would have happened."

Her hand cupped my cheek, and I found myself staring into her deep brown eyes.

"You can't be responsible for everyone, Jackson. I know you have this innate sense of duty to protect those you love, but don't be pulled down by the actions of others. Each of us makes our own path."

"I hated her for what she did to me and to Noah. But seeing her break in front of me…I only wish things had worked out differently for her. I don't long for the life we could have had, but anything is better than where she ended up," I said, nuzzling my head close to hers.

"You're a good man, Jackson," she whispered.

"Would you think less of me if I told you that I never want to leave this bed again?"

"Considering the barrage of concerned calls we'll both have to face all over again tomorrow and the police coming back for our statements once again, I wouldn't blame you one bit."

I smoothed down her dark hair, loving the way it almost seemed to glimmer under the light coming through the window. It had been a long day. After we'd rescued Noah, everything had seemed to unfold in a great blur of events. We'd received endless phone calls and questions, and an onslaught of media attention had swarmed the house when word had gotten out that a suspect was captured.

At least my embarrassing statement on the news was now nullified. Dozen of hate messages had begun pouring in from concerned citizens over the misuse of tax money over my faulty AMBER Alert.

Liv's father had helped where he could, fielding questions and issuing blanket statements for the family as a whole. The assistance was greatly appreciated. It hadn't made up for everything in the past, but it certainly left the possibility of something more between Liv and her parents open in the future.

While the world had exploded around the three of us, we'd tried to focus on each other. The phone rang, the door bell rang and sometimes it seemed like peace and quiet would never come.

But none of it mattered because we had him back.

The phone would eventually quiet, the media would find something else to talk about, and our lives would return back to normal with just the three of us.

"Dad," a small voice uttered from the doorway.

"Yeah, buddy?" I replied, lifting my head to find him slowly walking toward us.

His hair was a mess, and he looked so much younger in his sleepy state. "Can I…I mean, would you let me—"

"Come on, get in here," I said, answering the question he was so scared to ask.

He gave a relieved smile as I lifted the covers and scooted over, so he could crawl between us. He nuzzled into my pillow and curled slightly onto his side. I looked over to find Liv watching him, her hand reaching out to push away the loose piece of hair that had fallen into his face.

Our eyes met, and in that moment, I knew that I not only wanted this woman for my wife, but I wanted her to be the mother Noah had never had.

He deserved a mother like Liv.

Following the incident, Noah stayed home from school the first few days, but eventually returned and he began to adjust. His biggest fears were resolved when the kids all rallied around him, giving him support and love, rather than contempt and indifference. The lack of friends was a nonissue, and Noah suddenly adored middle school. It could have something to do with the female attention he'd been receiving since his harrowing adventure.

He took it in stride though and didn't let the extra attention go to his head—much.

Despite my best efforts, I couldn't keep my parents from flying in immediately, so the first few days were spent with them, catching up with Noah and me. Also, they were finally able to meet Liv.

Having grown up in Richmond, my mom and Liv made a great pair. Mom took a tour of Liv's house, and told her stories about the previous owners and how she used to play in the attic as a girl. Still recovering from everything that had happened, we stayed close to home, eating like kings as my parents showed off their new culinary skills they'd learned from a cooking class at the retirement center.

As their time came to a close and we pulled up to the airport, my mom turned to me, her blue eyes shimmering.

"She's lovely, Jackson. Don't wait too long,"

"She's a tricky one, Mom. I don't want to scare her away," I replied.

"Just trust me." She winked.

After saying farewell at the airport, I thought about what she'd said the entire way home. So lost in my thoughts, I ended up passing both houses completely, Minutes later, I found myself driving through Carytown, walking by many of Liv's favorite stores and restaurants. I decided to park and walk a bit. I wandered through some of the shops and even stopped for a cup of coffee at a small café. As I was turning the corner back toward my car after my impromptu afternoon walk, a small boutique caught my eye, begging me to take a look.

I doubled back and walked through the old antique door, knowing Liv would have a million adjectives to describe how much she loved this place.

It was small and cozy with mismatched furniture and display cabinets that all somehow seemed to go together. Local art hung on the walls while beautiful pieces of jewelry sparkled and shined under the glow of the warm lights.

"Can I help you?" an older woman asked.

She could have been Liv's mother in another lifetime. Dressed in boho chic, she had a long brown braid going down her side with tons of bracelets and rings adorning her skin.

"I don't know. I just kind of stumbled in," I admitted, looking around from one case to another.

"Well, anyone in particular you had in mind when you stumbled in?" she asked, smiling.

"My girlfriend."

Her playful grin grew warm as she watched me consider each piece with interest.

"A pair of earrings perhaps?" she suggested.

My eyes settled on the one thing I knew I wouldn't be leaving without. "This," I said suddenly, pointing to the emerald ring below.

"Good choice. Would you like to know how much it costs?" she asked warmly.

"No," I answered honestly.

It wouldn't matter. Now that I'd seen it, nothing else would match it.

"Well, at least let me tell you a bit about it. It was handmade by a local jeweler, so it's one of a kind. The emerald is about a carat... maybe slightly more. White gold, vintage setting with pave diamond accents flanked on either side."

"It's perfect."

She smiled and lingered a moment. Then, she turned to the cash register to ring me up. I handed over my credit card without a second glance at the total.

Now that I had a ring, I just had to find the right moment.

I just hoped it wasn't too much of a wait.

It was already starting to burn a hole in my pocket.

~Liv~

"Clare, you really need to stop bringing me baked goods. I'm fine, I swear. It's been two weeks," I said, opening my front door wider so that she could enter.

"I know. I just can't help it. Something happens to someone I love, and I bake. When my father died, I think the local grocery store was out of sugar for an entire week. It's the only way I know how to deal."

I took the mammoth plate of cookies from her hands, and it only revealed her belly to me more.

"Holy shit! Look at you!"

"I know," she answered. "Apparently, with the third one, there's no stopping it. That stick says positive, and bam, here comes the belly. I thought I'd have a little bit longer before I had to pull out the granny pants."

"You look great," I said, sneaking a few steps forward to run my hands over her swelling stomach.

It wasn't as big as she thought it was, but she was definitely showing. As my fingers ran over her taut rounded belly, I felt longing rather than relief for the first time in my life.

"I feel awkward and large, but enough about me. I came here to shower you with sugar and see how you were doing."

Setting the cookies down on the counter, I pulled out two mugs for tea. "Chamomile or peppermint?" I asked, lifting two small tins from the pantry.

"I want coffee," she whined, taking a seat at the center island.

"You get chamomile or peppermint, preggo." I laughed.

"Okay. Let's go with peppermint."

"Good choice."

I heated up the water and insisted Clare first update me on her life.

"Maddie is in four dance classes. Four, Liv. I think I might go insane." Her head dropped into her hands.

I couldn't help but laugh. "You're officially a dance mom now! We should make you a shirt or something."

"Please don't."

"Just be glad she's found something she loves, and she is passionate about it," I reminded her as I poured the hot water into the mugs and left the tea to steep.

"I am. Truly. It's been amazing to see how far she's come since that first year when she was practicing all her positions on the new ballet barre Logan built for her. It's just a huge commitment."

"For everyone," I added.

"Yes," she agreed. "I'm hoping Ollie's passion will be a little less involved."

Dividing the tea into two cups, I gave her a discouraging look. "I doubt that."

She sighed. "Me, too. He's already learning guitar chords while sitting on Logan's lap and throwing footballs in the backyard with Uncle Colin. I'm screwed."

"You're blessed," I said, handing her a cup.

"Yeah"—she smiled—"I am."

We sipped our tea in comfortable silence, both sneaking cookies off the tray to nibble on. The heat of the tea warmed my chilled hands, making me appreciate the crisp chill in the autumn air.

"Ever since that day, I find myself hugging my children a bit tighter in the morning and kissing them a few more times at night. It's—"

"Scary," I said, finishing her sentence. She nodded as I continued, "When my fingers wrapped around the door handle and it opened without force, I immediately knew something was wrong. I don't know how many times Jackson has told Noah to make sure he locks the door the instant he gets home. Hell, he's yelled at me about it a time or two. But nothing compares to walking into that house and finding his things scattered about while the house is completely empty."

"How is Noah coping?" she asked hesitantly.

"Better now that the media attention has died off a bit. Seeing his mother's mug shot splattered everywhere was hard, and there were nights when he woke up crying, frightened he was going to lose us."

"Both of you?" she asked with a warm smile.

"Yeah," I said. "His words, not mine."

"And how does that make you feel?"

"Cherished," I answered.

"And?" Her lips pressed together as she tried to look innocent.

"Oh my God, Clare, you have the worst poker face ever."

"What? I was just trying to see how things were progressing."

"Then, ask!"

"Are you…I mean…do you think he's going to…"

"Spit it out." I grinned. I loved watching her squirm.

"Propose?"

"Yes."

"What? Are you serious? When?"

"As in a specific date? I have no idea, but I do know for a fact that he intends on asking me—someday," I added with a sigh.

"How?"

"I found the ring."

"Shut up! Are you serious?"

"No, I'm just making all this shit up to screw with you, Clare."

"Well, that's not very nice." She smirked. "Hold on." She reached into the large mommy purse next to her on the counter and pulled out her cell phone. She began rapidly dialing and pushing buttons.

Within seconds, Mia and Leah were on speaker.

"Hello?" Clare said excitedly.

"Good afternoon," Mia said softly. I heard Asher cooing in the background.

"What's going on? Why are we conference-calling each other? Is someone pregnant again?" Leah asked.

"No, but Liv has some news!"

"I do not!" I squeaked.

"I was just about to hump my husband when Clare texted me, saying I had to answer my phone stat, so spill it, hippie chick." Leah said, as Clare and I laughed.

"You guys suck," I lamented, folding my hands over my chest.

"Well, no, not right now I'm not," Leah chimed in.

Male laughter followed.

"Ew…gross, Leah," Clare said.

"Hey, you called."

"It's the afternoon!" Mia said. "Who does it in the middle of the afternoon?"

"Um…do I need to remind you about the events that took place last April, Mrs. Finnegan?" I giggled.

"Shh…not around the baby!" Mia whispered.

"Wait—I need to hear this," Leah said.

"Me, too!" Clare agreed.

"Let's just say, after I was done shopping one beautiful spring afternoon, I decided to drop in for an unexpected visit, and I got quite the eyeful. Mia is one lucky lady. Her man is hung like a horse."

"Why, thank you, Liv. Hi, ladies," Garrett deep voice suddenly said, nearly startling me.

Female laughter roared through the phone as I watched Clare's cheeks go pink with embarrassment as she covered her ears and began to hum loudly. I batted her hands away as she laughed.

"We've seriously gone off topic, and shame on you Mia for putting us on speakerphone," she said, trying to gain control of herself. Tiny giggles still erupted from her lips every other word as she took deep breaths. "Liv, tell the ladies...and my disgusting brother what you told me."

"Do we really have to do this?"

"Yes. This is what friends do. Share, so we can all squeal like schoolgirls. It's our God-given right."

"Okay, but first, let me say, you guys are ridiculous, and this is all a bit premature."

"That's what she said," a male voice chimed in.

"Zip it, Declan." Leah chimed in.

"Sorry." He half-laughed.

"You're on speakerphone too, Leah?" Clare sighed.

Leah laughed, "Sorry."

She was not sorry. At all.

"Okay," I started, wanting to get this over with as soon as possible. "It appears that I might have, while putting away groceries the other day, found an engagement ring Jackson bought."

"Holy shit! Are you serious?" Mia yelped at the same time Garrett said, "In the groceries?"

"Yes, I'm serious, and no, it was not in the groceries...well, not exactly. I was helping him put away some things, and I needed to make some additional room in the cupboards, so I started throwing out some of the older things. There was an old canister of oatmeal. I knew it was old because I remembered seeing it there when Mrs. Reid was still up and around baking cookies. For some reason, I opened it before tossing it. It's a good thing I did because inside was a dark blue velvet box."

"Who hides a ring in an oatmeal container?" someone asked.

"Jackson obviously," I answered.

"And when was this?" Mia asked.

"Nearly two weeks ago."

Silence.

"See? This is why I didn't want to tell you guys!" I said, throwing my hands up in the air.

"I'm sure he's just waiting for the perfect moment," Leah suggested.

"Maybe he has cold feet," Declan said before he cried out in pain. "Ouch! My nipple is still attached to my body, Leah!"

"Not for long!"

"Oh my God, please stop! Too many images in my head. And maybe Declan's right. What if Jackson has changed his mind?"

"I think we need another opinion," Clare suggested, pressing another button or five on her phone.

Suddenly, Logan was joining us. "Hey, babe. Are you okay?"

"Yes, I'm fine. We're fine. Say hi to everyone."

"Who's everyone?" he asked in confusion.

"Hi!" we all shouted together.

"Oh, okay…so everyone. Is this some sort of club meeting I wasn't aware of? Can I nominate Declan for President?"

"President of Awesome," Declan added.

"Oh my God, you guys are children. I called because Liv found an engagement ring at Jackson's place."

"That's great! Congratulations—early, I guess?"

"Well, that's what she's worried about. Apparently, she found the ring nearly two weeks ago," Clare said, looking up at me as she spoke into the phone.

"So?" Logan said. "Do you know how long I had Clare's ring in my pocket? Months. Sometimes, it's not a matter of knowing if the person is right, but if the timing is. He bought the ring, so he's got the first part figured out. It's all down to timing now."

I looked at the phone, like it was my friend standing in front of me. "Are you sure?"

"Positive."

"Thanks, guys."

"Anytime," Clare answered.

"Can we go now? I have important things to take care of, Liv," Declan chimed in. "Oh, and let's do this more often. But not in the afternoons…or mornings…scratch evenings off the schedule, too."

"Mental images!" I screeched.

"You're welcome! Good-bye!"

The phone clicked, and slowly, we said good-bye to the rest, leaving just Clare and me once again.

"When—not if—he asks, what will be your answer?"

I smiled sheepishly. "Guess you'll have to wait and find out."

~Jackson~

"It's been a month, and I still haven't asked her," I admitted as Declan and I wasted away an afternoon playing pool at a local sports bar. I had yet to nail down a job, finding one reason or another to turn down every respectable offer I'd received. I had plenty of money to float us for as long as necessary, but I hated sitting around, doing nothing all day. Especially when I had Liv's ring constantly reminding me of the many possibilities the future held.

"Why the hold up?" he inquired.

I watched him line up his shot and sink three balls with ease.

"I have no clue. The words are right there on the tip of my tongue, and every time she walks through the damn door, I think, *This is it. This is the exact moment I've been waiting for.* Then, nothing. I end up asking her about her day or if she thinks my flowers are being properly watered."

"You're not getting cold feet, are you? I mean, you love her, right?" he asked, standing up straight to meet my gaze.

"God, yes. Jesus, calm down. You look like the Hulk, about to go postal."

"Just looking out for my family." He shrugged. His shoulders loosening, he grabbed his beer from the nearby table.

"I honestly don't know what it is. I mean, Noah is doing great, better than great actually, which is amazing considering everything we went through. And yeah, things with her father still aren't fantastic, but I know that will take some time. I just keep waiting for the perfect moment."

Setting his beer down, he turned to face me. "Did you ever think that maybe that moment doesn't exist?"

"What do you mean?" I asked.

"I mean, maybe it's not about how you ask. Do you really think five or ten years down the road it's really going to make a fuck-ton of difference if you asked her while you were cuddled on the couch in front of the TV or by some waterfall three months from now because you were waiting for the perfect opportunity?"

I rolled my eyes. "Says the dude who had his wife's initials tattooed on his chest as part of his marriage proposal."

Declan's cocky grin lit up his face. "Well, we all can't be as awesome as me."

"Clearly."

"Dude, I'm going to do you a favor, a huge and epic favor. It will break about a million friend laws that I don't even know exist, but Leah will cite me for them, if she ever finds out."

"I have no idea what the hell you're talking about," I replied in confusion.

"She knows."

"What? Who knows?"

"Liv. She knows. She found the ring in the pantry, like, a month ago. By the way, who in his right mind hides a diamond ring in an oatmeal container?"

"It's not a diamond. It's an emerald."

"Whatever. Same question still applies."

"I don't know! I got home with the ring and panicked. It was the only place I could think of."

"Well, it was a shitty idea because she's known about that little hiding place for a while now."

"She knows I'm going to propose?"

"Yep."

"Fuck."

"Yep. But hey, now, you don't have to worry about that perfect moment, right? Hell, you could ask her while you're making dinner or brushing your teeth. See how much stress I just saved you?"

I didn't answer. My mind was reeling with this new information, and then a sly smile spread across my face. If Liv had known all this time and not said a word, did this mean she was ready to say yes? Or maybe she was worried I'd become too complacent in our relationship and that I didn't want to propose anymore.

Well, I couldn't have that.

"Oh, fuck. What are you planning, Jackson?"

"The best *worst* proposal ever."

~**Liv**~

Dress fancy, he said.

We're celebrating, he said.

As I stared at my closet, I found myself wondering what one wore to a proposal dinner. Having never imagined myself being proposed to while at a stuffy restaurant, I really didn't know.

Honestly, I didn't expect to ever be in this position at all, stuffy restaurant or not.

Should I trust a man who thought a fancy dinner out was the perfect way to ask me this very important question?

Taking a deep breath, I reminded myself that it didn't matter where or when, only that I would be marrying the right person.

And I would be, regardless of what I wore or how much I hated the restaurant.

I pulled out three dresses and laid them out on the bed, trying to decide which would be more flattering. I decided on the sexiest of the three, and I squeezed myself into the little black dress that made my boobs look amazing and gave the illusion that I actually had a little junk in my trunk.

By the time I'd finished spritzing lavender perfume in the air around me, the doorbell rang, marking the arrival of my very punctual date.

"Holy shit, you look amazing," Jackson said, his eyes roaming my body. He handed me a huge bouquet of red roses drowning in baby's breath.

I hated baby's breath.

It was the thought that mattered, right?

"Thank you!" I smiled. "They're lovely. Let me put them in some water."

His face broke out into a cocky grin as we walked into the kitchen.

"What?" I asked.

"Nothing." He nearly laughed. "Just happy to be spending a night out with you."

Pulling out a large vase, I quickly arranged the flowers in a few inches of water.

Then, we proceeded to make our way to the restaurant.

"Fancy," I remarked as we pulled up to the valet at the entrance.

"Well, it is a special night." He smiled.

I gulped in response, hoping he hadn't seen my nervousness.

The restaurant he'd chosen for the night was new and hip. It was all anyone could talk about in the city. A well-known celebrity chef had moved in, taken over a run-down building right on the banks of the James River, and transformed it into one of the finest places to eat on the East Coast.

I should have been excited.

I should have felt flattered.

Instead, I was nauseous as I looked over the menu and saw nothing but meat and fish.

"Do you think they could make something special?" he asked. "I'm sorry. I didn't even think to ask about vegetarian options when I made the reservation over a month ago."

"I'll figure something out. Don't worry about it." I smiled lamely.

The waiter was extremely accommodating, and the chef was indeed able to whip up a vegetable risotto that was to die for. I just hoped it didn't come with a killer price tag to match.

"Isn't this nice? Just the two of us, all dressed up for a night on the town," Jackson said, smiling from ear to ear.

"Yes, it's lovely, really. Thank you, Jackson."

"Anything for you, sweetheart."

A table next to us erupted into shrieks of joy and clapping. I looked over to see a young man on one knee, holding a ring box above his heart.

"Yes! Yes!" the young girl answered with enthusiasm.

The entire restaurant melted into oohs and aahs for the happy couple.

I resisted the urge to roll my eyes.

"I hope you don't mind, but before we arrived, I took the liberty of ordering dessert for us. I wanted to have them make something special."

Of course he did.

"And I also ordered some champagne," he added with a wicked grin.

"Are you going to make a toast?" I asked, feeling my anxiety rising higher and higher.

"I guess you will just have to wait and see." He winked.

Oh, please, someone make him stop.

Our luscious chocolate torte was served, and I noticed Jackson watching me intensely.

"Something wrong?" I asked, dipping my fork into my dessert once again.

"Nope. Happy as a clam."

The champagne was served, and as Jackson held his glass up in the air, his eyes drifted down to my glass.

"Here's to our happy life," he said.

I lifted my flute and touched his. Our eyes locked as we tilted the glasses to our lips, and I felt a spark of heat zing down to my core. My eyes looked down at the table as I set my glass on the tabletop.

"Something wrong?" he asked.

"No, absolutely not. You?"

"Still happy."

I covered my laugh with a fake cough, bringing my hand up to my mouth as a diversion.

He thought he'd won this round, but what he didn't know was that I had been winning all along.

~Jackson~

Every last detail of my plan had been orchestrated flawlessly.

From the bouquet of flowers I knew she'd hate to the overly fancy restaurant, Liv was having the worst night ever.

And the best part was, she was biting her tongue to stay quiet about it.

When I'd announced the special dessert and champagne, I'd thought her eyes might explode out of her head as she waited for the horribly cheesy moment to come.

The added bonus of the couple next to us getting engaged had been like icing on the cake.

When the ring hadn't been on the torte or in the champagne, I'd seen her growing restless, waiting for the big flashy moment to come.

She was exactly where I wanted her to be.

"Are you ready to head home?" I asked cheerfully.

"Home?"

"Yep, it is getting late. I figured you'd want to get home and maybe watch a movie."

"Oh, um…sure," she answered, a hint of surprise in her voice.

I held out my arm as she rose from her chair, and I took a moment to admire the way the fabric of her dress clung to her breasts. That dress was definitely an extra perk to my plan.

She was quiet as we waited for the car to be pulled around. I could almost see the thoughts swirling around in her head as she wondered what the hell had just happened.

In that one second when Declan had spilled the beans about Liv knowing my intentions to propose, everything had come together for me.

It wasn't the moment or the place—it was about who would be there to celebrate it with us.

But how could I orchestrate that many people and keep Liv out of it?

Give her the worst almost proposal of her life.

Everything I knew she'd hate, I'd given her tonight. Liv was simple, earthy, and one of the most carefree people I knew. Stuffy restaurants and grand gestures were great and romantic for some, but Liv needed something less grandiose.

That was where our family and friends came into play.

As Liv and I had been away, having dinner and not getting engaged, the gang had been busy setting up a backyard proposal that would blow Liz away.

There would be candlelight, flowers, and not a bit of baby's breath for miles.

I was the master of proposals. After tonight, even Declan would have to acknowledge it.

Liz and I held hands on our way back to the house, and I brushed my thumb over the spot where her ring would sit in just a few short minutes. I couldn't wait to place it there and see it exactly where I knew it belonged since the moment I'd seen it.

From the outside of our houses, everything appeared normal and just as boring as any other Saturday night. As I took her hand and pulled her down the path to the fence separating the two houses, she began to see the first flicker of candlelight.

"What is that?" she asked.

"You'll see."

We walked farther, and as we rounded the corner to the backyard, it was me who gasped in surprise.

Pink flamingos encompassed nearly every inch of the border of the fence, creating a vibrant pink outline. Big boldly colored balloons were tied to everything, and potted plants were everywhere.

"What the hell?" I said, seeing the faces of our friends and family smiling back at us.

We entered the backyard, and Liv turned to me.

"See, your first mistake was trusting that the blabbermouth over there would keep your secret." She grinned, pointing at Declan.

He had his arms wrapped around Leah. He gave me an apologetic look and then laughed.

"You mean, you knew that I wasn't going to propose the entire night?"

"Yep."

"Damn," I said. "I've been duped."

"You know how much I like to win." Her hands rested in mine as she dropped to one knee. "And there is no greater prize than you, Jackson. I never expected that I'd be here, in a moment like this, ready to share my heart and soul with another. You showed me that love isn't about giving up any part of yourself. It's about sharing the best and worst of yourself and trusting that the person will love you through it all. Will you share your life with me?"

I kissed her softly, then kneeled down before her, as I reached into my pocket to pull out the ring that I'd been dying to give her for over a month since I'd first laid eyes on it.

"Only if you share yours with me," I answered, opening the box.

Tears cascaded down her cheeks as her fingers touched the smooth metal.

"Will you marry me, Liv?"

"Yes," she managed to say through the tears.

I slipped the ring onto her finger. Everyone in the backyard clapped and cheered.

Hands wrapped around us as Noah joined in on our tight hug.

Sometimes, what you needed in life was waiting for you where you'd least expected it. Sometimes, it was right next door.

Now that I had Liv, I knew everything I'd ever need was already in my arms. Nothing else mattered.

"So, where are we going to live?" Noah asked, poking his head out to look back and forth between the two houses.

Okay, so, sometimes, some things mattered.

We'd figure it out eventually.

~Liv~

"Liv, you look beautiful," Mia said, standing behind me as we both looked at my reflection staring back at us.

I looked like a bride—sort of.

Forgoing tradition, I'd chosen a simple bohemian-style dress in blush rather than white. The soft pink lace reminded me of vintage lingerie, so delicate and soft. It gathered above my natural waist with an ivory-colored sash, and it flowed gracefully to the floor.

It was the only dress I'd tried on. When I'd stepped into the tiny consignment store days earlier, I'd known the minute the woman brought it out that it was exactly what I had been looking for.

"Let's touch up your hair," Leah suggested, adjusting the crown of flowers she'd placed there minutes before. She sniffled and quickly dabbed her eyes.

"Are you getting misty-eyed, Leah?" I asked.

"No," she answered swiftly. "Allergies. I'm sure of it."

"Okay."

I gave Mia a sideways glance, and we both smiled. Signaling to Mia, I rounded my hand and moved it over my belly. Then, I looked back to Leah. She snorted in response.

"I am not pregnant!" she said, obviously catching the silent conversation between Mia and me. "Well, I mean…not much. Just a little," she amended.

We all looked at her, dumbfounded, and she crossed her arms in front of her.

"You guys can squeal now. I'm ready," she said before raising her hands to her ears.

Girlish cries of joy filled the room as we all ran over to hug her.

"Well, don't squish the poor little guy," she said, laughing.

"It's a boy?" I asked.

"Hell, I don't know. It's a tadpole right now, but Declan's hoping for a boy."

"We're going to have our own football team soon," I commented.

"Better start catching up." Mia winked.

"One step at a time I think. I just got engaged a week ago."

"You know, you could have waited. That is the idea behind the term, *engagement*." Clare laughed.

"I never was one to follow directions. So, how much longer?"

"About ten minutes," Leah answered, checking the clock on her phone.

A knock sounded at the door. We all turned to find my father walking in.

"Sorry to interrupt, ladies. I was hoping to have a moment alone with my daughter," he said.

I sat down on the small stool in front on the vanity in shocked silence as my friends scattered like flies.

Traitors.

"My Livvy Lou, all grown-up," he said with a note of sadness in his voice.

"It was bound to happen."

"You look radiant. Truly."

"Thank you, Daddy," I answered, fidgeting with my fingers, as I looked around the room.

"I know I don't deserve anything, considering everything I've done—or not done—but it would be my great honor to be the one who walks you down that aisle," he said softly.

"Dad—"

"I'm dropping out of the race. I'm retiring from politics," he announced, taking a step forward.

"What? Why? I thought—"

"I've been fixated on the wrong set of goals in my life for far too long. It was so long that I missed watching you grow up, and I ignored your mother. I gave up my life for my career. I need my family back. I can't do it anymore."

Tears stung my eyes as I looked at the man who'd once meant the world to me. He'd been my fairy-tale prince and forever hero.

Finally, he was back.

"Yes," I said.

"Yes what?"

"Yes, I would love to have you walk me down the aisle, Daddy."

We met halfway, and as his arms wrapped around me, I finally let go of the lost and angry girl I had once been. I would have been fine without him. I knew I would have gone on, knowing sometimes you had to make your own family and let go of your past.

But having him here beside me was like a cleansing for my soul. I didn't feel the need to show him everything I'd accomplished and achieved. It was about making sure he understood I'd survived without his support. It was simply holding his hand and knowing he loved me.

He always loved me.

"Let's go get you married," he said, taking a hold of my hand.

He led me toward the backyard where my new prince was awaiting.

"I'm ready." I grinned.

~**Jackson**~

I knew marrying someone like Liv would make for an interesting life.

I just hadn't realized how soon that would happen.

"Let's get married next week!" she'd announced minutes after our backyard proposal.

"Next week? Don't you need to plan stuff? Isn't there a girl code involved?" I'd asked.

Nope.

No plans. No waiting.

Liv had wanted to keep everything simple and small, so there had been no reason to wait.

Honestly, as I stood there, greeting guests dressed less formally than I had for work most days, I couldn't agree more.

We'd only invited close friends and family.

When I'd called my parents the next day to inform them that I would be getting married—and oh by the way, it was next week—I was met with sheer excitement.

I was starting to wonder if they had been scared that this day might never come.

The topic of Liv's parents hadn't gone over nearly as well. She'd argued with herself over and over regarding the topic, and finally, she'd decided to send them a handwritten invitation. She hadn't expected anything to come from it, and so far, I hadn't seen them arrive.

The wedding was to take place where it had all started—home.

Chairs and twinkling lights had been beautifully arranged in my backyard, which was now ours. We'd decided if we were going to join households, we'd do it here. Leaving Liv's house behind had been difficult, which was why we weren't selling it. We were just waiting to find the right person to rent it to. Until then, we'd slowly move her things over and settle into our new life.

Besides, she wasn't the only one moving. Next week, I would officially be moving my office next to hers. The old dentist was retiring, and I'd managed to swoop up the location for a steal. After a few long weeks of remodeling, I'd be in business for myself. Family law sounded hard, laborious, and completely awesome. The added bonus of a built-in lunch date and a sweet little garden to chill in didn't hurt either.

The backyard sparkled, looking elegant and ethereal. Hanging plants dotted the walkway, and people sat on benches and wicker furniture that we'd borrowed from friends. A small dinner was planned afterwards. We couldn't decide on what to cook, so I was firing up the grill, and we were calling in a large order of Thai food. Bets had been placed on whether either of us would venture out of our comfort zones.

The pot had grown pretty damn large. Even my own father had placed a bet. He wouldn't say who it was against.

It was the perfect wedding and exactly what I'd envisioned when I thought of the day I'd marry Liv.

Now, all I needed was my bride.

Noah, standing in as my best man, walked behind me as we took our places in the front.

Mia would serve as Liv's matron of honor, and that was as elaborate as our wedding party got.

The music started, and I saw the back door open.

Out came Senator Douglas, and as everyone rose, I saw him escorting the most beautiful creature I'd ever seen.

My breath caught, and my vision blurred at the mere sight of her. *My wife.*

Our eyes met, and in their depths, I found the missing piece of my soul.

As our fingers touched and we spoke the words that would bind our souls together for eternity, I knew every decision in my life had led me to this moment and the path we were about to create together.

"You may now kiss your bride," the minister announced.

Our new life had just begun, and it was time to start living it.

Coming Soon

Happily ever after.

That was what we were supposed to have.

Pudding cups, sandy toes and a lifetime of making each and every one of our dreams come true—that is the future I'd promised her.

I could see it in my dreams, hold it in my hands, but then I watched as all of our hopes and wishes suddenly slipped through my fingers like sand.

I thought the worst was behind us, but what if we'd just delayed the inevitable?

They say love can overcome any obstacle. But can it survive death?

The breathtaking love story of Lailah and Jude concludes in **Beyond These Walls.**

Coming March 2015

The Ready or Not Playlist

Natalie – Bruno Mars
Not a Bad Thing – Justin Timberlake
Latch (Acoustic) – Sam Smith
Before I Ever Met You – Banks
Stay With Me – Sam Smith
(You Drive Me) Crazy – Britney Spears
She's So Mean – Matchbox Twenty
Daughters – John Mayer
Boom Clap – Charli XCX
Flowers in Your Hair – The Lumineers
Lost Stars – Adam Levine
Aint Nobody – Jasmine Thompson

Acknowledgements

Right after I made the decision to move ahead with *When You're Ready*, I came to my husband in a panic (this is normal in our household) and asked, "What if I can't write another one? What if this is my only idea?" He pulled me into his arms (or at least that's how I remember it now…he may have just looked at me strangely) and said, "Then make it a good one."

Luckily, like most authors I know…the ideas didn't stop after that first book. In fact, they just kept coming. Some are great, others are well—not so great. But, the point of this really long, seemingly pointless intro is that I followed a dream. And it led to such an amazing new life—one that I would have never imagined.

Like most dreams, I couldn't have done it alone. So, let's started with the acknowledgments!

First and foremost—my husband. Chris—I don't know how you've managed to put up with me all these and stay sane, but thank you for figuring it out. I love you.

My girls—You always know the perfect ways to make me laugh—thank you. Oh and stop growing. Seriously, stop it!

My family—Thanks for being your weird, awesome selves. It's great inspiration for writing.

Leslie—I love you. Hard. Oh and I just have one thing to say—Birthday Weekend 2015. It's happening.

Melissa and Carey—There are too many reasons to list. You keep me sane.

Jovana and Ami—You are my editing wizards and I can't imagine working with anyone else. Thank you for your devotion and love of my work.

Beta readers—Thank you for always being there to eagerly read my horribly unedited manuscripts and offer feedback and advice. Your help means the world to me.

Bloggers—I wouldn't be where I am if it wasn't for bloggers reading, sharing and loving my work. I appreciate each and every one of you more than I can say.

Tara Gonzalez—Worlds Greatest Publicist. That is all.

Kelsey Keeton—Shut up. Just shut your face. Every time I think there's no possible way you could do any better, you manage to blow my mind again. I love you.

Sarah Hansen—Every day I get a cover from you is like Christmas, and you're the grumpy little elf that delivers them. P.S. Jamie is mine.

Gabriella and Dusty—Thank you so much for bringing my characters to life. You truly are Liv and Jackson on this cover and I can't thank you enough.

Stacey Blake—As always, thank you for making the inside of my book look amazing. You are a formatting guru.

Berg's Book Junkies—You guys bring a smile to my face everyday. Thank you for your neverending support and constant love.

Last but not least, a huge thank you to my readers—both new and old. Thank you for falling in love with my characters, becoming part of their lives and walking this crazy journey with me.

Until next time,

JL

About the Author

J.L. Berg is the USA Today bestselling author of the Ready Series. She is a California native living in the beautiful state of historic Virginia. Married to her high school sweetheart, they have two beautiful girls that drive them batty on a daily basis. When she's not writing, you will find her with her nose stuck in a romance novel, in a yoga studio or devouring anything chocolate. J.L. Berg is represented by Jill Marsal of Marsal Lyon Literary Agency, LLC.

CPSIA information can be obtained at www.ICGtesting.com
Printed in the USA
LVOW08s0002020915

452388LV00005B/558/P